THE INDIGO STONE

Simone Snaith

For my family of musicians, artists, and dreamers

ONE

The rain on the tin roofs of Thela was a symphony of pangs and crashes, a dance of tiny knives, an army advancing down from the sky. It was always the first sound Eine heard in the morning. It interrupted a dream this time, a dream she'd had a few times before. There was a feeling of urgency, almost like a voice calling her, and there were trees looming out of the night. She was moving slowly among them, with the sense that her feet were not touching the ground.

She had never seen trees in real life, except for the one scraggly specimen she had glimpsed the time she'd followed two Dredges that had stolen from her, all the way to the factories, and then raced back, frightened. She had never quite built up the courage to go back again.

The trees in her dream were deep green and indistinct. Like ghosts of trees.

Eine opened her eyes to a tilted view of the world, since she lay on her side under an old cart, curled up in her long gray cloak. The rain appeared to fall from left to right, and the mouth at the end of the brick-walled alley was a dim rectangle, blurred by passing people on the street. She was long accustomed to sleeping in the cold and the damp, with water sometimes puddling around her head, soaking her hood. She sat up now and hugged herself in her cloak, surveying her surroundings from underneath the cart. Her stomach rumbled.

She still had some dried meat in her cloak pocket and she pulled it out now to chew on a tough piece, her mind still hazy from the dream. She'd been having it for weeks now, off and on, this dream of wandering through dark trees. And the voice... She thought it was a woman's voice.

She frowned and swallowed the hard meat. She had seen old, malnourished Dredges become delirious before, and develop visions. She had seen one standing in the middle of the market once, railing at the Indigo like a lunatic. She heard later that he was taken, and never seen again. Like the others.

She'd been living off dried meat and stale bread for days. Maybe she needed fruit. She crawled out from the stall and stretched her stiff limbs, the rain greeting her with an icy thrill. The good thing about the near constant rain in Thela was that it kept her and all the other Dredges fairly clean. She was tempted to throw back her hood now and rinse her hair out in the downpour, but someone could be watching. Someone could always be watching. And there was a reason she never took down her hood. She hunched herself against the chill and started for the end of the alley, stepping over broken bits of wagon wheels, apple cores, discarded boxes. She had chosen this alley for its amount of trash; it was less desirable, and there was plenty to hide behind.

Out on the street, Eine pulled her hood low over her face and stepped out into the stream of Thelans trudging through the rain. They were a swarm of ragged, hooded jackets in mostly dark colors. Eine concentrated on moving like them, swinging her arms harder and stomping her feet. She had to pretend that her limbs were heavy, and that the ground pulled at her just as hard as it did everyone else. She had to remember this always, just as she constantly had to pretend that large objects were heavy.

Because walking as if she weighed nothing, and lifting things twice her size, was what came naturally to her. And that was bad. It wasn't so difficult to hide, however, to just be invisible. She remembered the Dredge woman who had covered her head with an old blanket, when she was very small. Eine had brown eyes dark as mud puddles, but her hair was strikingly white-gold. It was a combination that didn't seem to exist among the other Thelans that Eine had seen, and she remembered well the old woman's words in her ear.

"Hide your light, child."

Eine stopped now, at the edge of the alley, to study her reflection in a puddle. A barefoot waif wrapped in a tattered cloak gazed back at her. She looked younger than her age, which she was only scarcely sure was seventeen. Her face was still small around her deep-set eyes, like a little girl, with a round nose and a full bottom lip. Time was beginning to blur together, and it scared her.

The merchants were hawking their goods when she reached the marketplace, which was not much more than an enlarged intersection of roads in bad repair where a large ring of carts were set up each day. The carts bore bread, fruit, dried meat and rain-collecting canteens. They bore yards of mostly threadbare and dull-colored clothing as well, but when the sun occasionally broke free of the clouds, the whole market was momentarily transformed. That was when the entire place seemed to glitter with Thela's own home-manufactured goods: glassware and tin. The carts would suddenly sparkle with their lamps, spectacles, magnifying glasses, binoculars, even decorative spinning glass discs.

The Thelans that wandered through it all were the family members of the factory workers and tin miners. They shopped quickly with wary faces, and the mothers kept their children close. The old men were silent and watchful. Then they disappeared into their brick houses, closing their window shades tight.

Eine was quick and silent, snatching an apple from a fruit cart, unseen. She slipped behind a large barrel and crouched down to eat it, crunching, and savoring the sweet juice. She turned and peered out at the crowd. There were no indigo-colored, hooded uniforms in sight, at least for now. It was said they could appear out of thin air, and then disappear in a flash. The thought made Eine shudder.

She ate the apple down to the core and then darted out again. The sun was casting meager rays once more and the rain was slacking off into a drizzle. She stopped near a stall selling dried fruit, and casually wrung out her long sleeves and the bottom of her cloak. In another moment, she was crouched behind a large cart with a handful of raisins. She glanced up at the mounds of tin plates and goblets in the cart over her head. There were tin styluses and ink wells, bookends and lidded jars, all of them glinting in a faint stream of sunlight.

7

Not for the first time, she wondered what was beyond the tin mines. Her heart pounded at the memory of the giant factory buildings that had risen into the sky, over the heads of the thieves in front of her. Sand had blown across the cobblestones at her feet. The one naked tree had been visible in the distance, beyond the factories. Dry sand and leafless trees were bewildering in a city where it was always wet. A horn had sounded then, different from the Hunters' call, but equally as terrifying, and Eine had turned on her heels and run, faster than she'd ever run, back to the safety of her dark alley. Afterwards, she realized the sound had probably just marked the end of a shift for the factory workers.

Thela was laid out like a giant wheel, with the center marked by the marketplace and the nearby platform where the Hunters made their announcements. Eine recalled asking someone as a small child if the Hunters' platform had been there before the Indigo had taken over the city. She had been promptly silenced by the alarmed Dredge. 'Before the Indigo' was not a phrase to speak aloud.

If Thela was a wheel then its spokes consisted of the long winding alleys between the low brick buildings where the Thelans lived. The windows were always shuttered, which gave them an abandoned look. Beyond the factories, and the tin mines, somewhere, there were merchant roads that Eine had never seen. She only knew from eavesdropping that they led to a place called "The Docks" near the city walls.

No one was allowed to leave the city and no one entered. It was forbidden by the Indigo.

Eine put the last of the raisins into her pocket, turning away from the cart. It was better to save a little; she never left the market without a bit left in her pocket. She sighed and steadied herself, feeling anxious just thinking about the factories.

That was when she heard it, a voice in her head: *"It has got to stop raining at* some *point."*

She stumbled backwards, startled. It was the same reaction she always had when someone's stray thoughts hit her.

"My gun is rusting."

Eine knocked the side of the cart in her surprise, and a large tin urn tumbled straight down from the load, narrowly missing her head. It crashed to the ground and she scurried away, before the cart's owner could investigate. She ran back into the market crowd, unnerved and shivering, her eyes darting from face to face. She never knew how close the thinker was; she had no idea what her range was. The flashes came and went, like lightning across the sky:

"My leg is killing me in this cold."
"I'm late again. Stupid, lazy boy!"

They were like random snatches of conversation, except they were feelings and images that she sorted into words somehow, instantly, instinctively. It was just another thing she had to hide. It should have been the easiest thing to hide, in fact, except that there was never any warning and sometimes people noticed her surprise.

'My gun is rusting.' Eine frowned, following the others in the crowd. It was a man's thoughts, that much she could tell. The images she'd gotten had been rain and metal, but the words she'd formed were confusing. What was a 'gun'? She clenched and unclenched her fists in her pockets as she walked, regretting having let the thoughts startle her so much. Maybe the man they belonged to had been right nearby. She would never know if she took off and ran every time, instead of holding her ground and studying the faces of those around her.

Eine turned against the tide of people and ducked behind a wagon full of wooden crates. Maybe a gun was something made in the factories. It was obviously metal, but in the quick mental image, it hadn't looked like tin.

"What are you doing back there, you little rat?" A merchant suddenly grabbed Eine by the cloak, yanking her forward. He gave her a shove and she fell hard, since she weighed so little, sprawling on the ground. She glared back up at the man in his merchant's tunic, anger burning in her chest.

"What did you take?" he demanded, his hands on his hips. Eine leapt to her feet and darted under his arms, too quick for him to react. But she ran smack into another man, and cursed her luck as he grabbed her by the shoulders. This was a bad day. She needed to get back to her alley.

The second man's weathered face bore down on her with steel-gray eyes. Eine sucked in her breath, staring back. The color of his hood…!

"Oh!" the merchant exclaimed behind her. His voice was suddenly nervous, wobbly. "Thank you for catching her, sir. I hope she didn't bother you, sir. Just a Dredge!"

The man's cold eyes stared into Eine's as he stood there, clenching her shoulders like a vise. She winced and looked away, her heart thumping. How had this happened? Where had he come from?

"The Indigo doesn't tolerate thieves." His voice was thick and gravelly. Eine felt a strange sense of dread building up inside her chest. She couldn't bear to look at him. She stared at the building across the road, over his shoulder.

"She was lurking about behind my crates," the merchant said. The Indigo man straightened up and studied him over Eine's head. The hood of his blue uniform framed a sharp, hooked nose and a thin-lipped mouth. He gave Eine a rough shake, rattling her teeth. She closed her eyes.

"What's wrong with you?" he demanded.

"They're all sick, sir," the merchant piped up. "You know, from the rain and the cold... Maybe she was just resting," he added guiltily. Eine felt a small rush of gratitude. The Indigo gave her another penetrating gaze. Then he dropped his grip on her abruptly, turning away from them both as if in disinterest. He stopped, however, and looked back at Eine, a surprised expression on his face. She stared back at him, afraid to breathe.

"Why are you so light?" he asked, his voice calm. She swallowed.

"I don't eat," she whispered. Her voice sounded odd and raspy. She realized it was the first time she had spoken aloud in a couple of days.

The merchant nodded timidly. He was thin as well and his tunic was ragged. The Indigo knew well that no one was prosperous here. After another agonizing moment, the man turned and strode off as before, his head turning from side to side, surveying the crowds. Eine hesitated for a few seconds, unable to tear her eyes from his blue uniform. It was all in one piece and it cinched at the waist, with long sleeves that stretched tight over the backs of his hands, the pants over the tops of his boots.

Then she took off, running as fast as her light feet could carry her.

TWO

Eine woke the next day to a crack of thunder and realized she had slept much later than usual. She'd had difficulty falling asleep, her mind refusing to settle down. She'd had small run-ins with the Indigo before, but they always left her shaken. It would've been nice to just stay where she was, curled up safe, but her stomach was already growling. The watery sun was high overhead as she crawled out from under the cart and stretched. She dug the raisins from her pocket and ate them, crouching in the light rain that dripped from above.

'It has got to stop raining at some point.' It was an odd thought to 'overhear', considering how constant the rain was. As far back as Eine could remember, she was cold and wet, just as she was now. She remembered other Dredges taking pity on her and slipping her food, and she remembered the old woman who had covered her head. She had stolen her gray cloak from a stall not long after, and had never exposed her head since. The cloak was much too large for her at the time, but it was comfortable now.

She closed her eyes and tried to remember more, reaching further back. There were fleeting sensations that touched her sometimes, when she was half asleep or daydreaming. Occasionally, something would seem familiar. She heard a melody sometimes, when she really concentrated. A humming. It was a man's voice humming, soft and low.

Something brushed against Eine's fingers. She whirled and caught a tiny wrist just as it slipped into her pocket. She jerked hard, and there was a loud yelp as she flipped its owner over his head, onto the ground.

She had let her guard down for just one moment. She gritted her teeth.

"Wha' are you, Laxen?" the small boy exclaimed, staring up at her. Eine caught her breath at his words. Her mouth fell open and she stared down at him, wild-eyed, absolutely astonished. *That word!*

"What did you just say?" she whispered. The boy blinked up at her, just now taking in her features. His own face was pale and peaked, with a pointed nose and green eyes under messy brown hair.

"You're a girl?" he shrilled. "You're a girl and you threw me up and over?"

She stared at him for a few more moments, still amazed at what she'd heard. "...You're all skin and bones," she said finally, and pulled her hood lower. "This is my alley. Go out and steal from the market." The boy got to his feet, frowning. He wore what looked like a discarded black sweater that was too big for him. Eine guessed he was about nine.

"Diden know this was your alley. I don' see a sign anywhere," he said grumpily. Eine cocked her head at him, confused.

"Why are you talking like that?" she asked.

"Like wha'?" he demanded.

"Like someone knocked out your teeth." She peered closer at him and he glared back with his mouth closed. Then she dug into her pocket and handed him the raisins, at which his green eyes doubled in size. He grabbed them and shoved the whole lot into his mouth, revealing plenty of even teeth. They were straighter in fact than most Dredges' teeth.

"You don't say the T's on the end of your words," Eine said, watching him. Maybe he didn't know. Maybe he had never learned to speak correctly. He ignored her, swallowing and smacking his lips.

"Oh, you saved me. I was abou' to die from hunger," he said solemnly. Eine rolled her eyes.

"It takes a lot longer than you think." It struck her then how odd it was to be talking this much to someone. She turned towards the entrance to the alley, her own stomach growling again. "Come on, I'm going to get more." The boy's eyes lit up like green glass and he smiled. It was much more pleasant than the scowl, which Eine had imagined was permanent.

"You're nice," he said, following. "Even if you *are* like a Laxen."

"Hey!" Eine spun around and grabbed his arm. "What's wrong with you? Don't say that!" The boy cringed.

"Wha'? Don' say wha'?" he cried out.

"*Laxen*," Eine hissed, in disbelief. How had he survived this long? "Didn't anyone tell you not to say that?" she demanded. He shook his head, confused, still cringing away from her. For one moment, Eine considered attempting to explain something as commonly known as the rising and setting of the sun. She felt exhausted at the thought of it and shook her head.

"Just don't say it, ever," she said, sharply. "Or the Indigo will suspect you. Got it?" He nodded, but he looked bewildered. She let go of his arm, worried, and began to pick her way out of the alley. She heard the boy following and stopped to wait at the entrance for him to catch up. Maybe he was not right in the head somehow.

The two of them moved out into the street and walked quietly towards the marketplace. Eine wondered if he would be a hindrance at the stalls and cause her trouble. She frowned and considered whether she should even be letting him follow her. He wasn't anything to her; he wasn't hers to take care of. But she had not meant anything to the old woman who had covered her head, to keep her safe.

…Or *had* she? Considering what she was?

"Wha's your name?" the boy asked suddenly. Eine looked back down at him in surprise. It was something she was rarely asked. She only knew the answer from faded memories, faded voices.

"Eine," she murmured, feeling shy.

"Mine's Graf," he chirped back.

They reached the market a few moments later, and Eine ducked her head down to whisper to him, "Don't say a word. Just stay behind me." To her surprise, Graf reached out and took her hand. Then he nodded, blank-faced. Eine curled her fingers around his awkwardly and surveyed the stalls. The boy probably needed meat. She crept towards the dried meat cart and squeezed Graf's hand to signal him to stop. She let go of him then and, in a flash, snatched a piece of meat while the merchant was busy.

She was hidden behind the cart in another instant and peered back out at Graf, who stood hopelessly where she had left him. She caught his eye and waved him over.

"I diden even see wha' you did!" Graf blurted out. She clamped a hand over his mouth and darted around a street corner as he followed, panting. "You're fass as a L-!"

Eine slapped her hand on his mouth again, groaning. "I said don't talk! I said don't say *that!* You did both!" she said, despairing.

"Oh." Graf looked guilty. "Did you geh any food though?" he whispered loudly. Eine almost laughed. The poor boy was surely blest, if he'd survived this long. She pulled the piece of dried meat from her pocket and tore it in half. Graf reached for his half greedily and Eine took a bite of hers.

The sudden, loud blare of a horn tore through the air, and both of them flinched. Eine glanced up at the crowd in the market and saw that everyone had frozen, a familiar look of dread on their faces. It was the Hunters' horn, which meant a new announcement from the Indigo. Graf choked on his meat as the horn blasted again, a deep, harsh sound that split the damp air around them. The Thelans began to turn slowly and shuffle in the same direction, towards the Hunters' square.

"Wha's tha noise?" Graf asked, choking.

"The Hunters," she said and took his hand again. There didn't seem any point in asking him how he could possibly not know about the Hunters' horn, especially not now.

If she had been close enough to her alley, she would have hidden under her cart and ignored the horn, with her fingers in her ears. But in the dead center of the market, someone would surely see them moving in the wrong direction. She pulled Graf with her, out into the steadily growing throng of grim figures.

The Indigo had two reasons for making an announcement: to set new laws, such as the last one which had forbidden anyone to bring meals to the workers during the day, or to simply read out a list of those who had been recently captured. They were never charged with being anything other than simply "enemies of the Indigo". But everyone knew what they were.

The Hunters' horn was blaring again, sounding like the roar of a beast, as Eine and Graf reached the square. The sky was a flat gray over the heads of the crowd, low with heavy clouds. Several people stomped on her bare feet, but Eine barely noticed. She did feel Graf squeezing her hand. Then her stomach suddenly ached as the giants rode out onto the enormous platform, thundering across the planks of wood on their large shaggy horses. For as long as Eine could remember, proximity to the Hunters caused her stomach pain and nausea. It gave her plenty of warning when they were near, so it was useful, but it certainly added to her disgust. She felt Graf cowering against her now at the sight of them.

The Hunters were two heads taller than the tallest Thelans, and so muscled and broad-shouldered that they were nearly as wide across as two men. They had long, tangled dark hair much like their horses, and they wore brown helmets and brown pants only, their broad chests blindingly white in the sun. They carried whips and chains, and their dark eyes were humorless, feral. No one knew where they had come from; Eine had heard that they'd just appeared the day the Indigo had taken over. It could not have been long afterwards that she'd lost her parents.

The Hunters rode to a stop at the edge of the platform and reared their horses, which uttered short, awful cries and shook their heads as if half-crazed. Eine clung to her stomach, watching, as the Thelans near her shuffled nervously on their feet.

The Indigo had a leader, Eine had heard people say. But no one had seen him. The Hunters and the men in blue came out to do his work.

One of the Hunters wore a necklace of animal teeth and carried the long, conical horn that announced their arrival. He dismounted and stepped up to face the crowd. There was no roll of paper in his fist this time and Eine squinted up at him, apprehensive, as the dried meat she had just eaten seemed to roll over inside her. No list of names? Had something new become forbidden?

There was never any preamble to these announcements. "The Indigo has determined that there are new enemies in Thela," the Hunter bellowed. Eine frowned. This, she hadn't heard before.

It was always the same enemy, the Indigo's one true target, of which nearly all had disappeared.

"There are spies among us. Foreigners have broken into our sealed city, and they must be found!" the Hunter continued. The crowd broke out in gasps, which echoed Eine's own. *Foreigners?* People from outside of Thela? Her eyes flashed towards the faces around her. She saw that everyone else was doing the same. Their eyes met hers and then tore away to examine others.

Eine suddenly felt like laughing. The idea was absurd. Who in the world would want to sneak into Thela?

"All Thelans who find evidence of someone from a foreign city *will* report them to the Indigo. Anyone caught aiding a foreigner *will* be put to death! All foreigners will be found and *destroyed!*" Saliva spat from the Hunter's mouth as he barked the last words, running out of breath. Most of the announcements were delivered this way, spat out as quickly as possible, and with very few details, as if the Hunters could barely stand to be amongst them. But this time the air had begun to feel very thick in the square, fear and excitement mingling like smoke over the heads of the crowd. Eine felt smothered by it.

The Hunter turned and mounted his horse as if he'd been born to ride. Almost as one, the rest of them whipped their giant steeds around, leading their heavy hooves away from the platform's edge. The horn sounded again as the Hunters thundered away, their horses smashing through whatever carts and shelters might have blocked their path out of the square. Eine did not even know where they came from, or where they went. The ground shook in the square as they rode away, and the crowd broke into a hundred frightened factions, jabbering to each other about the strange news.

Eine stood there in a daze as the people brushed past her. There were spies from other cities inside Thela. Or at least there was one, who had either been seen or captured. But why were they here? Was it possible that someone was trying to stop the Indigo? The idea was so incredible, so impossible and wonderful that Eine was afraid to even think it. Were there people out there, somewhere, who were not afraid? …Who were trying to help? Graf tugged on her sleeve, nervously. She pulled him away from the crowd, feeling dazed, and leaned against a low wall, overwhelmed.

"Eine, wha' happened?" Graf whispered. She turned to look at him absently. If other cities were planning to attack the Indigo, did they understand how powerful it was? Did the outside world even know what it had done?

The Indigo murdered Laxens. They hunted them down and made them disappear, along with anyone who helped them, or anyone who disagreed.

The only things Eine understood about the world were hiding, stealing, sleeping and keeping to herself. She knew what she was, and that it was a secret to keep safe. She knew she was only half - a Demi, as the Thelans called it - and that this was the reason why she could blend in as easily as she did. She knew that her parents were gone, and that one had been a full-blooded Laxen. That was really all there was.

The Laxen were gifted. They were humans, but they had many special abilities, varying widely by individual, that set them far apart. Eine knew little of their abilities in general, because she had never, in memory, seen a full-blood Laxen in her life. But it was that side of her heritage that gave her unusual strength, impossible weightlessness, and her unlikely mix of dark eyes and light hair. It was the Laxen blood that caused her to hear others' thoughts, however quick and intermittently.

Eine slid slowly down the wall into a slump on the ground, thinking. She hugged her knees. She had to keep her eyes open, even wider now. If there were foreign spies here, in Thela, then she had to find them. And she had to help.

"Eine..!" Graf was whining now, peering into her face. She shook herself and stood up.

"It's okay," she said. "Let's get out of here."

***

They walked hand in hand back towards Eine's alley, as if they were brother and sister, she imagined. She wondered what had happened to Graf's family, and how he had not learned on his own about the way things were. She glanced down at the boy again as they walked and wondered if he had any Laxen blood. She didn't think so. It was more likely that his parents had abandoned him because they had too many mouths to feed. Or perhaps they had just fallen sick and died, leaving him alone. A small pang struck Eine's heart at the thought.

"Graf, where did you sleep last night?" she asked.

He looked up, surprised, and then appeared to think about it for a moment. He frowned, as Eine watched him, and finally shook his head.

"I don' know," he said, sounding worried.

"You mean you don't know which street?" she asked. They had reached her alley now and she turned in, scanning automatically for any intruders.

"Yeah…" Graf said, thoughtfully. "I mean I don' know *if* ih was a stree." It took Eine a moment to understand, and then she looked back at him, startled. "I don' remember ih ah all, actually." He frowned again and looked around the alley's afternoon shadows. "I remember being here and being hungry. I remember wandering around for a long time before I saw you," he finished.

"And before that? In the morning?" Eine asked, suddenly uneasy. He shook his head. "You don't remember how you got to my alley?"

"No," he said, sounding irritated. He looked like he was opting for anger over fear. "Diden I juss tell you?"

Eine studied him for a long moment. "Did someone hit you on the head?"

"I don' remember!" he yelled.

"Shhh!" she hissed back. He sat down on top of a box in a huff while Eine stared at him. A nameless worry was beginning to settle in her gut. Something was wrong here but it was beyond her comprehension, and that made her nervous.

At that moment, someone's thoughts interrupted hers: *"This place is like a maze. How can there be mines here?"*

Eine gasped and spun around. There was no one in sight. The voice belonged to the same man she had heard before, she was sure of it. It was a young man, older than her, but not by very much. He had to be nearby.

"Wha'?" Graf asked, alarmed. "Wha' is ih?"

'How can there be mines here?' Eine turned and stared down the opposite end of her alley, the dark end. It stretched on ahead through the close brick buildings. It was in that direction that she had followed the thieves to the factories, and along the way, the alleys had turned and widened and narrowed, between the staggered houses with their shuttered windows.

This man was wandering through the alleys, looking for the mines.

"A foreigner," Eine murmured.

"You're always saying things I don' understand," Graf said wearily. He yawned and Eine turned back to look at him, her thoughts spinning. If a foreign spy was out there, lost among the alleys, then she could find him. She could head for the mines right now, and maybe, if she got closer to him, she could hear his thoughts again.

"Wha you gonna do now?" Graf asked. Eine considered, watching him with her dark brown eyes. She couldn't leave him on his own while his memory was gone. He would never survive alone. "Why are you juss staring at me?" he exclaimed.

She shook herself out of her reverie and then strode over to him. "Let's go," she said, pulling his arm.

The rain began to fall once more as she pulled him after her, leading him away from the safety of her overturned cart and the surrounding debris, into the yawning shadows of the city beyond. She was leaving all that was familiar, and this time she would not run back, afraid.

THREE

"So why can' I talk abow… the Laxens?" Graf whispered the last two words, dramatically.

Eine glanced around at the walls on either side of them, but she saw only the usual shuttered windows. She hesitated and then whispered back, "You *must* know that the Indigo killed all the Laxens." Graf stopped and stared up at Eine, his mouth open. She shook her head in disbelief. He really didn't know!"They're still hunting Demi's, and anyone trying to protect them."

"Killed the Laxens?" Graf hissed. "They're stronger than Laxens?!" Eine shushed him and shook her head again, continuing on.

"You have to know this, everyone does," she insisted. "Something happened to you and you forgot." He shook his head at her, his green eyes huge.

"Buh why?" he whispered.

"No one knows why, or how."

Graf was quiet for a moment. "Grey gods," he muttered. It took Eine a moment to recognize that he'd meant to say '*great* gods', the common expression. She thought of something then and turned to face him.

"Is your name really Graf or is it *Graft?*" she asked.

"Wha'?" he asked, bewildered. Eine laughed suddenly, and both the sound and the feeling surprised her. Her laugh was out of use. It was scratchy and hollow-sounding, but it felt somehow nice, and Graf took her hand again, companionably.

"You laugh like my sister," he said.

Eine's ears perked up, encouraged. "You have a sister? Where is she?"

Graf's brow wrinkled up in thought. He seemed to almost have it for a second, but then he shook his head. "Nah here," he said.

"What's her name?"

"Grissa," he replied, automatically.

Eine looked up and saw that the alley turned sharply just up ahead. A building on one side was wider than all the ones before it, forcing the bend. The rain had ceased again but the path ahead remained cast in shadow. In truth, what she always thought of as her alley had only been hers on one end. The rest was unknown and unsafe.

Her imagination tried to furnish an image of someone from another city, traveling through here. What would a foreigner look like? Was he a giant like the Hunters? Was his hair some strange color?

"Where's your family?" Graf asked. As he spoke, his little fingers reached into her pocket and pulled out the piece of dried meat again.

Eine flinched automatically and then relaxed. He tore off a chunk and handed it to her first. She still felt odd about having laughed. "I don't think I have brothers or sisters," she said, biting into the meat. "My parents died."

Graf gasped and looked up at her, his mouth full. She shook her head, embarrassed. "It's okay. I don't remember."

"Buh you're all alone then," he said, sounding worried. *So are you...?* Eine thought, and then wondered if he'd forgotten that as well.

"Well...you seem to be hanging around," she said, as sternly as she could. Graf looked up again, startled. Eine smiled in a stiff sort of way. Then he saw that she was teasing and he grinned, showing his straight teeth. He held her hand again and she squeezed it. It was different being with someone, Eine realized. It was better somehow.

The rain started up again, as was inevitable, and it came down harder, tap dancing across the tin roofs on either side of them. Eine felt lulled by the familiar sound, but Graf shivered and put his hands over his ears.

"Why does ih keep raining?" he wailed. Eine gaped at him.

"Sometimes, I swear…" she said, shaking her head, "it's like you've never even been here before!"

And then a man appeared in front of them. Eine flinched and Graf shrieked. One moment they'd been alone and now he was standing there, so close that he could touch them. A man in a deep blue uniform.

Eine grabbed Graf's shoulders and whirled around, but the Indigo man was faster. He threw his arms around Graf's waist and lifted him off the ground. Eine cried out as he turned and ran with the boy. She dashed after them. Then they disappeared.

Eine stopped short and stared into the semi-darkness. There was no sign of either Graf or the Indigo. She spun around wildly, looking for doors in the brick walls around her, but there were none. Horrified, she dropped to her knees on the wet ground. The Indigo man had appeared out of nowhere, out of thin air. He had grabbed a harmless little boy and then vanished. *Why??*

Eine's heart pounded against her chest as she realized it could have been her. In fact, it should've been her! Graf wasn't a Demi; he was just a little Dredge who didn't know anything. He didn't even know… She gasped, as she knelt there in the rain, her own words coming back to her. *'It's like you've never been here before.'*

Graf was a foreign child! The way that he talked…! It was an accent! Eine stared around her in astonishment. She had been leading a foreign child around the city, right under the Hunters' noses! But who would bring a little boy into Thela with them? Surely not someone trying to infiltrate the Indigo? Was it possible that Graf could be a spy himself? Was he just pretending to have lost his memory?

A crazy thought struck Eine as she sat there. Was Graf somehow not actually a child? Her imagination failed her after a moment, and then she snorted, getting up.If he was a spy, he wasn't a very good one. No, Graf was truly a little boy, lost and hungry, with no idea what was going on. And now, he was in the hands of the Indigo. Her heart sank as she stood there with the rain soaking through her cloak. She had been his only friend and she had failed to protect him. He had been her...friend. She had had a friend.

She felt her eyes sting as she trudged forward. There was nothing she could do for him now. If only she could hear the foreigner's thoughts again; if only she could control it! Was he the one who had brought Graf into the city? Maybe he'd lost him and was trying to find him. She started walking faster, dragging the back of her hand across her eyes. Whatever the result, finding the foreigner was the only real option now. It was a far cry better than running back to her overturned cart and hiding from the world.

***

Eine walked for a long time along the passage, following its turns. Sometimes there were small piles of debris under the dark windows, as if the people inside had thrown their garbage out into the alley. Sometimes rats scuttled across the ground and into the shadows. The rain slackened off again and she wrung out her sleeves and the end of her cloak.

She came across a pile of broken furniture and picked through it, finding a loose table leg that seemed useful. It was made of solid dark wood and it had a knobbed end that made a good handle. She wondered briefly who traded such materials with Thela, and how. Somehow, at 'the Docks', outside goods were brought in and collected by the merchants. She wiped the table leg clean and tucked it into the cord that kept her cloak tied around her. She felt better with the wood tapping against her leg as she walked. She would not be caught unaware again.

It was not long afterwards that Eine heard noises up ahead. She froze and listened, her hand resting on the table leg at her waist. The sun was beginning to set behind the alley walls and she felt a sudden quake at meeting anyone now, just as it was getting dark.

There was a scuffling sound in the near distance, as if around the next bend. She heard a voice suddenly, cursing, and her heart beat faster as she realized it was some sort of fight. She darted forward, hearing another voice cry out as she rounded the corner quickly.

There were two Dredges fighting in the middle of the alley. One was thin and wore a tattered gray cloak and the other was tall and broad-shouldered, wearing a much nicer brown cloak. Eine watched as the tall one shoved the other to the ground. He fell clinging to something tightly in his hands.

The man in the brown cloak spotted Eine and turned back to the one on the ground. "What is this, your partner?" he growled. Eine gasped, staring at him. His voice!

The tattered man leapt up and ran towards Eine, clearly attempting to pass her. She saw that what he held was a small loaf of bread. Without hesitation, she yanked the table leg out from her cloak and struck him across the head. The man yelped and stumbled, dropping his prize. He gave her one astonished look – she ducked under the shelter of her hood - and then he ran pell-mell back down the alley.

Eine sighed and retrieved the bread from the ground. She had no sympathy for Dredges who stole from each other, even if this one was not truly even Thelan. She glanced at the man in the brown cloak now, warily.

He was motionless, watching her. "Now I guess it's yours, huh, boy?" he said, irritated. It was indeed the same voice she had heard in her head. It was raspier aloud, but it came from the same mind. Eine smiled.

She had found him.

"I'm not a boy." She tossed the bread to the foreigner and he missed it, startled. In the growing dark, and with his hood pulled up, she could not make out his features, but she could see he was not frail at all like a Dredge.

"…And not a thief," he commented, bending down slowly to pick up his food.

"Dredges aren't really thieves," Eine told him. "They're just starving."

He looked at her for a moment. "*They're* just starving? What are you?"

She hesitated. Then she looked around at the quiet alley, all her senses alert. "I'm like you," she said softly.

The foreigner stiffened immediately. He turned on his heel, striding away. "I don't know what you're talking about, kid," he said over his shoulder. "But you better stay away from me."

Eine hurried after him, her heart leaping into her throat. They hustled down the path in silence for a few moments before he spun around again.

"Why are you following me?" he demanded. His hand was inside his coat, and Eine realized he must have a weapon as well.

"I need to talk to you," she said, and as soon as she spoke, she suddenly knew how to tell him.

"I'm not talking to anyone," he said, with clenched teeth.

Eine stepped forward boldly and he tensed. "Where are you going?" she asked, raising her voice.

"None of your business," he hissed, stepping forward as well.

"What business could you possibly have out here? In the evening?" She kept her voice pitched just loud enough so that she knew he would be paranoid about it.

"If you don't stop asking questions, little girl, I'll be forced to shut you up." His voice was steadier now and fierce, and Eine felt a small pang of intimidation, despite her ability. Perhaps he was a Demi like her. Perhaps he could hurt her.

She stepped forward regardless, prepared to find that out. "I'm not a little girl," she retorted. "And I'd like to see you try it."

To her surprise, the foreigner launched himself straight at her. His shoulder met her neck, and she hit the ground hard, her head banging against it painfully. The foreigner's weight was heavy on top of her, but he made a strange sound and sat up quickly. She knew why. They had fallen further away than he'd expected – and harder - because she weighed so little.

She sprang up then, knocking him over. She swung a kick but he caught her foot, surprising her; the force of the kick still knocked him onto his back and Eine fell with him. Then they were in a heap on the ground, Eine sprawled across his long limbs.

The foreigner scrambled to his feet a moment later and stared down at Eine, his mouth open. She got up more slowly and shook some of the dirt from her cloak. The back of her head was pounding and she had pulled a leg muscle. The foreigner stepped closer to her and she flinched. Then he flinched. The two of them stared at each other in the dark. Up close, Eine could just make out his face: he was square-jawed, dark-eyed, and scarred. Several long scars ran down his cheeks and his jaw line. His skin was darker than hers, tanned from the sun somewhere where it didn't rain so much.

"What are you?" he whispered. He was studying her face as well and Eine felt suddenly shy, as she had when Graf had asked her name.

"I want to help," she said quietly.

The foreigner straightened up, which made him two heads taller than Eine. He kept his eyes on her. "You must be a Fourth," he muttered. A Fourth was someone who had a Laxen for a grandparent. Eine didn't correct him, afraid to speak the truth out loud. She had never said it aloud. No good could ever have come from it.

The foreigner turned away, muttering to himself. He turned back again in a moment, his arms folded across his chest. "How did you know what I am?" he asked softly.

Eine tapped the side of her head and whispered, "I can hear things...sometimes." His eyes widened. "I heard you earlier today and I came looking."

He nodded and started to walk forward again, continuing down the alley. Eine picked up her fallen table leg and followed, tying it back into her cloak cord. He stopped before long and turned to her again, as if undecided. "Listen, it's not safe for you to travel with me," he said, sincerely. "You're better off hiding."

"It's not safe for me anywhere," Eine told him. "I'm tired of hiding."

He studied her again, frowning. "How old are you?"

"Not much younger than you," she retorted. She wasn't sure of that at all, in fact.

The foreigner snorted and started walking away again. "I can't protect you and I don't have supplies for you." He didn't stop this time or look back at her.

"Supplies?" Eine asked, mystified.

"Food, water," he snapped.

Eine almost smiled. The idea of needing someone to bring those things to her! "I can get my own," she told him.

"Is that right?" he said, in sheer disbelief.

"I've been doing it my whole life."

The foreigner stopped and stared at her again. "You've lived on the street your whole life?" he asked, his tone altered.

Eine nodded. "I don't need you to help me," she said, as clearly as she could. "I want to help *you*." She thought he smiled then but she couldn't quite make it out in the dark.

"I appreciate it, kid," he said. His voice sounded kinder now. "But I don't need your help."

Eine folded her arms and met his gaze, despite his greater height. It was her turn to project disbelief and she launched into it.

"What is your story for being down here? What are you going to say to the workers if you run into them near the factories? What about the tin mines? Are you going to cross them? Because I've heard there's quicksand. How will you get yourself out of it alone?" She stopped and coughed, her throat feeling scratchy. It was the longest speech she could ever remember making. And it felt good.

FOUR

The foreigner was visibly startled. He stared off down the alley, and scratched his head through his hood. Eine felt hopeful while he muttered something to himself. It was in another language, she realized, and she strained to catch it. The words sounded gruff, guttural, with a hard clicking sound.

"People *never* go beyond the alleys at night?" he asked, ungraciously.

"There's no reason to," Eine said, hugging herself. "But maybe a worker could go back if he left something behind. I think we could use that as a reason, if someone asks." She hadn't yet heard that one declared forbidden by the Hunters.

"Who's going to ask?" the foreigner queried. She shrugged. He stared at her for a long moment, considering. Then he began walking again, as if resigned. Eine followed, flooded with relief. She had done it. He was letting her come with him.

They walked side by side for a long time, in silence. The foreigner's steps made little sound and Eine wondered if he'd been trained to be so quiet. Her own light steps were naturally silent. The night deepened around them and Eine peered into the darkness ahead, worried. They had come a long way already.

She suddenly thought of Graf and turned to the foreigner eagerly. "Did you have a boy with you, who got lost?" she asked. He looked at her, surprised, and shook his head.

"What boy?"

Eine frowned, feeling more confused than ever. At that moment, they both heard a faint clanking sound in the distance and the foreigner's head jerked up.

"The factories," Eine said, nervously.

"Have you ever been this far?" he asked. She nodded. "What happened?"

"I ran back," she said, her chin jutting out defiantly. He said nothing, but her heart sank as she followed him, knowing he probably thought she was a coward. She struggled silently to find the words to tell him that the fact she'd gone at all already set her apart from most Thelans.

But with his scarred face, she wasn't sure he'd understand such a small feat of bravery. The clanking grew louder very quickly and soon Eine could see smoke rising above the tin roofs ahead of them. She glanced at the foreigner and saw that his hand was resting on something at his hip again, under his coat. He met her eyes, expectantly.

"We could be brother and sister," she said, thinking quickly. Although she looked like a Dredge and he didn't, not quite. "I could be keeping you company, while you go back to get your..." She wracked her brain for another moment.

"Spectacles," he finished. "I can't see without them. You're my eyes." Eine nodded, impressed. "What's your name?" he asked.

"Eine." It was already less strange to say it aloud, after the first time. "What's yours?"

"Give me a Thelan name," he said. She tried to remember a man's name she had heard recently, other than Graf.

"Weil," she said, hesitantly. She was sure that was the name she had heard an old woman using, while scolding a child. The alley turned again, and then ended abruptly, opening up like a wide doorway. A tall building rose up into the night sky on their left, and another one rose up on the right. Even in the dark, she could see that they were uniformly built and window-less. Smoke drifted from one of the roofs, high above, but everything was now silent. The clanking had stopped.

Eine wasn't sure when the day ended for the workers. It was a blessing that they hadn't run into any of them going home through the very alley they were in. The foreigner stepped out from the shelter of the alley's brick walls and surveyed their new surroundings. Glancing down, Eine noticed sand scattered lightly across the smooth cobblestones. She felt her heart begin to beat faster. She tiptoed after the foreigner, her hand on her own 'weapon'.

It felt very much now like the buildings and the dark sky had eyes.

"Which way are the mines?" the foreigner whispered. Eine pointed past the two buildings that loomed ahead. She knew only that the tree she had seen was beyond them, but it was too dark to see it now.

The sudden sound of a door slamming made them both freeze in place. They listened for a moment, as faint footsteps sounded on the cobblestones and then faded away. Someone leaving work late? There was so little that Eine knew, she wondered now how much help she could really be. The foreigner was striding forward and she rushed to catch up to him.

Suddenly, she felt a lurch in her stomach that stopped her in her tracks. She spun around, eyeing the two dark buildings and empty stretches of cobblestones. All was quiet.

"What is it? " the foreigner asked.

"Hunters," she muttered, putting a hand on her stomach. He tensed and listened.

"I don't hear anything."

Eine didn't either. She looked around again, wondering if she could be wrong. "Let's hurry," she said and started to run. The foreigner followed.They dashed around the corner of the building on the right and then Eine caught her breath as she spotted the tall, straggly tree, silhouetted against the sky. Empty, black sky. There were no more buildings beyond it. Turning, she saw the foreigner standing with his coat drawn back, revealing the weapon at his belt. It was an odd, angled object. He was staring back behind them.

Then she heard horses. The sound of giant hooves crashing against cobblestone broke through the stillness, and Eine jumped in her skin. The foreigner turned towards her, his arm outstretched. A light flashed on in a distant window, as Eine spun on her heels. He grabbed her arm and they ran together, the thundering sound of the Hunters' horses loud and clear behind them.

Eine suddenly stumbled into sand and the foreigner fell into her, almost knocking them over. Her brain was spinning desperately. Where had they come from? How did they know the two of them were here? Had the Indigo been watching?

They couldn't outrun them. They had to hide. They could hide here in the mines, where the Hunters would at least fear falling into a mine shaft, or quicksand.

She spotted a low-lying cluster of thickets in the distance, across the sandy ground. Beyond it was darkness. She ran for it, leaping over any patch of ground that seemed unbroken and smooth.All she knew about quicksand was what she'd overheard in the market. She ran past the entrances to mine shafts, blurred and dark, gaping like open mouths in the sand. She was out in the unknown now, leaving walls and paved ground behind her. She had plunged into a great wide blackness!It was as exhilarating as it was terrifying. The ghostly shape of the thicket ahead was zooming closer when the foreigner let out a sudden cry. She spun around to see him floundering in the sand, oddly reduced in height.

"Stop moving," she hissed and he froze, his arms up in the air. In the fading light of the city behind them, she could see the massive shapes of the Hunters on horseback, thundering across the cobblestone courtyard. She knew they couldn't make her out among the vague shapes of thickets and scattered trees in the sand, not just yet.

"How do I get out of this?" the foreigner hissed back. He had grabbed hold of a thorny bush that dangled over the smooth pocket of quicksand. The ground shuddered as the Hunters surged closer. Their horses' hooves were now pounding on sand.

Eine took a breath and acted on impulse. She slid feet-first into the quicksand with the foreigner. She sunk in to her waist. Barely registering his look of shock, she grasped the branches of the overhanging bush and pulled the thorns and leaves down over the two of them. She hoped the branches were enough to cover them up in the dark.

The foreigner was motionless next to her as the Hunters crossed the sand. Eine listened to the muted footfalls of the horses. Her fingers were stinging from the thorns she gripped tightly. Her legs and hips began to feel numb from the tight suction of the sand. It was a gradual, slow squeezing. It was a vacuum, she had heard people say, but it was triggered by movement.

The Hunters barked at each other in a strange language, the sounds coming closer. Eine's heart pounded in her ears. She flinched when the foreigner suddenly placed his hand over her bleeding fingers. He took hold of the branches himself and she exhaled silently in relief.

A horse's high-pitched cry went up among the Hunters, much closer than Eine had even imagined. A deep voice gave a yell and others responded. The sounds of thrashing in sand and brush followed, and Eine knew one of them had stepped in quicksand. A long moment of what sounded like orders and argument followed, punctuated by the horse's cries and more thrashing.

A sudden blaze of light filled the sky around them and Eine's heart sank. A torch. They would be seen now.The foreigner tensed next to her. The light moved towards the sound of the frightened horse, followed by a heavy thump as its rider leapt to the ground. There were more arguments and shouts, and then dragging, scraping sounds as they tried to pull the horse from the sinking sand.

No one shone the light in their direction.

The poor beast shrieked terribly as it sank lower into the sand. Eine closed her eyes, her stomach feeling sick. The ground began to shake with the sounds of the other horses moving again, pounding away. They were leaving the trapped horse behind. It screamed again as the Hunters rode past Eine and the foreigner, lighting up more torches as they went.

The giant horse screamed and then made a choking sound. After a few agonizing moments, it suddenly went silent. Eine gasped and tried to see its dark shape through the branches. The foreigner slowly released them, clearing her view. There was no sign of the horse. She turned her head and saw the Hunters' torches blazing in the distance.

"It only sucks you in if you move?" the foreigner whispered, startling Eine. She nodded. He turned his head carefully, surveying the sand that was now up to his chest. "But we have to move to get out."

"Hang on," Eine said. She reached for a stronger branch near the base of the bush hanging over them. The movement sank her slightly deeper. She remembered the conversations she had overheard, both out loud and internally.

'You have to pull yourself out slowly, inch by inch. You have to be very strong.'

She took a deep breath and pulled with all her strength, for just one moment. She felt a pop somewhere beneath her and slid just a little out of the sand. She took another breath and did it again, this time emerging further.

Watching her, the foreigner followed suit and braced himself to pull with all his might. He rose an imperceptible amount as Eine hauled herself halfway out of the sand. She was shaking now, feeling the strain in her arms. She grasped onto another bush further away.

"How are you doing that?" he demanded.

"Hang on," she repeated. The plant nearly came uprooted as she peeled her legs inch by inch from the vacuum of the quicksand. She rolled onto the ground afterwards with a sigh of relief and lay there for a moment, feeling overwhelmed. She was covered in fine sand and grit.

A vast, clear sky full of stars greeted her as she looked up from that position. It was a shock. The sky had always been cloudy, as long as she could remember. She could usually only spot a few stars at night.

"I really don't want to end up like the horse," the foreigner said, sounding grumpy. Eine sat up and offered him her hand.

"You won't." She closed her fingers around his hand, which was large and tough, and got to her feet to brace herself. In a few quick pulls, she had hauled him out with much more ease than she had rescued herself.

The foreigner slid out of the sand with a startled expression. Eine let go and he leapt up into a crouch, staring at her. She gazed back at him, exhausted, and then looked off into the distance towards the tiny dots of torch light. The terrified scream of another sinking horse shot through the night.

"They could come back this way," she said. The foreigner nodded.

"We need to keep out of that torchlight." He stood up and brushed some of the sand off his coat. "Can we get to the Docks before dawn?" he asked. The Docks! They were going to the Docks? Eine shook her head, wide-eyed, staring at him.

"I don't know," she said.

"All right. Let's find out."

***

Sleep began to tug at Eine's eyelids as they crossed the sands in the dark. They lost track of the Hunters' torches after awhile, and she kept her ears strained for any sounds. She led the way, carefully searching the ground for large smooth patches of sand. The foreigner was stepping on as many rocks and plant life as he could find, just to be sure. He showed no signs of fatigue, so Eine pushed herself.

The night was very still and the stars were infinite overhead. She glanced up at them as often as she could without slowing down. There was something so fascinating about them. She would have liked to lie down on her back and lose herself in the sight of those ghostly, impossible lights. She ate the last of her dried meat instead and squinted into the gloom ahead. Somewhere out there was the city wall. The idea of reaching it took her breath away.

The darkness was beginning to fade into gray when Eine suddenly stumbled, half-asleep. She realized she couldn't keep her eyes open. The foreigner caught her arm.

"Are you tired?" he said quickly. She nodded and murmured something she wasn't sure of herself. She had never felt so tired. She wanted desperately just to crawl back underneath the cart in her alley. The foreigner said something low that she couldn't hear, and then suddenly strong arms were lifting her up. She felt herself cradled like a small child. It was the oddest sensation, to be carried along, with no effort on her part at all. She struggled for a few seconds against a wave of sleep, but the warmth of the foreigner's arms and chest seemed to swallow her up. She closed her eyes.

Almost instantly, it seemed, she was dreaming again of drifting among the same dark trees. She felt the urgency; she felt rather than heard the woman's voice calling her. Her arms floated out to her sides, and her fingers brushed against the rough bark of the trees.

Then suddenly, tiny white lights burst into being beside the trees. They sparkled like stars, but they swirled about in the air like flies. Eine watched them, astonished, enchanted.

She awoke abruptly to a cold breeze across her face. Confused, she found herself surrounded by leaves and branches. Not her vague dream trees; these were very distinct and sunlight filtered through them. Was she still dreaming? Weren't they in the tin mines?

Eine sat up quick and then gasped. She was in a tree. She was high up in the air, in a tree, sitting in the yoke of several branches. Seized with dizziness, she looked down, and saw the sandy ground far below, barely visible through a thick mat of fat, succulent leaves. This tree was entirely different from the bare one on the edge of the tin mines. It was enveloped by a shield of the thick leaves and its trunk was covered haphazardly in spines. It dawned on Eine suddenly that she must be well-hidden here. She also realized something was around her ankle.

The foreigner gave a small snore from nearby. He was sleeping in an awkward position between two other branches, and there was a long rope tied around his waist. It stretched from him to the tree trunk where it was secured in a large knot. Then the remaining end of it was tied around Eine's ankle. Eine felt a sudden horror as she imagined waking up, hanging upside down by her foot. It was better than rolling over and dropping to her death…but still!

Feeling indignant, she leaned her head back against the rough bark of the tree, and listened carefully. After a long moment of stillness, a distant clanking sound reached her ears. She felt a small surge of excitement. The factories were carrying on as usual, far behind them. She heard no horses' hooves or Hunters' voices. She wondered how far the Docks were now, and she peered through the leaves carefully in that direction but she couldn't see anything.

Eine realized that the foreigner was lucky to have found this tree, stumbling around with her in the dark. How had he climbed it and carried her at the same time? He must be very resourceful. He must have been carrying the long rope somewhere under his jacket. She gazed at him now and he snored lightly again, his hands resting folded in his lap. He had pushed back his hood, and even though the light under the leaves gave his face a greenish tint, she could see his features now better than before.

She had been right about his skin; it was very brown from the sun.His jaw was square and his nose was round, kind of flat. His short-cropped hair was dark brown and his mouth was a thin sharp line. One long pale scar ran up each side of his face, asymmetrical to each other. Another short scar ran diagonally across his chin. Eine could not imagine how he could've been cut that way and not killed. Unless the attacker had not meant to kill him.

When he didn't move for several seconds, she sighed again to herself. It was a truly odd feeling to think that no one could see her. She was perfectly hidden. She raised a tentative hand and pushed back her gray hood, feeling the light breeze stir through her hair. It felt wonderful. She brushed the remaining sand from her hands and then ran her fingers through her hair, letting the nearly white strands fall loosely. A sigh escaped her lips and she glanced at the foreigner again to reassure herself that he hadn't moved.

They could spend the day here peacefully, and then head out again after nightfall. Eine's stomach rumbled with hunger and she felt in her pockets. They were empty. She felt eyes on her suddenly and she glanced up, tensing. He was awake now, and he was staring at her. His brown eyes were wide. Eine snatched up her hood and pulled it low over her face, her heart pounding. She pulled her legs up carefully and hugged her knees for a moment, calming herself. Then she met his eyes again. This time he had an odd expression on his face, one that she couldn't read.

He blew his breath out slowly. "You're light as air, but strong enough to pull me out of quicksand, and you look –" He stopped then and seemed sheepish. "It's a good thing you keep your hood up," he finished. He averted his eyes and then suddenly cracked a huge yawn, leaning his head back precariously. "Been a long time since I slept in a tree," he said. "I bet it's your first time."

Eine nodded emphatically and peeked down through the branches again, down to the ground.

"Bet you're scared, huh, kid?" he said, grinning. Eine gave him a withering look.

"Thank you for tying me by the *foot*," she said coldly. He smiled, splitting the scars across his face and revealing crooked teeth. It gave him a much younger look. Eine nearly smiled back.

"It was too hard to reach your waist. I was tired." He dug in his cloak pockets and produced a packet of dried meat and the bread that had almost been stolen before. Eine's mouth immediately watered at the sight of it. "I'm surprised you didn't wake me up with a drop and a shriek." He glanced up with another grin and caught her expression. She swallowed and looked away quickly. "Here, I'm not going to starve you," he said. His voice was suddenly softer, and Eine turned to see that he was holding out the packet of meat to her.

"Thank you," she muttered, reaching across. She stuffed a piece into her mouth and tasted an unfamiliar flavor. She glanced down at the meat in surprise. It was spicy and a little sweet. It was wrapped in a translucent paper, and it was definitely not from the Thelan market.

"Lucky we found a water-tree. I can squeeze some juice out of these leaves," the foreigner was saying. "No sign of the Hunters, at least while I was awake. Maybe they think we got caught in the quicksand. We have a few hours until sunset, so you better get your rest while you can."

Eine took another bite of the good meat and studied him. Her mind was spinning with a thousand questions, with excitement, with disbelief. Where did he come from? Why was he here? How old was he? What was his life like?

"What is your name?" she asked, chewing. The foreigner gave her a wary look and folded his arms across his chest.

"Nevermind. You couldn't pronounce it." He closed his eyes. Eine stared at him, surprised.

"How do you know that?" she asked.

"No one can. No one outside of Creede," he told her. *Creede.* Eine turned the word over in her mind, greedily. It was another city. It was part of the outside world. She folded the meat packet back up and kept it in her lap, listening to the breeze rustling around them.

"Then what do I call you?" she asked, after a moment. The foreigner stirred, sleepily.

"Whatever you want," he mumbled. Eine actually smiled at that, thinking it wasn't likely to last long.

"How about Scar?" she said and his brown eyes snapped open to glare at her. She felt herself grin wider than she thought she could. Her dry lips cracked. She closed her mouth quickly and licked them.

"If I didn't know better, I'd guess *your* name means 'rude'," he said casually, and closed his eyes again. Eine looked up, confused.

"Does that mean you do know what it means?" she asked. He gave her a surprised look.

"Eine? Yeah, it's like 'a crossing', or 'passage'." He resettled himself as Eine stared at him, turning over the words. She had never known that before. She rested her head against the bark again and thought about her dream of lights in a forest. Then she sighed and closed her own eyes. Maybe she would just call him No-Name.

FIVE

Eine awoke to the sound of a long, far-off whistle. She sat up with a jerk and caught hold of a small branch near her, to steady herself. Noname was shadowed now in the semi-darkness of evening. He was peering out through the leaves back towards the factories.

"The workers must be going home," Eine said, her voice gruff with sleep. Noname turned to look back at her.

"It's time to move," he said.

They began a careful descent down the large tree, both of them glancing around frequently for signs of movement in the darkness. The tin mines spread out around them once more in a grainy expanse, broken by vague shapes. The tree trunk was tough and spined, so it was difficult going. Eine used her toes to help her cling to its surface. She was almost to the ground when she heard Noname swear softly in his own language. She looked over at him and saw that he was staring at her bare feet. He must have been too tired to notice how tough they were when he'd tied the rope around her ankle. He gave her an amazed look and then dropped the rest of the way to the ground.

Eine had noticed that he wore boots like the Thelans, but she could see that they were different: thicker, with buckles on the sides. A few Dredges managed to salvage boots but most of them lived on their rough-soled feet. She half-scrabbled and half-slid down the last of the tree trunk and landed on the ground. Ahead of her, Noname began to pick his way carefully across the sand. Eine squinted around them in the dim light, still feeling a little groggy. Despite being in a tree, she couldn't remember the last time she had slept so deeply. Perhaps because she had felt safer.

It wasn't long before Noname stumbled into quicksand again. Eine smiled as the foreigner struggled silently for a moment, sinking a bit. Then he stood still, as if in defeat, and reached out for help. She caught his large hands and planted her feet, drawing him slowly out. She stumbled backwards then, and they sprawled in the safer sand for a moment. Noname sprang up and brushed himself off. Eine got up and stepped in front of him, pointedly, to lead the way.

She heard a quiet snort behind her.

They continued on that way for what felt like a very long time. Eine chose each step carefully as the sky grew darker above them. Once or twice she thought she spotted the shape of another water-tree. She listened to Noname whispering occasionally to himself, in his coarse language.

"What was it like here?" she asked him, after awhile. "Before...?"

Noname looked up from watching his feet, but in the dark, she couldn't make out his expression. "Before the Indigo?" He said it so casually. She nodded. "Thela was a trading hub. And a leader in tin, unfortunately," he grumbled. "That's why Thelan's the most commonly spoken language in the world."

Eine stopped, surprised. "It is?"

He nodded again and cupped his hand around her elbow, guiding her forward. "That's why I speak it. This was a prosperous city, just fifteen years ago. I remember, when I was a kid, the women in my village made trips to Thela, to visit the markets. My father used to complain that my mother spent too much money here. All her glass ornaments." He was quiet for a moment, as if wistful. Eine envisioned the market as it was now, and frowned in disbelief. "There was a gate in the wall then, of course, and it didn't use to rain all the time either," he added, and she glanced up at him.

"What do you mean?"

He shrugged. "It started raining after the Indigo took over. No one knows why. Look, it's all dry out here. It's just in the city center." He stopped suddenly, and dropped her arm. Eine saw that he was looking up, staring out ahead of them. She followed his gaze and saw the enormous, looming dark shape of the city wall. It seemed to rise up taller than the factories behind them, but it was hard to tell, because the top of it faded uncertainly into the night sky. It stretched out in either direction, dwindling away again into the darkness.

"The wall," Eine breathed. They were at the edge already, the very sharp edge of her entire world. A strange tingling spilled over Eine as she stared at it. Her skin prickled with awareness.

"Good," Noname said simply. He started forward again and Eine walked hesitantly after him, still staring at the ominous shape. What would they find at the base of the wall? Where were the Docks?

"Did you say there's a gate?" she whispered after the foreigner.

"There was. The Indigo filled it in. We've got to meet my contact there. He'll help us get out."

Eine thought about that for a moment. "But how did you get in?" she demanded.

"It's a long story," he said, suddenly impatient. "No more questions, I'm concentrating on walking." He stumbled even as he spoke and grabbed at a nearby shrub for support.

They carried on in silence again for awhile. Eine concentrated on the nervous tingling she had felt a moment ago, dredging it up again, dwelling on it. It was excitement, a powerful new feeling that she wanted to hold onto. It was intoxicating when she focused on it.

"Did I leave the door unlatched?"

She started violently, and grabbed hold of Noname's coat. In a flash, the foreigner spun around and pulled out his weapon. He crouched, motionless, gripping the strange object in both hands, the long end pointed forward. The 'gun'? What did it do? Eine held her breath, staring at him, afraid. He was definitely a fighter, a soldier.

They stood that way for one long moment. Then he asked, barely audible, "What is it?"

"I heard someone," Eine whispered, shakily. *Someone's thoughts*, she added silently. "Someone is nearby." Noname cocked his head in the darkness, listening.

"Are you sure? I don't hear anything."

She looked around them, recalling the strange voice. It had sounded a little bit murky. Sleepy, even. She gazed over the foreigner's head at the wall. There were smaller shapes visible now, near the ground. Were they houses? "Do people live near the wall?" she asked, surprised.

Noname straightened up and studied her for a moment. "You couldn't possibly hear that far, kid. There's a merchant camp, but it's at the base of the wall."

Eine realized she had caught the stray thought of someone half-asleep, someone in the camp. "Nevermind," she whispered. They were getting close; it was no time to stand around now. She hurried forward, staring at the wall. She heard Noname mutter something behind her, and stow his weapon.

The moon was low in the sky by the time they reached the long row of shacks that stretched along the bottom of the city wall. These buildings were dwarfed by the vertical mass of solid pavement that rose up behind them. They were also roughly built and falling apart. Eine understood that they were temporary homes for the merchants who traveled here to purchase their goods. But how did they receive the goods from the outside if there was no entrance through the wall?

Noname stepped out of the sand and onto the paved ground with an obvious sigh of relief. No more quicksand.

"Where do we meet your contact?" Eine murmured. Dawn was not far away now and the thought made her nervous. They would not fit in here at all with traveling merchants. Suspicion would arise immediately. She had also never been so close to anything as tall or nerve-wracking as that dark city wall.

"I hope he's all right." Eine flinched and glanced at Noname, realizing she had just 'heard' his thoughts. He reached inside his coat and pulled out a small object. He raised it to his lips and made a small, hollow sound, a bit like the wind tunneling through an alley way. Eine stared up at him, fascinated. A few seconds later, an answering sound blew towards them. Noname set off at once in the direction of the noise, shoving his hood back at he went. Eine followed, breathless.

They crossed a dark courtyard that faced a row of the merchants' huts. Here and there a shabby tent was pitched, as if by poorer merchants. Noname stopped short by one of the tents that was set apart from the others, and gestured for Eine to stay back. Then he whispered, "Anda?"

The tent's door flap opened promptly and a peculiar face peered out at them. The face was long, thin, and wrinkled, with graying, reddish hair cropped close. A pair of bright eyes belied the age of the other features. The man smiled and his eyes seemed to dance for a moment. Then they fell on Eine and the smile disappeared.

"She's a friend," Noname whispered and pushed gently past the older man, into the tent. The latter gave Eine another worried look and then disappeared after him. She lifted the flap and saw the two of them crouching inside, patting each other on the back.The tent seemed just large enough for three people to lie down side by side and the roof was drooping onto Noname's head. Eine crawled in and tucked herself up as small as she could, just inside the door flap.

The older man wore a white collared shirt and black pants, with sturdy boots much like Noname's. He turned his brilliant blue gaze back on her and she saw comprehension in his expression. She looked away nervously.

"Anda, she's a Fourth," Noname said. "She's been hiding out in the city."

"No, Ney," Anda said softly. His voice was lighter, almost wispy. "She's more than that. At least half."

Eine saw, from the corner of her eye, Noname turn and stare at her. "Why didn't you tell me?" he demanded. She gave him a wary look and said nothing. Anda smiled and thumped Noname on the shoulder.

"In times like these, we don't go around volunteering such things. Besides, Ney, I would've thought you'd notice."

Eine looked up, realizing she'd heard what must be Noname's name twice now. She frowned at him. "I can pronounce *Ney*," she said, indignant. The two men looked at her blankly for a moment and then Noname laughed, a nice husky sound. He said something to Anda then, a long string of alien, melodic syllables. Eine listened, fascinated. It wasn't the guttural language he'd spoken to himself before. The older man chuckled and winked at him.

"Ney is a nickname for my young friend here," he told her.

"It means 'little one'. Creedens have rather melodramatic names, you see. Entire phrases, very indulgent."

"What?" Noname exclaimed. Eine was already grinning at the thought of him answering to 'little one'.

"I am Anda Leona from Enahala, which is where we're headed." He spoke more formally than Noname, and with a sing-song rhythm that was soothing. "What is your name?"

"Eine." It felt like a short, rough name compared to his.

"And are your parents alive?" he asked. She shook her head. Anda nodded wistfully and glanced back at Noname. "It's a wonder she's alive, Ney. She must come with us. We can learn more from her than any of these mind-sent missions."

"Well, I wasn't gonna leave her stranded outside the city wall," Noname said, grudgingly.

"I *have* been a big help," Eine reminded him. His face turned an embarrassed, red-brown, and Anda grinned.

"What do you call him, Eine?" he asked.

"Noname."

Anda chuckled. His friend jerked his head up in surprise, and Eine realized that she hadn't yet spoken it aloud. He gave her a half smile. Perhaps he didn't mind it.

"Well, rest up, both of you. We've got about an hour before the market begins stirring," Anda said. There was nowhere to stretch out, while anyone was sitting up, but Eine did the best she could, touching her toes to the rough material of the tent. She couldn't be tired now, anyway; her mind was whirling.

"What's the plan for the Docks?" Noname asked, folding his arms.

"All I've been able to come up with is the simple diversion plan. We've got to make a diversion, something very loud, and then hop down in through the grate.It sounds childish but from my observations, I think it's our best bet."

"How does the grate work?"

"Rather crudely," Anda said. "The merchants lift it up and drop their goods in. On this end, that is, for exports. There's another 'dock' about half a mile that way where goods are brought in. Several dock workers are assigned to fish out the goods from that grate, with long, hooked poles. A Hunter is stationed at each dock, of course, keeping a dull eye over the affairs…"

"The Hunters are here?" Eine exclaimed.

"There are four of them that guard the docks, yes."

"But what are the docks? What do the goods fall into?"

"Into the water," Anda said, surprised. She looked at him blankly. "There is an underground river, child, which forms a manmade loop under the city. It carries the objects in under the wall and passes underneath one grate, where the objects are retrieved. It turns the loop and then passes under the other grate, where objects are dropped into it to go back out." Eine stared at him, unable to imagine it. "The Indigo built this system the year after their coup."

"She's never been away from the city center, Anda," Noname said quietly.

"The Dredges don't know how things work," Eine said.

"Dredges?"

"Street people," Noname filled in. "Anda, look at her feet." The two of them gazed down at Eine's sandy feet, pressed against the inside of the tent. They were dark and leathery as they'd always been. She suddenly felt ashamed of them.

"Indigo is a monster," Anda muttered. Eine glanced up at him. She hadn't heard of the Indigo as an individual before. Was that what their leader was called? "Letting children starve in the streets."

"I'm not a child," she protested, but the word suddenly reminded her of Graf. "But there *was* a child with me and he wasn't Thelan. I think he was a foreigner!"

"What?"

"When I was looking for you, in the alleys," Eine told Noname, her spirit sinking. "I was helping him because he was so…confused. He didn't seem to know anything at all about Thela, or how he'd gotten here."

"A foreign child?" Anda said, frowning. "Who would bring a child here?"

"What happened to him?" Noname asked, catching Eine's long face.

"The Indigo took him. Right in front of me in the alley." She shook her head. "The man appeared out of thin air!"

Noname scowled at Anda, and the older man looked very surprised. "Fading?" he murmured.

"He grabbed Graf and then they were gone," Eine finished. "I couldn't save him."

"What is this, Anda? What kind of trick is that?" Noname asked. Anda shook his head, his brow furrowed.

"What kind of name is Graf? Or Graft?" Eine asked them. She wondered if it meant something, since hers apparently meant 'passage'.

"A common one. Could be from anywhere," Noname told her. Anda nodded unhappily.

"The Indigo have no real magic, of course, without any Laxens," he said. "So a trick indeed it is. But the boy did not remember how he came to be there?"

Eine shook her head, wondering what he meant by magic and Laxens.

"A memory drug," he said, and gave Noname a serious look. "That kind of thing, Ney, is very Enahalan. I'll have to investigate back home."

SIX

"How did you two get here?" Eine asked Anda. "Through the river under the wall?" Perhaps Graf had somehow gotten in that way too.

"Oh no, it would be much more difficult to hide someone coming *in* that way. We were sent here through the mental powers of one Laxen named Oln. I was sent to this particular area in order to investigate the ins and outs, while Ney was sent straight into the heart of the city. Oln must be present to mind-send, of course, and he is very occupied in Creede these days, otherwise he could get us back home." Anda turned to Noname and shook his head. "You know there are *still* Creeden battles taking place? Do you think even Oln can restore peace?" Noname frowned and said nothing.

Mind-send? A Laxen had sent them into Thela with his "mental powers". Eine was stunned into silence as the two of them exchanged unhappy looks about Creede. There was fighting in Noname's homeland, that much she understood. But now the gulf of what she did not know about her own kind was suddenly vast and alarming.

"How does anyone know who's trading for what, anyway?" Noname asked, changing the subject.

"That's why the merchants camp here for several days, you see. It's a slow process. First, they make lists of the goods they require and what they can offer. They then give these to the dock workers who insert them into canisters and drop them into the river. On the other side, from what I've overheard, there is an indoctrinated market, where traders do the same," Anda explained. "In the morning, the workers pull out the canisters and read off what is needed and available on the other side. The merchants speak up when there is a match and goods are sent out with notes attached. It's all rather primitive. Sometimes arguments break out and then the Hunters step in and everyone scatters."

"How did you figure all that out?" Eine asked, looking at his clothes. He was not even wearing a merchant's tunic to blend in.

"Oh, I have my ways of not being seen." Andy gave her a mysterious smile.

"What about this diversion we need?" Noname asked. "Did you have an idea?"

"Well, I thought perhaps we could make use of all the glass and tin. They both make an unearthly racket when they fall off a cart." He smiled at Eine as if to say, *'Surely you agree?'*

Noname nodded and scratched his head. "It would have to be close-range to have enough time for us to slip under the grate…" Eine listened, watching him and feeling mystified. "If we could position ourselves close to the grate, without being noticed, I could shoot down a pile of tin goods about ten feet away. Make them all turn their heads for a second."

Eine wondered what he meant by the word 'shoot'. Was he going to throw something?

"Perhaps we could hide inside a merchant's cart?" Anda offered. "They push them right up to the grate, and they're often covered."

"Right, maybe we can bribe one of them to take us. Have you got Thelan coins?" Noname asked him. Eine shook her head, amazed, and they both looked at her.

"You can't bribe anyone here. No one would do it. Everyone is afraid."

"But they're so poor," Noname argued. She shook her head again.

"You don't understand. We don't even *speak* of the Indigo. …Or the Laxens." She stumbled over the last word.

The two were silent for a moment, watching her. "No wealth is worth the risk of capture," Anda mused. "Well, can we sneak inside a cart, do you think?" Noname sat back a second, considering.

"What we need to do is grab a merchant, and take his clothes and his cart," he said. Eine was startled. "Anda, you'll have to dress up and push the cart. Eine and I'll hide under the cover, and then you give me a signal at the grate, so I can poke my head out and take a shot."

"Excellent," Anda said. "Don't worry, we won't harm the fellow," he added to Eine, catching her look.

"I better know what I'm aiming at," Noname told him. "I'll have to pick a target beforehand, one that won't move."

"What are you going to shoot at it? A stone?" Eine asked Noname. He raised his eyebrows.

"I'll shoot it with my gun, kid."

"…Oh."

"A gun creates a small combustion inside, like an engine," Anda explained. "And that generates an energy force, which fires out of the barrel end." Eine blinked, completely at a loss.

"She's never even heard of it?" Noname exclaimed.

"How would she, Ney?" the older man reminded him. "Indigo banned all technology back when she was an infant."

Noname shook his head. He pulled back his brown coat and showed her the weapon that was strapped to his belt. It was made of a polished, silver metal with sections of brass, and the handle was wrapped in dark leather. She could see now that the longer end narrowed and that there was a hole in it at the end. There was a switch at the back and a switch on the handle. It had grown lighter inside the tent since they'd first arrived, and she could make out decorative swirls, scratched into the metal.

Eine heard a faint sound outside, a distant rustling.

"Early risers?" Noname said, peering out through the tent walls. "We'd better find our merchant." He pulled his hood up over his head and Eine followed suit, feeling worried and excited. "Oh no, you're staying here," Noname said. She stared at him, surprised.

"Why?" she demanded. Had he gone back to treating her like a child again?

"You can guard the tent," he said, with a sly smile.

"I'll return in the merchant's disguise and then help you

into the cart," Anda told her. "Don't worry. We will return shortly!" They lifted the door flap and slipped out into the early morning. Eine curled up and waited, feeling tense and anxious. What happened if they didn't succeed? What if the two of them were caught and she was left here, with no idea of what had happened? She wondered how long she should give them, before deciding that something had gone wrong. What she would do afterwards was too difficult to think about, so she set that aside for the moment.

Anda had left a small bag behind, with straps that looked as if he wore it on his back. There were markings on the cloth, small printed words that were probably in his language, Enahalan. Eine decided that if he and Noname didn't return before the sun became bright enough to see the markings clearly, then she would go after them. She set her jaw and waited.

How far away she suddenly felt from her alley, from the cart under which she slept on the damp ground. One thing was certain: even if she lost her two new companions, she had come too far to go back there now. She would stay here at the Docks and try to make her own way out.

It turned out that she need not have worried. Just a few moments later, the tent flap was thrown open and Eine froze, alarmed. But it was only Anda who pushed his head through, and he smiled at her, his blue eyes even brighter in the morning sun. "Come out quietly, child, and climb into the cart," he whispered. She was up in a second and crawling out, not even minding being called a child.

Anda stood gripping the handle of a large, wheeled cart, covered in a heavy brown cloth. Eine could see now that he was tall and willowy, and the gray merchant's tunic they had scavenged only just barely fit him, falling short of his pale bony wrists. He lifted the cloth that was over the cart and Eine saw Noname folded up uncomfortably inside, with his gun drawn. He jerked his scarred chin at her. There wasn't much space left over but she crawled in as best she could, and Noname pulled the cover back down, cutting off most of the light and air. Eine lay almost on her side, with her knees tucked up close, and listened as Anda collected his bag from inside the tent. Then the cart began to move.

It rumbled jerkily over the pavement, knocking her head against Noname's shoulder. "What did you do to the merchant?" Eine whispered.

"Knocked him out and hid him. Left him Anda's clothes." The answer was very matter-of-fact. Eine listened as merchant's voices and sounds of a market began to grow around them. A loud voice called a greeting, possibly to Anda, but she heard no reply. It would be wise of him just to nod. They rolled along almost peacefully for several moments. Then suddenly her stomach lurched. She clenched up tighter and cringed against that familiar pain and fear.

"Hunters," she whispered. Noname tensed but said nothing. She knew he was wondering how she knew they were close. The cart rumbled on, and Eine felt sorry for Anda, so exposed in the middle of this. He had the most difficult part of the job.

The cart stopped after a moment, and then the ground suddenly shook with the thundering of Hunters' horses. Was it the four guards just arriving? It sounded like more than that. Eine listened as the horses rode past, not very far off. The sound of their hoof beats was interrupted by high-pitched cries, and hoarse calls from their riders. The cart remained still and Noname shifted behind her. Why were they stopped?

A voice nearby said, frightened, "Those aren't the guards." Eine felt a small prickling of fear.

"Leed said they're looking for someone," another voice said.

Eine dug her nails into the palm of her hand, listening. Would they search the covered carts? A Hunter barked a hoarse command, and there was more murmuring from merchants around. Anda must be in with a group of them, although he was wisely keeping quiet.

"What do you think they're after?" a voice asked. Eine strained to listen as an even lower voice replied.

"What do *you* think?"

"…Surely there aren't any left?" the first one muttered.

Noname placed a hand on her arm and she felt a wave of sympathy in his touch. The merchants thought the Hunters were after Demi's and Fourths, not foreigners. In truth, they were mere feet away from two out of the three.

The cart began to wheel forward slowly. Eine closed her eyes, willing them to make it to the grate somehow. Voices flitted past them: "Don't cause trouble, just line up with the others…They're calling for carts now…" Anda started moving a little faster. "…Over here…" How far were they from the grate now? Was Anda in a line with other merchants or was he sneaking away?

"Come, old man!" someone was calling. Anda was surely not where he was supposed to be. "Come this way!" The cart was moving faster, knocking Eine into Noname and rattling her teeth.

"Where is he going?"

"What's going on?"

Then suddenly, there was a terrible roar from one of the Hunters, frighteningly close by. "Get in line, you fool!"

A low whistle sounded overhead and Noname grabbed the bottom edge of the cart cover. He raised it just enough to slide the very end of his gun through. Then, squinting, he peered out beside it. He whispered something to himself, then he pulled in the switch on the handle. Eine heard a quick, sharp sound.

An incredible clatter suddenly rang out across the air. Eine gasped as the cart's cover was yanked away, and bright sunlight blinded her. The racket of plummeting tin continued as the cart suddenly tilted violently. Noname grabbed her hand and she saw, just for an instant, a great metal hash of bars overhead. Then she was falling, out of the cart and straight down into blackness. Down through the yawning mouth of the Dock.

Eine screamed. She was in weightless blackness. Overhead there were shouts and a loud clang of metal. There were the Hunters' roaring voices. She heard a great splash below, and then she plunged deep into water. A cold she had never felt before swallowed her up whole. She swallowed and choked, sinking into ice-cold darkness. She struggled, kicking her legs, plowing upwards through the water.

Air! She burst up through the surface and gasped. Then she was down again, thrashing her arms. She surged upwards again, gulping another breath.

"Eine!" She heard Noname's voice - hollow, echoing. She tried to hurl herself towards the sound. So much water! She had never seen so much water. In another moment, someone was grabbing her hand, her arms. She felt a rough wall suddenly dragging against her and she clasped onto it. The water was rushing past her, pulling her with it. She was horizontal, clinging to the hands that had grabbed her.

Then Noname was pulling her up over the edge, onto a dirt

floor. "Are you all right?" he asked, as she choked and coughed up painfully from her lungs. The cold in her bones was unbearable.

"We must get further away," Anda said, more quietly. He caught hold of one of Eine's arms and Noname took the other, and they ran, half-dragging her along the ground. She spluttered and gaped at her surroundings. The blackness was beginning to turn gray, as her eyes adjusted to the dark. She could see the water now, alongside them, wide and flowing ahead in the direction they were walking. Across it were another dirt ledge and a wall, which curved overhead and disappeared into a shadowed ceiling.

The underground river. It was a tunnel with a river running through it.

Eine looked back over her shoulder and saw a block of light up high in the dark ceiling, slatted with bars of shadow. She realized now that Anda had pushed them into the opening, and then jumped in afterwards.

"Were you seen?" Noname was asking him. The two of them were just as soaking wet as she was, trailing streams of water along the ground around them. Her hood was hanging down her back, but if Anda noticed anything odd about her hair, he said nothing.

"A young man saw me," Anda admitted, sounding tired. "I doubt he knew quite what he was looking at! Here is this deaf, mute merchant, dumping his cart and then leaping into the Dock like a lunatic." Noname laughed and Eine steadied herself, pulling her arms free of their grip. She could manage to keep up now. "And that noise! That cacophony is still ringing in my ears," Anda grumbled.

"What was it?" Eine asked, hoarsely. She coughed again.

"Tin bars, stacked high up on a wagon. There were hundreds of them. I saw it earlier and knew it would work." Noname sounded cheerful.

"What on earth do they use tin bars for?" Anda asked.

"I've seen some framing windows. Looks nice, I guess," Noname said with a shrug.

Eine hustled along with them in silence, feeling very overwhelmed. She had never been inside an enclosed space before, albeit a very large one. There was no sky above. The air smelled of damp earth. The water was rushing along loudly and steadily, and

Eine stared out over it, impressed by its sheer force and immensity. How deep was it, she wondered? What if Noname hadn't found her, and she'd been carried off, or drowned? She shuddered.

"Are you cold?" Noname asked. "We'll dry off soon. We can get new clothes on the other side." Eine stared up him, her dark eyes enormous. On the other side. They were leaving Thela. They were underneath the wall.

"What about…the Hunters?" she asked.

"They didn't see us jump," Noname explained.

"But they'll come looking for us," she insisted.

"They have no authority on the other side," Anda told her, confidently. "They can't follow."

"But they can," Eine said, confused. "They can go anywhere."

Noname looked down at her, and even in the dim light, she could see that his brown eyes were soft. "They would be taken down, Eine. People outside of Thela have weapons and many ways of fighting back," he said. "And the Laxens thrive."

SEVEN

They travelled through the tunnel for what felt like an entire day. Without the sun, however, there was no telling the passage of time. Eine listened to the water rushing, and to Noname and Anda discussing the politics of the great, wide world awaiting them. She couldn't shake the feeling that this could still be a dream. She could still wake up back in her alley, hunger driving her back into the market.

A sudden thought struck her then. Now that she was alone with these two - and especially in the dark - she didn't have to pretend. She didn't have to walk as if she were heavier, and she certainly had already stopped hiding her strength. She felt an unexpected rush of relief. She took a deep breath and tried to relax, but it was hard to just let it go.

Could it be possible that she never had to pretend again? She didn't quite believe it.

"…I don't see what all the fuss is about. The Laxens can't risk getting close to Thela, so obviously it's the humans who have to fight," Noname was saying.

"Ah, but Ney, there are so many who believe it is none of their concern. If the Indigo is only a threat to the Laxens, then why should humans get involved?" Anda said.

"So they should just let them die out?" Noname demanded.

"And who's to say the Indigo will stay in Thela? Why would someone with that much power stay in such a small place?"

"The world would be a rather dry place indeed, without the Laxens," Anda muttered.

"Why?" Eine asked. He gave her a surprised look, as if he'd forgotten she was there. Or what she was.

"They possess all the true magic in the world, my dear. Everything impressive that we humans do is merely a clever trick, a way of getting around limitations, a manipulation of the senses."

Eine felt a peculiar kind of anxiety as she thought about his words. Were her abilities actually magic? Magic was a word she'd heard used to describe things that couldn't be explained. But this seemed like a more important use of the word. The idea that her kind could be so important to the world, when she had grown up unable to even mention them, seemed absurd.

She flinched suddenly, and stopped walking. Anda and Noname looked back at her.

"What is it, child?"

She had heard a stray thought again. But it had been unintelligible. Like a dark mental scrawl. "I heard something," she murmured. "Something's here."

"In the tunnel?" Noname asked, looking around. She nodded, hesitantly. It had been such a strange wave of thought. More like a feeling? A familiar feeling.

"Look, there are goods ahead, in the water," Anda said, pointing. "Perhaps that's what you heard." Eine saw dark shapes bobbing up and down a little further ahead of them. They were being carried along in the water, knocking into each other and splashing, tinking. Eine frowned. That wasn't it.

"You obviously have Laxen hearing," Noname commented. "You heard something out there in the mines too –" Eine gasped, cutting him off. The familiar feeling! It struck her again and she realized what it was. It was hunger!

"Something is here and it's hungry!" she blurted. As soon as she spoke, there was a scratching sound ahead of them in the darkness.

"Get down!" Noname pulled out his gun and stepped in front of them. Anda grabbed Eine and pushed her down to the ground, shielding her. The scratching became a scuffling sound. Something with claws was making its way towards them, moving faster.

"What is it, Ney?"

"I can't see it."

"It's an animal," Eine realized, astonished. "What kind of –
"

Something sprang from the shadows, straight at Noname. He fired and the thing landed heavily on top of him, its limbs striking Anda and Eine. They scrambled away as Noname roared and flung the creature off of him. Not until then could Eine make out what it was: a rat, just like the ones that scampered through the market. But it was the size of a grown man.

Anda exclaimed something in his own language. The beast had taken the gunshot in its shoulder. On the ground now, in pain, it bared garishly yellow, enormous teeth. Eine stared at it in horror. It was covered in matted, shaggy brown fur and the whites of its eyes glowed in the dark. Noname aimed at it again, but then suddenly two more of the monsters came barreling towards them.

"Look out!" Eine screamed. Noname whirled, narrowly missing the charge. One of the monsters skidded into a turn and made a leap towards him. The other headed straight for Eine and Anda.

Eine ran for the tunnel wall to avoid it and then towards Noname to help, as Anda vaulted neatly over the rat and ran back towards them, his blue eyes wide. "No one warned us about these!" he bellowed.

Noname was grappling with the other rat. It was up on its hind legs, digging its front claws into his shoulders, lashing its hairless tail behind it, while Noname held its face at bay. He struggled to get his gun in position to shoot the rat. Eine threw her arms around the lower half of the monster and pulled, hauling it backwards. She felt its ribs through her cloak and smelled a pungent, gamey smell. But the wounded first rat suddenly lunged for her, and she ducked underneath it. The weight of its belly crashed down on top of her back. Her nostrils were flooded with the same foul scent. She heard Anda cry out her name. But he'd forgotten her strength. She strained her leg muscles and bolted up into a standing position, knocking the thing off of her with ease.

A gunshot exploded afterwards and Noname was suddenly free. Anda was dodging the third rat at an impressive speed; Eine yanked out her table leg and smashed it down upon the animal's head as it passed. It shrieked horribly and stumbled to the edge of the walkway. Blood dripped from its giant ears. It slipped at the edge and then fell into the water. Eine gasped as it squealed and struggled to stay afloat. Behind her, Noname shot the first rat and it fell down with a thud.

He whirled around quickly, his gun raised, ready for more. Anda sighed and gestured to the final rat as it was carried away by the water. Noname lowered his gun. "Giant... *rats*," he spat. Anda harrumphed. The two of them looked quickly at Eine.

"I'm fine," she spoke up. Noname grinned in disbelief. The sleeves of his coat were rent almost to shreds from the rats' claws. He looked very tattered, but unharmed.

Eine thought about how any daring merchants who may have leapt into the dock would've been torn to shreds and eaten.

"How did you hear them, Eine?" Anda asked her.

"It's something that happens sometimes..." she said, shyly. "I can't control it."

"You could hear their thoughts?" he guessed.

"Well, it wasn't like a human's thoughts. I've never heard an animal before. But I could feel that it was hungry."

"You can't control it?" Noname asked. "So you can't read our minds on purpose?" Eine shook her head, and Anda gave him an amused look.

"Why, have you got something to hide, Ney?"

Noname scowled. "It's a reasonable question!" He turned and started off down the tunnel again, keeping his gun in hand. Anda smiled at Eine.

"That's certainly a gift from your Laxen blood. And you can send your thoughts as well, I'm sure?"

"No," Eine said, surprised. The thought had never even occurred to her.

"Really? That's unusual," Anda said. "I've never known a mind-reader who couldn't also send. Are there any other abilities that you haven't told Ney about?"

"Just a small one. My stomach aches when the Hunters are near," she told him.

"Hmm, that's peculiar," Anda mused. "You are receptive but not reactive."

"What do you mean?"

"Are you two coming?!" Noname demanded from up ahead. He had disappeared into the darkness, and Eine realized this with a sudden unease. It occurred to her that she didn't like him to be far away, and that was a strange thought. Was it because he was a soldier, who could protect her? But she herself was so much stronger than him.

"Well, you may have a few other traits that are yet undiscovered," Anda said. He waved a hand after Noname. "Let us continue on!"

***

The tunnel wound its way ahead as they walked, with the scenery unchanging. Everywhere there was dirt and blackness and water splashing. The three of them were quiet, listening for rats. Eine realized after awhile that the tunnel must go further than just under the Thelan wall, since the latter couldn't possibly be so thick. Her stomach rumbled again and she dropped a hand into her damp pocket, automatically, before remembering it was empty. Noname and Anda seemed lost in their thoughts as they trudged along. She frowned, hating to ask either of them for food. She was unsure even how to do it. Normally, she could just go and get her on.

After another minute, she cleared her throat. "I'm hungry," she announced. "I don't know how to get food here." Her companions turned to look at her, both of them amused.

"What are you going to do?" Noname said, with mock concern. She frowned at him, as Anda dug into the little back-bag that he'd managed to keep with him. He produced a very wet package as Noname pulled out his dried meat.

"I have some oat cake, although it's more meal now than cake, I'd imagine." They both handed her the food and Eine smiled, feeling embarrassed and shy. Her smile was beginning to feel more natural, easier. She accepted it silently and tore off several pieces, then handed it back.

"We'll have to get more of that and some water on the other side," Noname said. "How much further do you think?"

"We're more than halfway through. We must be..." Anda's words trailed off as he looked up ahead, and Eine followed his gaze. There was a faint light glowing further down the tunnel. It was bluish.

"Is that it?" Eine exclaimed, her throat suddenly tight. Had they come through to the end?

Noname stepped in front of them with his gun ready, peering towards the light. "What is it, Anda?"

"It's not the sunlight, that is certain," he said, surprised. Eine swallowed to calm herself and followed after Noname. He eased forward, keeping his gun trained on the strange glow.

Was it someone with a lantern? But the light was faint, and not flickering. It wasn't long before Eine could make out that it was coming from something on the tunnel wall. It was a thick blue mass of something. As they stepped closer, she saw that it was stretched out across the wall, almost like a web.

"Anda?" Noname asked, tense.

"Plant life!" the older man exclaimed. "Phosphorescent life, yes, of course." He pushed past them and strode up to the wall, his hand on his chin. Eine glanced at Noname and he shrugged. The blue web of spongy vines seemed to gleam back at them peacefully, almost pulsating. It covered the wall from roof to floor, and stretched about ten feet wide. "Very interesting. And perfectly harmless," Anda announced. With that, Eine approached the wall eagerly and studied the underground plants up close. The blue of the thin vines was like the color of the sky when there was a rare break in the clouds back in Thela. But it was more intense and it had more green in it.

Back in Thela. The phrase was wonderful. She was *outside* of Thela.

"They're beautiful," she said, smiling.

"Don't touch them," Noname said. "Could be poisonous or something."

"Oh, they're just feeding off the moisture," Anda said. "You see, Eine, life can grow anywhere, as long as it can adapt." She looked up at him and thought of all the Dredges, struggling to survive in the alleys. "Adaptation is the key…to keep from growing stagnant." Anda's expression changed suddenly, his heavy gray brows sinking. Noname gave him a knowing look, and he sighed and turned away.

***

It was a long time after that before Eine noticed that the dark was beginning to lessen. They had met no other rats, although they heard a few scratching away in the darkness. They had trekked past another mass of glowing plants, this time more green than blue, and growing on the other side of the tunnel. There was something about them that made Eine think of her dream, with the floating lights. She turned now, in the fading darkness, to look at the two men beside her, and she saw them in sharper detail. Anda blinked and looked around them, hopefully.

"We must be approaching the end!" he exclaimed.

"Thank gods," Noname said. "I feel like I'm turning into a mole." Anda laughed.

"What's outside, at the entrance?" Eine asked.

"A market, but very different from yours. We can walk right out into it without much trouble," Noname said.

"Yes, and we'll buy food," Anda said, walking faster. "And supplies for the rest of our trip. Let's make haste." He and Noname surged forward and Eine began to half-run just to keep up with them. The dark continued to disintegrate around them, and soon she saw a few golden rays peeking through from the left. It was brighter than she had expected. There were more objects floating ahead of them in the water, this time glinting in the sunlight.

The tunnel curved gradually towards the left, and they rounded the corner, catching up with the floating goods. Then suddenly Eine was blinded. Stunned, she gasped and closed her eyes. The sun! The outside world was on fire! Squinting through her lashes, she saw a yawning archway of piercing light. Filling the width of the tunnel, it greeted them with a welcoming warmth. Eine closed her eyes all the way again and felt the warmth wash over her.

"Here we are, safe at last," Anda said. Then there was a sudden, sharp blast. "Great gods!" he cried out. Eine's eyes snapped open. Noname crashed into her, knocking her down into the water, as something exploded again.

"*Thieves!* Smugglers!!" a strange voice shrieked.

The water was shallow now, and Eine hit the bottom only half submerged. Noname was lying across her, aiming his gun out into the sunlight. A canister splashed into Eine's head.

"Hold your fire!" Noname roared.

"I knew it!! I knew you'd take my pendant!" the voice screamed back.

Eine lifted her head out of the water to catch her first view of the world outside. The river spilled out through a cave and into the open air. Then it continued on, rushing shallowly through rows of carts and stalls, which even from her position, Eine could see were far more decorated and elaborate than the ones in Thela. There were people everywhere, stepping right into the river and grabbing the goods, checking things on slips of paper.

But a small group stood at the very mouth of the tunnel, staring inward, and one of them was a tiny, fierce woman with a very large gun. It would have been a comical sight, but she fired again and Eine plunged her head back into the water. Just before she did, she spotted a vast row of treetops over the market, sharp and clear in the bright sunlight.

"Madam!" Anda exclaimed, as she re-emerged. "You are *mistaken!*"

Noname fired his gun into the air – Eine couldn't tell where, but several people screamed and there was a bustling of some kind beyond the cave.

"They're fugitives!" a voice exclaimed. There were sympathetic murmurs from the crowd.

"Stop hassling them, you crazy woman!"

Noname stood up slowly and held a hand out to help Eine up. She accepted, keeping her eyes on the commotion ahead of them. Several people were accosting the woman now, and someone had taken her gun. She saw with a start that everyone involved in the scene was dressed entirely differently from everyone else. They differed in skin color - some were darker than others, much darker. The tiny woman who had shot at them stood only about four feet high, and she was squat and robust, with a long mass of reddish curls.

"But the Seer!" she shrieked. "The Seer said someone would take my pendant! From the tunnel!" Several people consoled her and she was coaxed away, out of sight.

Anda found his way over to Noname and Eine, and helped them both onto the bank. He was shaking his head. "The Meyjan. Always so dramatic," he said.

"I ought to find that *inuck* pendent and put a bullet through it," Noname snarled. Eine looked at him in surprise. It wasn't the first time she'd heard him swear in his language, but this was the clearest she had heard it, and it sounded like he'd clicked his tongue in the middle of it. What a strange sound.

"Mind your language, Ney," Anda said, mildly. "Now, let us go and get some dry clothing!"

Eine followed the two of them with a thumping heart, as they marched out of the tunnel's mouth. She yanked her sopping wet hood up automatically, as the people stared at them with open wonder. Her eyes flew over everything, as if she couldn't take it all in fast enough. The ground immediately softened into thick green grass, and she marveled at the feel of it under her feet. In the distance, to the east, she could see a separate gathering of people, and another yawning tunnel into the rock behind them. Into this tunnel flowed the original river, which wound towards them from a source that she couldn't see. This was the river that brought goods into Thela. A man with a bright-colored wrap around his head was sorting through the items and calling out names, marking things on paper.

Watching them, Eine understood suddenly that Thela was at a higher elevation than where they stood now. She looked behind, her heart in her throat, and saw that the tunnel emerged from a giant rock wall, that rose up above their heads. Somewhere beyond that was the Thelan city wall, but she couldn't even see it. It was gone.

Eine spun back around and gaped at the hectic sights and sounds of the strange foreign market before her. Then her eyes were drawn upwards to the tops of the massive trees that tossed in the wind, beyond the market. A forest. Just like in her dream. The source of the river was somewhere inside the woods. There was no city here, just a market. Perhaps that was what Anda had meant by 'indoctrinated'.

Smiling, almost delirious, Eine hurried after Noname and Anda. Merchants of all shapes, sizes and colors were hailing them to buy their goods. Eine was amazed to see stacks of sliced meat – fresh meat, not dried! Piles of fresh fruit, and yards and yards of cloth like nothing she'd ever seen. Here and there were glints of tin objects, and several merchants carried tin and glass in their arms from the goods collected in the river.

"Where...? How do they have these things?" Eine murmured. Noname glanced back at her, as Anda stopped to study some cloth at a stall.

"What do you mean?" he asked.

"Thela gives them tin and glass, but what are they trading for it? We don't have food like this! We don't have any of this!" She turned slowly in a circle, struggling to take it all in.

"Since Indigo took over," Noname said patiently, "he's

refused all goods except the basic necessities of life."

"He?" Eine repeated.

"The leader of the order," he explained. "We don't know who he is, so we just call him Indigo. So the people export tin and glass, and maybe a few other things, but they get very little in return." Eine's legs suddenly felt weak, and she slowly sank down into the grass, squelching into it in her wet cloak. Noname crouched down next to her and she stared at him. In the brilliant sunlight, she could see his face better than she ever had. His scars were not menacing. His eyes were a golden brown, and they were sad.

"Why?" she asked.

"We don't know. Just like we don't know why he's murdering Laxens, or how. It all started so quickly. His people took over the old Thelan order, and shut Thela down, almost overnight. The rest of the world heard the news and had mixed reactions." He reached down and snatched a blade of grass out of the ground, twiddling it between his finger and thumb. "At first it was just a coup and people waited to see what would happen. Then the stories began to come out. The Laxens in the old order had been killed, the Hunters had shown up and were rounding up the other Laxens... People didn't believe it at first, and then they just sat around and shook their heads." He tore the blade of grass in half and dropped the pieces. "Then we started hearing about the rain, how it started raining all the time in the city center. Some people say a Laxen who could control the weather must've done it before he died."

Eine felt numb, listening to him. "Then we began to take action," he said, meeting her eyes with a steady gaze. "Anda's people most of all, the Enahalans. They're the ones who sent me and him."

"Look, Ney!" Anda's voice called. Eine and Noname looked up and saw the older man standing with his arms out, draped in thick green and blue cloth. He had thrown off his hood as well and Eine felt heartened by his cheerful smile. "Good colors for the woods and very hardy. What money have you got?"

EIGHT

It wasn't long before they had made several purchases: a long blue coat with buckles for Anda, a short brown jacket with a high collar for Noname, and, to her surprise, a deep green cloak for Eine. They also bought some packs of ammunition for Noname's gun, which he strapped to his belt and slipped into his boots. Then there was a pound of dried meat and another of dried fruit, the latter twisted up neatly in paper, as well as a large canteen of water.

Eine studied the faces of the merchants who worked out their prices and measured out the goods. There was a woman with a golden-tinted skin, who wore long skirts sewn with glittering thread; a huge, fat man with a bald head whose skin was as white as clouds; a shrewd-looking man with darting black eyes who was nearly as brown as mud all over.

"Here you are, child, get out of that wet cloak and put this on," Anda said, handing her the long swath of dark green. He donned his coat, which seemed to match both his eyes and the sky, and began doing up the buckles. Noname peeled his wet and torn brown cloak off, and flung it away as if relieved. Without it, he stood in a tan-colored shirt that closed with clasps in the front, and his black trousers. Eine took the cloak Anda offered and watched Noname as he shrugged into the short jacket and pulled the collar up. Neither of their new coats had hoods. Eine stared at them both with wide eyes from under hers.

"I can't…take my cloak off," she protested. Noname gave her a questioning look and Anda cocked his head to one side.

"Why not?"

Eine hesitated, and felt her face suddenly grow hot, as she thought of the short, threadbare shift she wore underneath her cloak. It was the only underclothing she had ever had. Noname suddenly laughed, and she knew that she had turned a bright red.

"Anda, she's not wearing much else," he said, grinning. The Enahalan looked confused for a moment, and then flushed a bit himself.

"Oh, gods. Yes. Come with me, we'll find you a secure spot to change."

Eine followed him through the market, leaving Noname behind. She looked over her shoulder as she went, and saw him standing in his strange short jacket, in front of a stall that sold guns in different sizes and styles, as well as knives of various lengths. She stumbled and continued on, anxious not to lose sight of Anda. It was odd not to feel in control, not to know at all where her alley was, and that she could run back to it. It was also strange to have stood there while her companions *bought* things from market stalls, rather than slipping in and out of them, stealing a bit here and there.

Anda found a stall selling elaborate lacy dresses, which had a section curtained off for customers to try them on. Eine hustled in under the curtain, and then she hesitated, standing there with the new cloak in her arms. She could not remember ever taking the old one off. It had always felt dangerous. She had even washed underneath it, cleaning her skin and the shift as best as she could with rain water. She realized after a moment that she was trembling.

"Yes, yes, I'll buy this ribbon then, madam," she heard Anda saying outside. "Then we'll be customers and all will be right."

All will be right. Eine closed her eyes. Then she quickly untied her gray cloak and pulled it off. Shivering, even though it wasn't cold, she wrapped the other one around her and tucked her table leg under the new cord, which was thicker and stronger. The whole cloak was very warm and felt secure. It was thick and soft, voluminous. Eine sighed with relief and pulled the new hood up.

She took a moment to glance down at herself in wonder at being dark green, instead of threadbare gray, and fraying. Then she bundled up the old cloak and left it there, stepping back out to meet Anda.

He smiled and handed her a long piece of black ribbon. "Now you're a wood sprite instead of a street urchin," he announced. "Come along then." He strode off again and Eine followed, twining the ribbon uncertainly around her wrist.

They rejoined Noname and headed north through the market in the direction of the tall tree tops. Before long, they had passed through the last of the stalls and were approaching a dense wall of trees. There was a path that led into the woods between the great tree trunks; Eine looked up overhead as she followed Anda and Noname through them. She saw a sky of crisscrossed branches, deep green leaves and vines. The light softened immediately all around, and the sounds of the market seemed muted behind them. She felt suddenly in awe.

"Is this part of the Kalid country, these woods?" Noname asked Anda. Neither of them appeared unused to seeing so many trees.

"Technically, this is still part of Thela. It used to be full of cottages. But I believe it's a bit of a no-man's land now, which does mean we must stay alert." Anda gazed around him as he spoke. "But it should be no more than two days passing through."

"Two days!" Eine exclaimed, in a hushed voice. They looked back at her in surprise, a reaction she was growing accustomed to. "That's just...a lot of trees," she murmured.

"The path goes all the way through," Noname told her, as if thinking she must not understand how they were going to get around the trees.

"Yes, and by all accounts, these woods are still the best way through to Tobin. Then we'll take the train from there to Enahala," Anda said.

"I've heard the Hunters got their horses from Tobin. How do they breed them so large?" Noname asked him.

"The Tobins are great horsemen, but I certainly have no idea."

"Where are the Hunters from?" Eine spoke up.

"They're mercenaries, bred from a mix of peoples. They

have some obvious Calibreen characteristics, namely their height, but I'm not sure what other races are involved," Anda replied.

"Who bred them, originally?" Noname asked.

"I think they were an old experiment of the Pinnacle," the older man said, darkly. Eine listened intently, full of questions. Then a sudden rustling nearby made her jump, and Anda smiled at her. "Little things," he said. "The forest is full of little, living things." Eine nodded, uncertainly, and swept her eyes across the mass of green foliage all around them.

The trees grew in such a sprawled, wide-spreading manner that at first glance, it appeared to be utter chaos. But there was a design to it; Eine could see a strange kind of symmetry unfolding before them, a loose pattern. There were 'little things' using each nook and cranny for shelter, drinking water from the tilted leaves, and burrowing into the soft dirt. The undergrowth was high and thick, and it spilled over into the path where they walked. Into the cracks in the ground near her feet, Eine spotted ants and other tiny insects crawling eagerly. Leaves and petals fluttered down from above, alighting in her hair. She had pushed her hood back just to be able to see, because the sunlight was so scattered and filtered here.

Another rustle startled her, as a bird squawked and flew off from a tree above. Everything was alive. There was so much alive.

"Sometimes they're not such little things," Noname said, sounding unconcerned. "Let's have some of that dried meat, Anda."

Anda dug into his bag and produced several large strips of the spicy meat. Eine's mouth watered immediately at the sight of it. At the same time, it occurred to her that this was the most regularly she had eaten in as long as she could remember. It was an amazing thought. When he handed her a piece and she took a bite, she was surprised to taste spices different even from Noname's meat before. She chewed it, fascinated, and gazed up above them again, into the canopy of branches above.

"My mind keeps drifting back towards that child in Thela," Anda said, chewing on the meat. "Tell me, Eine, what was he like?"

Eine accepted the water canteen from Noname and took a long drink. Then she handed it back. "He dropped the T's on the end of his words when he spoke," she said. "So 'got' sounded like 'gah'. And 'don't' was 'don'."

"Like in Belgir?" Noname said, swallowing a mouthful of

water. "The servant class in Belgir talk like that, don't they?" he asked Anda. Anda nodded, frowning.

"Is Belgir working with Enahala? To stop the Indigo?" Eine asked, eagerly.

"No. They aren't. I'm afraid there is no reason in the world why a Belgin servant's child would be involved at all." He sighed, still looking perturbed. Then he yawned suddenly, a great cavernous yawn that had both Eine and Noname following suit. It had been a very long day, Eine realized, traveling through the tunnel. "It will be dark before too long, Ney."

"Let's go another mile and then make camp," Noname told him.

Eine touched the soft cloak wrapped around her and thought about how nice it would be to lay down in it. She yawned again and chewed on another piece of meat.

***

Someone was calling for her through the trees. A woman's voice, soft and low. Eine wandered through her dream forest, following the voice. The trees were much more distinct this time. She could see the knobs and crags of their trunks, the delicate stems peeking out of vertical hollows.

"Eine..." the voice said. "It's through you."

"Eine. Eine!" It was Noname's voice now. She awoke with a start, and found herself lying nestled in her green cloak, in the bottom of the small hollow where they had made camp. It was dark and there were insects singing. The forest loomed in great shadows all around, ghostly and dreamlike still. She turned her head and saw that Noname lay at her side. He was staring back at her.

"You were kicking me," he said softly. He was just a few inches away from her, lying there, but she couldn't quite make out his face in the dark. She couldn't remember sleeping so close to anyone before, and it gave her an odd, vulnerable feeling. She scooted herself over a bit, putting more space in between them. She had been dreaming the same dream again, but this time, the trees had seemed so real. Was it just because she knew what a forest looked like now?

She sat up, groggily, feeling thirsty and disoriented. She looked around in the darkness, listening. She could hear Anda snoring softly. She crawled forward, feeling for the Enahalan's

69

bag, which carried the canteen.

"What is it?" Noname asked.

"Just need water," she murmured. He propped himself up on one elbow and she looked back at him. "Sorry I woke you up."

"I was awake. I don't like sleeping out in the open," he said, yawning. He and Anda had set a few simple snares around them, and the hollow was very inconspicuous, but Eine understood how he felt. It was eerie not having the protection of something over their heads. They did not even have walls around them, or any remotely nearby.

"This is the way animals live," she said, thoughtfully.

"That's why they sleep so lightly," he replied. "What were you kicking about in your sleep?"

Eine found the canteen and took a sip from it. "I have this dream sometimes where a woman calls me."

"I have dreams where women call me too," Noname said, sounding like he was grinning. Eine was only half aware of what he meant, so she ignored him.

"It takes place in a forest, just like here, but I've always had it, even back in Thela."

"Hmm. Maybe it's your mother?" Noname said. Startled, she put down the canteen and stared at him.

"But she's dead."

He shrugged and lay back down, looking up at the dark canopy above them. "I sometimes dream about my father, and he's dead. Maybe it means something. Do you know which one of them was Laxen?"

"No," Eine said, wistfully. "I don't know anything about them." They fell silent and the night noises of the woods settled over them again. Eine lay back down on the grass and bundled her hood into a soft pile to rest her head upon. Noname was breathing steadily nearby, but she could tell he was not asleep.

"What happened to your father?" she asked. He cleared his throat.

"He died in the second war with the south. Creede is divided into north and south, but only by disagreements. The two sides have been fighting for generations." He stopped and Eine turned on her side to face him. "My mother lost her mind when she heard that he died. She gets taken care of by nurses now." His tone was flat and emotionless. Eine felt the weight of the grief underneath, and understood how much of a loss it was.

"Can you visit her?" she asked, her own voice sad.

"I can but I don't," he said, more quietly. "It's too hard to see her like that." Eine couldn't imagine having a mother to visit, and not doing so.

"But you have a sister," she said, remembering what he'd said in the tin mines.

"Yes, she married a man in the Kinimin Islands and never came back. I can't blame her, it's peaceful over there."

Eine shook her head, listening. "So many places I've never heard of. Where are the Kinimin Islands?"

"'No-Name, how big is the world?'" he asked back, in a small voice. Eine laughed, surprised. "I'm sure Anda has a map he can show you. I can't tell you how many miles away it is, but it's several week's journey, to the south, and that's by airship."

"Airship?!" Eine exclaimed. Anda snorted in his sleep and then turned over. "A ship that goes in the air?"

Noname shook his head, amazed. "Even living way out on the Ice Lands, you'd have seen one or two in the sky by now, but not in Thela, I guess. Nothing flies over that place. Nothing goes near." Eine just gaped at him.

"Flying?" she repeated. "Traveling in the sky?" Noname laughed.

"It's the only way to go."

She looked up eagerly but the stars were covered by the treetops and there was no sky to see. "I would like to try that," she declared.

"Maybe Anda can take you up in one in Enahala," he said.

"Won't you come?" she asked. Noname didn't say anything for a moment. She suddenly felt embarrassed for asking.

"I might go home for a little while, after the council. Unless they decide they need me right away," he said, sounding uncertain. Eine nodded, but she was struck by the phrase 'after the council'. What would happen to *her* after the council, whatever it was, exactly? Where would she go? There was a great, wide unknown now, waiting for her at every corner. It was so difficult for her to grasp, it made her dizzy. She was afraid to even mention it out loud.

"But what…why do you work for Enahala?" she asked, shaking off those thoughts. "I mean, *do* you work for them?"

"I don't have to, if that's what you mean. I'm a volunteer," Noname said. "I'm a soldier like my father, trained to fight in the stupid Creeden wars just like everyone else. And I did, for awhile. But I don't believe that either side is right, so I left." He yawned again.

"Is that why you have scars, from fighting there?" Eine asked. He grumbled something.

"You ask a lot of questions. I wandered around a bit, met Anda, and ended up falling in with his people when Indigo appeared and started his reign of terror," he announced. "I could help, and they needed me."

"Oh." Eine listened to him sigh and resettle himself in the grass. There were so many other questions she wanted to ask. How had he met Anda? What were the wars in Creede about? And what about the Laxens? Did he know where they came from?

"Noname?" she asked.

"What?"

"Just one more."

He snorted. "Go on then."

"Why won't you tell me your name?" She waited, as he was quiet for a long moment. It didn't seem like such a difficult question. Why was he silent? Should she not have asked?

"In Northern Creede, we don't tell people our names just…like that. Only people we love." His voice sounded gruff now. "Go to sleep now, Eine."

NINE

Eine awoke in the early morning to the sound of birds chirping and singing. She opened up bleary eyes to warm sunlight streaming through the branches above. She swallowed and sat up slowly, listening to the birds and the rustling of the trees. It was such a nice way to wake up that she found herself smiling. To hear such pretty sounds, first thing in the morning!

"Good morning, Eine!" Anda said, cheerfully. He was up and digging through his bag, setting out the package of dried fruit. Noname gave a snore and Eine glanced down to see him sprawled next to her in the grass. His expression while sleeping was peaceful and boyish. The boy who told no one his name. Eine wondered exactly how old he was.

"Ney is up and ready, I see," Anda said with a smile. "There's a small creek just past that fallen tree over there if you'd like to wash up."

Eine stood up and stretched, long and far. Her cloak still felt soft and clean, and it smelled of grass. She caught herself humming as she wandered off towards the creek, and she stopped immediately, surprised. She didn't know what she was humming. It was a tune that she knew somehow, but she couldn't remember how. She reached the small stream and knelt down to splash water on her face, the black ribbon from Anda dangling into it from her wrist. The water's surface was clear with tiny fish visible underneath, darting here and there. Eine watched them in fascination. Little things.

She realized with a start that she felt stronger. She had been feeling stronger, in fact, the last two days. Was it because of the food? Or because she was away from Thela?

She felt the sudden twinge of a foreign mind, and stood up straight, staring across the water. It was an animal's thoughts; she recognized the scattered feeling of it like the rats in the tunnel. A pointed face peered at her from the bushes on the other side of the creek. Large, dewy eyes, a black nose. Then a tuft of a white tale as it turned and darted away.

"Thirsty, water. ...People by the water! Go!"

Eine grinned after it.

Back at the camp, she saw that Noname was up and eating with Anda, but he looked puffy-eyed and tired. He had definitely not gotten much sleep. He was not as talkative either, mostly just grunting in response to Anda.

They set out shortly afterwards, after Noname and Anda had disabled their traps and gathered up the rope from which they'd been made. Eine had figured out that one was a tripwire, triggered to let loose a nearby branch that was pulled taut – to make a loud noise – and another involved a noose for a trespasser's foot, but she couldn't tell what happened once it was stepped in.

The three of them returned to the path and continued on. Eine thought about the tune she had hummed earlier, bewildered. What did she know it from? She tried to remember the whole tune for a few moments, and then suddenly a funny feeling took hold of her.

"'...and the light goes on further than eyes can see,'" Anda sang suddenly, finishing the tune. Eine stopped in her tracks and stared at him. "'And the light can return from beyond! To defend – '"

"Anda." Noname gave him an irritated look.

"It just popped into my head," Anda said mildly."And then there's that bit about the stone. 'The light from beyond will destroy the stone.' I never understood that. One of those legends…"

"What is that, Anda?" Eine asked, breathless.

"'Further Than Eyes Can See'," he told her. "The Old-World song."

"…Oh." Eine looked away down the path ahead of them. It

was an odd coincidence. "I know it but I've never heard it before."

"Maybe you did when you were very young," Anda suggested. Eine suddenly thought of her memory back in Thela, of a man humming. Had it been the same song? Anda began walking again and she followed. "Memory is an odd thing."

"But what does old-world mean?" she asked.

"The Old-World, goodness, let me see. It's just a measure of time, really, to mark history. Old-World is the time period before the Laxens arrived. So, therefore, it's the time before there was any magic, and we knew little about the world." Anda looked thoughtful. "It was a dark time, figuratively, or so the songs and stories seem to show us."

"But how did the Laxens arrive?" Eine demanded, stopping again. "Where did they come from?"

"They just started being born," Noname told her. "Some babies just started showing up with special abilities. And then more and more."

"Yes, it was as if they evolved. At first, people thought they were supernatural beings, or gods. That's why we still say 'great gods' and so on. But after we understood things better, much later, some began to call it a mutation, although that has negative connotations. But you see, there were no apparent connections between the families that produced Laxens, and the phenomenon spread," Anda said. Eine listened in wonder.

"But what kind of special abilities?" she asked.

"Oh, all kinds."

There was a sudden whistle and then a loud thunk. Eine jumped. She saw a very long dart, protruding from a tree trunk a few feet ahead of them.

Noname swore as two more darts hit trees very close to Eine. She dropped to the ground as he pulled out his gun. A second later, three men leapt from out of the bushes, landing right in the path before them. Eine peeked upwards and saw a tall, broad-shouldered man who wore tattered pants and carried a very long blade. Next to him was a huskier, dark-skinned man in a ragged brown suit who held a long, wide gun - very unlike Noname's - and had a short blade strapped to his belt. The third man, who had a shaved head and very few teeth, wore a kind of wrap-around garment and wielded the dart-launcher. It was a curved piece of wood with a wire that stretched from tip to tip.

"Ney..." Anda warned. Noname had not moved an inch, his weapon aimed directly at the man with the long gun. Eine supposed he was the one could injure someone the fastest.

"Your food and your money," the man said, in a voice that wasn't much more than a rasp.

"No." Noname's voice was just as rough.

"Don't be a fool," the man with the long blade told him. His voice was clear and he sounded very calm. "You have one weapon."

"One that you can see," Noname snarled. Both men who had spoken gave short, hard laughs. The bald man was quiet, tense.

"Is that right?" the man with the blade snorted. "Is your old man that good with his fists?"

"Never judge a book by its cover," Anda said calmly.

"I don't think they've seen many books," Noname told him. The bald man bristled, but the others didn't seem to notice the insult.

"Take the girl too," the dark man rasped. Eine raised her head, astonished.

"Just shoot them, Gaza," the first man ordered.

Noname shot first.Gaza collapsed and the bald man fired, but Noname whirled; the dart shot threw the corner of his jacket, knocking him backwards.

The man with the blade yelled something in another language and lunged straight for Noname. The bald man aimed his weapon again.

"No!" Anda cried. Eine shot forward on instinct. She threw her weight into the man just as he made his shot, sending the dart off target. The man crashed to the ground underneath her and Eine made a grab for his weapon, but he threw her off. She rolled away from him, hearing a clash of metal.

Noname had dropped his gun; he'd pulled the blade from the dead Gaza and was using it to block the other man's swings. The bald man leapt up near Eine and fired a dart straight at Anda. Eine screamed - a sharp pain in her throat - then Anda disappeared. The dart pierced only air and then fell, several feet past the spot where Anda had been standing. The bald man made a gurgle of surprise and swung his weapon towards Eine instead.

In a flash, Anda was back, leaping onto the man from behind. Both of them crashed to the ground, as metal clashed again in Eine's ears. She turned to see Noname deftly whirling and blocking as the other man's larger blade lunged again and again for him. Noname was incredibly fast. Eine scrambled for the fallen gun. She heard the bald man cry out behind her just as Noname leapt forward and slashed his attacker's blade straight out of his hands. Eine whipped her head around to see that Anda now held the dart weapon aimed at the bald man. She turned back to Noname, relieved. He stood straight and taut with the knife pointed at the other man's chest. Eine was astonished by how fierce he looked.

"Give me my gun, Eine," he said, sharply.

"Don't shoot!" his target yelled. "We're just poor men!"

"Oh, Mallid," a sudden voice spoke up. Eine started, nearly dropping the gun. "You are *noble* under fire."

A second later, a fourth man dropped straight out of the trees above, landing on the ground between Anda and Noname. He landed in a crouch and straightened up gracefully, unfolding long limbs and a long, narrow waist. The movement was weirdly fluid and effortless. He wore a dirty, white collared shirt and tattered pants like the man with the blade. Long brown hair was tied back from his face, which was pointed and sharp, and brown sideburns grew down to his chin. Eine took one look at his dark blue eyes and suddenly got a strange feeling. It was like a buzzing, a faint buzzing inside her head.

His eyes met hers for a moment, and then he spoke, his voice languid. "Mallid, Gunder, get out of here." Almost as one, the two men turned and ran off into the bushes, leaving Anda and Noname aiming at empty air.

"Who are you?" Noname demanded.

"I'm the boss. You've entered my part of the forest and killed one of my men, so you'll have to pay a price." His tone was not threatening at all, but rather amused. His voice itself was almost musical. Eine listened to the buzzing in her head and stared at him, confused. As she watched, he gave a little jerk of his head at Anda, and the dart-weapon leapt straight out of his hands. Eine gasped as the weapon hurtled into the woods and out of sight. She stared after it in utter disbelief.

Anda seemed less surprised, however. He dropped his hands and gazed steadily at the strange man in front of him. "What a waste of your abilities," he said with a sigh. The man chuckled, as Noname lowered his sword and rolled his eyes.

"They're my abilities, so I'll use them as I please," he said, pleasantly.

"When full-blooded Laxens turn into forest bandits, you know the world has gone to rot," Noname grumbled. The man laughed again, a ringing laugh that vibrated in Eine's head. *He was a Laxen.* She was in the presence of a Laxen. He was full-blooded and free, standing right before them. …Robbing them.

"Tell me, before I take your coins, why are you traveling with a little Demi?" the man asked. His sharp gaze penetrated Eine and she felt herself tremble suddenly, intimidated.

"A good question," Anda spoke up, stepping forward. The Laxen gave him a warning look, and he went no further. "She's an escaped Thelan."

The words seemed to strike the man like a blow. He took a step backwards, his whole manner of carrying himself suddenly altered. He actually cringed. Eine stared back at him, wide-eyed, wondering.

"It's true," Anda told him.

The Laxen shuddered. "I can't stand to hear that place even named," he said quietly. "It's bad enough being this close to the wall." He studied Eine with his intense blue eyes for a moment. "You've never even seen a full-blood before me, have you? They're all gone." She nodded.

"You're buzzing," she told him, and he suddenly smiled. His face was unexpectedly handsome then.

"Buzzing?" Noname said, frowning.

"How did this come to be?" the Laxen demanded. "What are the three of you doing in my woods?"

"We are part of the Enahalan campaign against the Indigo," Anda explained. "The Creeden and I were sent undercover into the city by the Laxen called Oln." The Laxen's eyebrows went up at the name, as if he recognized it. "There we found Eine and smuggled her out with us."

"Actually, Eine found me and wouldn't take no for an answer," Noname said. She glared at him.

The Laxen stood there silently, looking from one to the other.

"Will you let us pass?" Anda asked him. "We're returning to Enahala to report." The Laxen said nothing, but he stretched out his arms over his head, in an oddly elegant manner. Eine found herself admiring his graceful motions.

"What are you doing, robbing travelers anyway?" Noname demanded. "Looks like you could get money from wherever you want, with a flick of your head."

"Exactly, and I want to do it here. I love the forest, and you'd be surprised how laden down these travelers are, passing through after going to the market. Although not you lot from the looks of it," the Laxen replied.

"And you hire thugs that prey on women?" Noname said sharply. The Laxen cocked his head at Eine as she continued to stare at him, mesmerized. There were so many emotions and questions suddenly building up inside of her, that she felt like her eyes must be enormous.

"Some things never change, I'm afraid. I don't encourage it. However, I can't just let you go without payment -"

Eine couldn't hold it in any longer. "What's your name?" she interrupted, eagerly. The questions exploded from her: "Where are you from? Were you ever in Thela? Could you possibly have known my parents?" The man cringed again, overwhelmed. "Why do I hear buzzing in my head when I look at you? Do you get that from me?" she demanded. The Laxen glared at Noname as if asking him to make her stop. "How did you make that weapon fly away? What else can you do?"

"All right, get out of here," he muttered.

"No, I want to know -"

"I said, get out of here!" he roared. "Quick, before I change my mind."

Noname immediately slid his blade through his belt and walked over to Eine, grabbing her hand. She made a sound of protest, but he ignored it. She looked back over her shoulder as they joined Anda and hustled down the path. The Laxen stared after her for another moment. Then he crouched down suddenly and shot straight up into the tree branches above.

Noname continued holding Eine's hand as the three of them hurried away. She felt a great deal more like a child now than she had ever felt, being shushed and led away. She didn't really mind though, distracted as she was by the slow fading of the buzzing in her head.

"So I can feel them in my head," she marveled aloud. "I know when Laxens are near."

"If you've never felt that before," Noname said grimly, "then there definitely aren't any left in Thela." This was a sobering thought and Eine nodded, letting go of his hand.

"Well, Eine, I'm sorry your first experience with your own kind was with a bandit," Anda told her. He glanced back over his shoulder as well. "At least he's not following us."

"I did get a sword out of it," Noname commented.

"And you…killed someone," Eine said, as if she had only just realized it. She glanced up at Noname, feeling suddenly a little bit afraid. She wasn't sure if the fear was because he was capable of killing someone, or because he might be offended by what she'd just said. She had known he was a soldier. She certainly knew that people died.

Noname turned and stared at her, taken by surprise. Then his dark brows drew together in an injured way. He was hurt by what she'd said, and she felt a pang of regret.

"He would've hurt you," he protested. He frowned immediately afterwards and looked away. "…But I could've just wounded him." He sounded a little worried and Anda put a hand on his arm. He said something in his language to Noname, who didn't reply. Eine suddenly felt awful, intensely, hideously awful. Why had she said that? She was blurting everything out now, without even thinking! It was better to be quiet, like she used to be, always.

Anda was giving her a sympathetic look. "You both have grown up in a world of violence. But your only option was to hide from it, and to survive," he said. "Ney, here, has grown up fighting, and when you are accustomed to fighting…"His voice faded away for a moment and his blue eyes looked sad. "…Sometimes it becomes difficult to know where the line is drawn." As he spoke, a bird flew low over Eine's head and she ducked, half-heartedly. She turned to watch it flit off into the trees, thinking about Anda's words.

Noname was quiet, and she avoided looking at him.

"I've just never seen anyone killed before," she ventured. "I've only seen them taken away…to be killed somewhere else." She sighed, thinking of Graf. It must certainly be too late for him now. She had failed him.

"One never gets used to it, child," Anda replied. "And that

is certainly a blessing." Eine glanced up at him and suddenly remembered the way he had vanished when the bald man had fired at him.

"Anda!" she exclaimed. "How did you disappear like that? Like the Indigo!"

Anda scoffed and waved a hand at her. "Oh, I didn't disappear. I simply faded out for a bit and faded back. It's a simple trick."

Noname looked back at them and gave Eine a small smile. "He's explained it to me several times and I still don't get it."

"It's a trick of the eye," Anda said, smiling. "You just have to practice it. You just sort of side-step, just shift a little, right out of view." Eine shook her head, confused.

"I thought you said only Laxens had magic."

"This isn't magic, Eine, I promise you. Enahalans are very good at sleight of hand. But how that monster managed it in Thela, I have no idea," Anda said, his voice lowering. "It all comes back to us knowing so little about them."

TEN

The sun was setting when the trees and the undergrowth began to thin around them. Eine could see strips of rose-colored sky between the branches. She felt her heart begin to pound for a moment. Beyond the forest were new places she knew nothing about. She was going further and further out into the world.

"We should reach Tobin before too long. We'll catch a night train and be on our way shortly," Anda declared, walking faster. Eine wondered why she couldn't see any signs of a city wall over the treetops. Noname sighed and she glanced at him.

"I can never sleep on trains…" he muttered.

They walked for another hour or so, as the forest dwindled into a series of scattered trees and bushes. The path eventually widened at their feet, and soon the undergrowth looked as if it had been deliberately cleared. There were wild flowers growing here and there in the grass. Eine looked ahead of them eagerly as the sun slipped down behind the roofs of a huddle of buildings. They appeared to be built of planks of wood, instead of brick, and the roofs were made of black shingles. The walls had large windows, although most of them had curtains drawn over them now, in the twilight.

"Is this the city?" Eine asked, astonished, looking around.

"It's the outskirts," Noname said.

She stopped and looked up at him. "There's no wall?"

"Ah, that there isn't," Anda replied. "I think you'll find that most cities gave up the idea of walling themselves off from the world a long time ago. Although a few places still do, like Enahala."

"Enahala would never do without a wall," Noname said, drily.

"Hush, Ney."

Eine followed Noname and Anda off the forest path and onto a road of hard-packed dirt. The road led the way through the first group of houses and then gradually broadened out onto a wide thoroughfare. Eine stopped mid-step and stared at the scene ahead of her. A bustle of people and several rows of buildings stretched out before them. Women in long dresses were sweeping across the road, holding the hands of children, carrying packages, gesturing dramatically to companions. Men in both sharp suits and rough, rugged clothing stood on porches and chatted, or strode confidently from building to building. No one wore a hood – in fact, few people wore coats or cloaks at all.

These were not frightened, huddled people, passing through.

The women's dresses were a mélange of thick, sturdy swatches of cloth and pretty bits of lace. Some of them wore their hair coiled up very high, while others left theirs curling around their shoulders. The people here weren't as diverse as in the market; most of them had curly, blond hair and very fair skin, with only a handful of darker types among them. The men wore their hair cut short like caps around their heads, and several had beards. The ones in rough clothes reminded Eine of the forest thieves, but most of them didn't carry weapons. The finer ones who wore suits had buckles down the front like Anda's blue coat.

There were men leading horses down the road, horses so much smaller than the Hunters' beasts that Eine stared in disbelief. They seemed almost delicate, until one of them suddenly reared up and whinnied, knocking over crates and scattering people around it.

Eine realized then that Anda and Noname had gotten ahead of her, and she hurried after them anxiously. "The last time I was here," Noname was saying, "I had to stop a fist fight that started up over a woman. She wasn't interested in either one of them." Anda chuckled.

"Was she interested in you instead?" he asked, grinning. Noname grinned too and shrugged. A clattering sound interrupted them and Eine looked out into the street. Then she gasped. A leather and metal contraption was moving down the street on wheels at a fast, even pace. It was box-shaped with gleaming metal and bits of flapping canvas. There was smoke puffing out the back in white clouds.

"Look!" Eine exclaimed. "There's someone inside it!" The machine was open in the front and she could see a man riding just inside, staring out at all the people in the road. The machine made a loud croak and several people scurried out of the way as it rattled by.

"It's an auto-car," Noname told her, smiling.

"It's a vehicle, Eine, made for carrying passengers about," Anda explained. "Someone has to drive it."

"Oh." Eine turned around and watched the auto-car make its way quickly to a street corner and swing around it.

"Wait till she sees the train, Anda."

She heard the croaking sound one more time and then the auto-car was gone. "Did we ever have those in Thela?" she asked, catching up to the others.

"Of course. Indigo banned everything. Now let me see, the train station was north, I believe... This way!" Anda waved a hand and they turned down a side street. This one turned out to have children playing in the road, kicking a leather ball back and forth to each other. A few of them stopped and stared as Eine passed, and she stared at them back from under her hood. They wore short dresses and pants, and their fair faces were freckled. Their critical stares made her suddenly very nervous.

"Why's she wearing a cloak? It's not raining."
"She's pretty."
"That man's got a lot of scars!"

Eine flinched at the strange thoughts that sprang from them.

"Come in, boys! It's getting dark out!" a woman's voice called, from one of the houses. Two boys turned and ran off towards the voice, and the rest of the children began to scatter. Eine watched them go, unable to imagine what their lives were like.

A loud whistle burst through the air, drawing her attention back towards Anda and Noname, and the direction they were headed. She could see smoke rising up into the evening sky, and for one instant, she remembered the factories. She sucked in her breath, the old fear suddenly striking her. What was this? Where were they going?

Noname turned back as if to make sure she were following. He was smiling at her, in his boyish way. She smiled back automatically, feeling her fear subside.

"Come see, Eine," he said.

They were approaching a long dark building, beyond which strange rumblings and roarings were bursting forth, and clouds of smoke puffed upwards into the sky. Eine felt her senses overload as they stepped inside the building through a tall, arched entranceway. Her head fell back as she looked up at the vaulted ceiling. From it were hanging hundreds of lamps which filled the building with both bright light and shadow. Up high on the wall directly ahead were two black boards scrawled upon in white letters. A man stood on a tall wheeled ladder, rubbing out some of the words and writing new ones. He was making lists of numbers next to letters, none of which meant anything to Eine.

19:30 MEYJA
20:00 KALID (DELAYED)
20:15 GUSSON, ON TO KINIMIN ISLANDS FERRY
21:00 KROLAND (FULL)

Below the boards, there was a long row of small gates, each marked by a booth and a person in a black hat, and each flanked by a line of people, passing through. Eine looked at Anda, mute with wonder, as he opened his bag and flicked through some coins inside.

"See, the trains are like very long auto-cars," Noname was saying. "They can carry a lot of people at once, and they go a long way." Eine nodded, uncertainly.

"We want that Meyjan train. Here, follow me," Anda told them. He led the way to one of the shorter lines of people, and stood behind the last person, which was a very fat woman who carried a small animal. Eine peered around Anda and stared at the little creature. It was bright-eyed and fluffy with fur, but very well-brushed. It stared back at Eine and yapped loudly, showing a pink tongue. She giggled.

"They better get moving or we're going to miss it," Noname told Anda. "When's the next one to Meyja?" Eine looked up with them at the boards above, not comprehending a thing. She didn't even know how to read Thelan, and she wasn't sure what language these letters were in.

21:20 CALIBREE
21:50 AXT (DELAYED)
22:00 BELGIR

"There aren't any others tonight," Anda commented. The line moved forward and the woman's pet yapped at them again.

Just as Eine was beginning to get tired of standing and shuffling slowly forward, they arrived at the booth at their gate. Anda purchased three tickets from the man there with the black hat, who pointed to the left; Anda and Noname set off down a hall in that direction and Eine followed, darting through other people. Only when the hall suddenly opened up to the night outside, did it start to make sense to her. They were only passing through this building; the trains would be outside like the auto-car, on a road…

She was startled to see several long, dark shapes that rose up above them, silhouetted against the night sky. She stopped in her tracks. The smoke in the sky was billowing forth from massive pipes set into the roofs of those looming shapes. These behemoths were the trains, the giant auto-cars! They were monsters of metal, canvas, and leather, with great, polished wheels and darkened glass windows. Beneath the smoke stacks at their front ends, the machines sloped down into long points, as if they had noses that would smell the way ahead.

The sky above was breaking out with stars, and the moon was visible and bright, just behind a stream of smoke. Eine hurried after Anda and Noname as they strode confidently toward the train to Meyja, wherever in the world that was. She felt a tingling all over as she stood with them at the foot of the train. Everything was happening very fast now. Anda passed over their tickets and soon they were being helped up several steps and into the belly of the train.

Inside, Eine found herself walking through a dim, narrow hallway with small doors along one side and windows on the other. Every now and then, a lamp in the ceiling marked their progress, and Eine could make out numbers on the doors. Anda stopped at one and slid it open. He ducked his head and stepped inside to a little room that held two padded bench-seats, facing each other.

"Here we are, 24," he said cheerfully. He sat down onto the padded seat with a sigh. Noname shut the door behind them and followed suit, stretching his long legs out across the middle. Eine stepped over his legs and went straight to the rectangular window, intent on staring out eagerly into the night. She could see another train outside beginning to move. Its wheels were grinding and churning, and distant voices were calling out.

Noname made a small, satisfied groan behind her. "So good to sit down," he breathed. Anda was dumping out the contents of his bag onto the seat next to him, sorting out the bread, fruit and meat. Eine sat down between Noname and the window, and felt herself sink into a pleasant softness. She glanced up at the low ceiling and saw a small lamp swinging slightly. There were other passengers thumping their way down the hall, past their door.

"So how can Meyja have a train station anyway? I thought it was just a little village," Noname asked Anda. Anda passed him the meat and handed Eine a piece of bread.

"In truth, it's just a platform with a sign and supposedly, the Meyjan object to its very presence," Anda replied. "But since the council won't allow a rail station to 'mar the beauty of our fair Enahala'…" Noname snorted. Someone was yelling outside, and more passengers moved past their door, swaying the room a bit. "Let me go and fill our canteen before we take off," Anda said and he went back out into the hall, sliding the door shut.

"I'll trade you meat for bread," Noname told Eine. She swapped with him quietly and he gave her a look. "You all right, kid?" She gazed back at him for a second, thinking.

"How does the train move?" she asked. "Why is there smoke? Is there a fire inside?" He groaned and stretched again, shaking his head.

"Anda's the one who can explain those things, not me. I know that it runs on steam. That's what the smoke is, actually, it's steam." He leaned past her and looked out the window as another train rushed out into the night. With his face that close to hers, she noticed absently that he smelled like grass and a little like sweat. It was somehow a pleasant smell. She noticed outside that there were metal tracks laid into the ground underneath the departing train. "I think the steam builds up pressure inside and that gives us the energy to move so fast. A Laxen first invented it, I think, so as far as I'm concerned, it might as well be magic." He sat back down in his seat, watching her.

"How long will it take to get to Meyja?"

"Probably all night. Meyja is just the closest station to Enahala, by the way. We can walk from there," Noname said, tearing off a bite of dried bread. Anda returned a moment later, just as the train began to tremble violently. Eine clutched the edge of the seat and looked out the window again, wide-eyed, as loud clanking and the hissing of steam reached her ears.

In a few more moments, the train began to crawl forward. Eine watched as the remaining trains at the station appeared to roll very slowly backward. The open night gradually filled up the window. She craned her neck to look back and watch as the train station shrank. They started to pick up speed then, and her heart pounded in her chest. It was so fast. How could they be moving so fast?

"How I miss my warm bed," Anda thought, surprising her. She glanced back at him and then back out the window, anxiously. They were leaving the buildings of Tobin behind. In a few seconds – impossibly fast - there was nothing but land outside the window. It was indistinct, dark, open land, apparently free of buildings.

"We're traveling over the Gold Plains, Eine," Anda told her, and then broke into a yawn. "No city lights to give you much of a view, I'm afraid."

The Gold Plains. Eine pressed her face up against the dark glass. "Does no one live out here?" she asked.

"Only a few scattered groups. It's rather rough living. The weather is terrible, lots of lightning storms and a powerful wind." He unbuckled his blue coat as he spoke and turned it around, laying it like a blanket across him. "I believe I will take a little nap," he murmured.

Eine glanced back at Noname. Slumped now, his legs reached all the way across the space between the seats and his feet rested next to Anda. She remembered that he had said he couldn't sleep on trains, but his eyes were half-closed now, his arms folded across his chest. She wrapped herself up tighter in her cloak and leaned her head against the window, watching the darkness flash by. They were flying along inside a giant machine that moved by steam. How could anyone sleep?

***

A crash of thunder snapped Eine awake. She sat up in pitch blackness, and then a flash of light appeared on her right side. It took her a moment to realize it was lightning, outside the train window. Thunder boomed again and she jumped, staring out at the rain that was streaming down the glass.

"Never fails," Noname muttered next to her. She turned to look at him in the darkness, and could only make out a silhouette. The lamp in the ceiling must have been extinguished.

"What does?" she asked, sleepy.

"I start to drift off, and then the train rocks or thunder crashes." He yawned and stretched, his right arm reaching past Eine's face, almost touching the window.

"It's so loud," she said, and glanced over at Anda, who appeared to be sound asleep. He snored to confirm it.

"Anda could sleep through a battle," Noname said. "Did you have your dream again?"

"No..." Eine said, thoughtfully. "I don't think I slept deep enough."Another loud crack of thunder made them both jump.

"Imagine that," Noname replied. "I dreamed about cheese toast," he added, sounding like he was smiling. "Guess I'm tired of travel food."

"What's cheese toast? I'm hungry too," Eine said, sitting up straight again.

"Cheese toast and warm honey water," Noname said, dreamily. "You melt the cheese on the bread and you spoon honey into some hot water. I used to eat that at night when I couldn't sleep."

Eine laughed and he turned to look at her in the dark. "I have no idea what you're talking about."

"Oh yeah?" He was definitely smiling. "Night trains usually have a late kitchen. Let's go see if we can find it." He stood up and slid open the door, as the train swayed slightly around them. Surprised, Eine jumped up and followed, feeling a little thrill inside. She didn't know why, but creeping out into the dark train felt exciting. Wide awake now, she followed Noname down the narrow hallway, holding onto the walls. Some of the lamps were still lit, but not as many, and in the moving train, they cast shadows everywhere.

The two of them tiptoed down the corridor until it came to an end where a door faced them. There was a window in the door, but a shade on the other side was pulled down; light was visible around the edges. Noname tugged on the door but it didn't open.

He tried again and grumbled, bracing against the frame.

"The stupid thing is stuck," he exclaimed. "Must be the damp." Eine nodded and reached under his arm. She grabbed the handle and pulled. The door unstuck with a small pop and slid open. Noname said something in Creeden and scowled down at Eine. She grinned.

Through the doorway, Eine squinted in surprise to see a room partially filled with people. Apparently, there were many other passengers who were hungry in the night. They were sitting at tables on either side of the train. A man with a cart was handing out drinks to a couple at the end of the aisle that ran in between. The wide windows on either side of the train continued to reveal gushing rain and bursts of lightning, but the passengers were talking and eating, ignoring the weather.

Noname slid into a seat and Eine sat down across from him, studying his scarred face in the brighter light. His brown eyes were tired, slightly puffy, and he was beginning to grow the shadow of a beard, which made him seem a little older. He smiled wide, however, and she smiled back, as if it were contagious. "Now we'll get some real food. Let's see what they got," he said. He dug into his pocket and pulled out a few coins.

The man with the cart wheeled over to them and nodded his head, looking tired. He greeted them in a lisping language, and Noname replied in the same. Eine watched, fascinated, as he made his order and the man replied, turning the cart around. Noname drummed his fingers on the table happily as he went.

"Is it really that good?" Eine asked.

"Right now it'll be, I'm sure of it." He looked at her more closely then and his smile faded a little. "I guess you've never had a favorite food," he commented.

"A favorite food…" Eine hadn't thought of that before, since she had always eaten whatever she could get. "I liked apples the best, in Thela, but now I think I like that spicy meat we bought better than anything."

Noname nodded, watching her. "Why do you keep wearing your hood?" he asked.

Hide your light, child. Eine blinked, and looked away from him, staring around the train at the other passengers. Their clothing was widely varied but no one was wearing a hood. None of them were paying her or Noname any attention. Eine reached up hesitantly and pushed her hood back, glancing around again. She looked back at Noname and his eyes darted away quickly, almost nervously. It gave Eine a funny little feeling in her stomach.

The man with the cart was returning down the aisle, and something smelled incredible as he rolled up to their table. He lisped at them again and then passed out slices of bread that had been cooked with a creamy substance on top. To that he added two mugs of steaming water and a small jar with a spoon.

Eine examined everything closely, as Noname counted out his coins and paid the man. Then he scooped up his cheese toast and took a big bite. He yelped right afterwards and waved a hand in front of his mouth. Eine grinned and blew on hers, inhaling the wonderful smell. Hot food. Just cooked, very hot food. She shook her head in amazement, and lifted the lid of the little jar, to see the honey inside.

As another roll of thunder shook the room, the door slid open and two tall, thin women walked in. The train rocked to one side as they entered, but neither of them stumbled. Eine looked up at them curiously as she took a bite of her cheese toast. Then she stopped, as her head began to buzz.

Both women turned and gave her a short stare. Then they continued on down the aisle. One of them had very blue eyes and long red hair that curled in ringlets; the other had black hair tied up in a bun and slanted dark eyes. They both wore patterned tunics over trousers, and they had soft-looking slippers on their feet. Eine turned in her seat, watching them as they sat down at a table and looked expectantly at the cart.

"What is it?" Noname asked. She turned around again to see him scooping the honey into his mug and stirring it up.

"They're Laxens," she said softly. He glanced at the women and then nodded, putting honey into her own mug.

"They look like Inowens. Probably scholars." He stirred her water and slid it back towards her. "There's a university in Inowa, and I doubt anybody else but a student would go around in flimsy shoes like that. They're for somebody who stays indoors and reads."

Eine had a peculiar feeling as she listened to him, almost as if a very thin thread were sliding through her ears. "She can hear you," she said, wonderingly. "The redhead."

"How do you know?" he asked, staring at her. She shook

her head and rubbed both her ears, and then suddenly the feeling was gone. He looked over at their table and smiled a polite smile. Eine glanced over at the women, intimidated. What had just happened? The brunette was reading a folded packet of papers, but the redhead gave Noname a tolerant nod.Had she somehow used Eine's hearing for a moment?

The food cart rolled over to the women and they both ordered. Eine watched as the man explained something, and the brunette shook her head. She held out her hand, and he placed a bowl of soup into it, looking confused. Then the Laxen stared down at the bowl for a moment, until steam suddenly rose from the top.

Eine smiled.

"How do you like it?" Noname asked, bringing her back to her own food. She settled back into her seat the right way and took another bite of the cheese toast. She nodded enthusiastically, and he looked pleased. "I can't imagine growing up without cheese toast."

"What do you call it in Creeden?" she asked.

He made a series of clicking syllables that sounded something like '*bikikuckni inick*'. She stared at him and he laughed. "How are you doing that?" she demanded.

"You have to be a Creede, kid," he said, looking smug.

"It's your tongue. You're doing something with it."

"Yes. Talking."

Eine set down her toast. "Let me see," she insisted. Noname stuck his tongue out at her. She squinted at it, leaning across the table, but it looked like a very ordinary tongue. He started to laugh and leaned away from her. She liked how he looked so micheivous, with his brown eyes twinkling, and his boyish grin.

"Wait a minute, why does everyone say Oln's name? The one who 'mind-sent' you. Isn't he a Creeden?" Eine asked.

"Oln is a nickname too, but it's widely used," he told her. "Because he's widely known for his mind-sending. It means 'sender' in a couple different languages."

Eine shook her head, still awe-struck at the idea of anyone who could move a human being with his mind. The thought occurred to her suddenly, that some would consider it very threatening. Was that why the Indigo wanted to kill Laxens? Did it have to do with fear?

"Is that why…?" she began, with her mouth full, and then hesitated, chewing slowly. "Is the Indigo just afraid of Laxens?" she asked, almost as if to herself.

"That is one theory," a woman's voice said. Eine and Noname both jumped, as the red-haired Laxen suddenly appeared at their table. Noname choked on his hot water and heaved, pounding himself on the chest. Eine stared up at the woman, astonished. Up close, she could see that the pattern on her tunic was of tiny, embroidered stars, and that she had a sprinkling of red freckles. She saw with a start that her eyes were violet. "I heard him through you," she said, studying Eine's face.

"What?" Eine asked, bewildered.

"You are from Thela," she continued. Eine nodded. "What is it like?" Her expression was pained suddenly, and her voice fearful. Noname cleared his throat with an annoyed sound, but she ignored him.

Eine picked up her plate and held it up towards the Laxen. "We don't have this," she said, with a small smile. "We don't have hot food."

"Or shoes, or shelter, or any knowledge of the world," Noname said, sipping his water. Eine stuck her chin out. The woman's mouth twisted and she made a fist with one pale hand.

"How did they not find you?" she asked.

"I looked like one of the people that live on the street. They don't know, the way that we do," Eine said, feeling the gentle buzz in her head. "But they keep looking. I guess they would've found me after awhile." A weight she hadn't felt in several days now settled back onto her shoulders. She understood why perhaps Noname hadn't wanted her to talk about Thela. She had been enjoying herself very much just a moment ago.

"Especially if I had left you there," he muttered. Eine realized with a start that he was absolutely right. He looked grim now.

"My colleague and I have been following the theories…" The Laxen sighed and looked back over at the table where the dark-haired woman sat, watching them now. "There are some who suspect that Indigo may be a survivor of Andliss." Noname stared up at her, and she nodded intently. "It doesn't do much to explain his power but perhaps it gives insight to his motive." She gave

Eine a sad look. "And the new science on our kind suggests that we may all share a certain gene, which means that something toxic to us all could, in theory, be created." She turned away, looking thoughtful, and then floated down the aisle as if her feet barely touched the floor. It was much more weightless than the way Eine moved. It was ethereal.

Eine looked back at Noname's stunned face. "What's Andliss?"

"It was a city." He ate the last of his cheese toast and sat back, frowning. "There's a story from back when my parents were young, about this great city of Andliss and how it was destroyed by Laxens."

Eine gasped. "Why?"

"There was a small group of very powerful Laxens, ones like Oln, who…got a little carried away," he said. "They got together and called themselves the Pinnacle. And then they decided that they were gods. Like Anda said, people used to think Laxens were gods, when they first started showing up." Eine sat back in her seat, confused. "The Pinnacle decided that there was nothing stopping them from *being* gods, and when people refused to treat them that way, they destroyed the city of Andliss, as punishment. They set the whole place on fire, in a single instant." He drank the last of his honey water and wiped his mouth on his sleeve. "Andlissians were a very talented group of people. It was a place where a lot of artists, inventors and scholars came from. So it was even more terrible… Afterwards, other Laxens broke up the Pinnacle, and its members were imprisoned or put to death. Some people blame them for not acting sooner."

"But there were survivors?" Eine asked. He shrugged.

"My father used to say there must be. And imagine if there were, how much hatred they would have for Laxens."

Eine nodded and stared down into the murky water in the bottom of her mug. If the theory were true, then the leader of the Indigo was a talented, intelligent person with a vendetta. The thought weighed heavily on her. She realized a second later, incongruously, that she felt very, very full.She had eaten the whole cheese toast and drank most of the sweet water. Noname sighed and stretched his arms over his head.

"What are scholars?" she asked, and he groaned. She frowned. "How am I supposed to learn anything if you're too impatient to tell me?"

"That's what scholars do, all right? They learn," he told her. "Do you know what reading is?" She nodded slowly.

"I've seen books but I can't read."

"Well, maybe I'll teach you in Enahala. If you stick with me, I'll teach you all kinds of things. But we'd better get back," he said. "Before Anda wakes up and thinks we got into trouble."

ELEVEN

"It will be a blessing to see the towers of home," Anda's voice said, over the rumble of the train. Eine opened her eyes and was nearly blinded by bright sunshine streaming in through the window. Anda and Noname were sitting up, eating the dried fruit and bread. She glanced at them and then squinted out the window again, at the immense flat land that was rolling past. It was a sea of tall, yellow grass – the Gold Plains - that stretched straight out to the horizon, where an intensely blue sky curved down to meet it. Here and there were clumps of large boulders, but there were no houses or other structures. The tall grass seemed blown back, as if by a great wind.

Eine had never seen such a sky. It was so amazingly bright and clear.

"Aha, she's awake," Anda declared. Eine looked back at her companions and saw Noname give her a quick smile. "They'll pull the sails out in a moment, to catch this wind. It saves the engines a bit," Anda told her.

"Sails?" Eine asked, reaching for the canteen.

"Like on a boat, which you've never seen either," Noname said, chewing. "Look." He gestured out the window and Eine turned just in time to see a flutter of white cloth suddenly block the view. It whipped straight forward, billowing out full of air, and then Eine could see how large it was. She was only seeing a portion of it; the length seemed to stretch from the roof to the wheels. The train lurched forward and she gripped the seat. They were riding on the powerful wind.

"I just hope the poor folks riding on the back can hold on," Anda commented and Noname nodded. Eine choked a little on the water from the canteen.

"There are people riding on the back?" she exclaimed. "On the outside?"

"Not everyone can afford a ticket, I'm afraid."

"Not everyone who can gets private seats either. Enahala pays for the best," Noname said, with a smirk. Anda made a tsk tsk sound at him.

Eine craned her neck, trying to see out the window towards the back of the train. Noname laughed. "You can't see them, Eine," he said. She frowned, embarrassed, and passed back the canteen.

"But how do they hold on?" she asked.

"You get a good leather strap and tie it to a rail. I've done it a couple times, as a kid," he said, grinning. "Not all the way across the Plains though. I'm not crazy." Anda snorted.

"That is a matter of opinion."

They rode along for another hour or so before the train let out a fierce whistle, and Eine jumped in her seat. Anda began to stuff the food and water back into his bag, as Noname stood up and stretched for the hundredth time, holding onto the door frame. The train's sails had retracted several moments before, but Eine could still see only the yellow grass. They were slowing down now, inching along towards Meyja, the village closest to Enahala.

After a few moments, the train came to a halt with a heavy, grinding sound. Eine stood up and followed them out into the hallway, heading towards the front of the train. Peering out the windows as they went, she could see nothing but grass on this side as well. As they reached the door, she spotted a large sign outside. There were three unfamiliar symbols painted on it; underneath them, it said MEYJA.

The three of them stepped down through the open door, onto a low wooden platform which held up the sign and nothing else. The boards were very warm from the sun under Eine's bare feet. She shaded her eyes and saw to the right a small huddle of thatched roof houses. But beyond them was an entirely different sight, one that took her breath away.

A cluster of tall spires rose up into the sky, brilliant and sparkling like glass ornaments in the sun. Eine stared at the distant spectacle, as a strong wind swept over her, blowing her green cloak back. Someone on the train behind them slammed the door shut and another fierce whistle burst from the looming machine.They were the only people getting off.

"And there it is," Anda was saying, as the train shot steam into the air overhead. "Home sweet home!"

A shrill cry erupted from the village, startling the three of them. Six small figures suddenly came running out from between the thatched houses, just as the train slowly chugged away.

"No strangers! No foreigners!" the villagers shrieked. Eine could barely hear them over the noise of the train. She could see that they were no taller than she was, even though four of them were men. They were broad, squat people in rough clothing, and their skin was tanned a light brown from the sun. The two women had curly hair that they wore in braids. At that moment, Eine realized they were the same race as the little woman who had shot at them at the end of the tunnel. She hadn't remembered what Anda had called her.

"Go back!" one of the Meyjans hollered. "No foreigners!"

"Great gods," Anda muttered, glancing at Noname. He pulled out his gun. "I hadn't realized it was this bad." He addressed the closest Meyjan, who had a short gray beard and looked much older than the others. "My dear sir, forgive the intrusion. We are on our way to Enahala, and won't trouble you."

The man looked him up and down, unimpressed, as the others fell silent, watching him. "We never gave them permission to build this train stop," he snapped. "Every time we tear it down, they put it back up!"

"The train is so loud!" one of the women yelled. Noname lowered his gun and gave Anda a knowing look. Eine glanced around them and saw that the train tracks curved away from the platform and headed west, where the train was still visible in the distance. All around the village of Meyja were large outcroppings of rock, and yellow grass waving in the wind. The noise of the engine carried very far in that stillness.

"I am so sorry," Anda said, sounding truly humble. "I will pass on your complaint once we reach Enahala." Almost as one, the Meyjans snorted and grumbled in disbelief.

"Why doesn't the train track go around the town?" Eine asked Anda. Another one of the men, one who wore a cap that tied under his chin, pointed at her and nodded.

"The Laxen makes sense," he said.

"She's not a Laxen," one of the women snapped.

"She's part Laxen!" he retorted. "I can always tell!"

"Don't be silly! She's just a plain little girl!"

Noname started to laugh. Eine felt herself blush and she elbowed him in the side. A baby suddenly cried from one of the nearby houses, cutting short the argument. The woman harrumphed and hurried away, her braids blowing in the wind. Anda cleared his throat, catching their attention again.

"Perhaps my people don't always make the best decisions – " he began.

"Anda Leona, you old trouble-maker!" a voice rang out suddenly. Eine jumped, and Noname swore, raising his gun again. A white-haired man was approaching from the village, tall and pale, and wearing a long white coat. He was certainly not a Meyjan. The group of small people snarled at him as he approached, but they parted to let him pass.

"Reen," Anda said with a smile. "What trouble am I making, old friend?"

"Criticizing our good council, apologizing to Meyjan, oh the shame," the man said, but there was humor in his voice. He passed through the Meyjans without giving them a single glance and reached out to clasp Anda's hand. He was older than Anda and his face was finely wrinkled, but he had the same bright blue eyes. The trousers he wore were fitted and buttoned up the side of each leg, and he wore a collared shirt like the one Anda had been wearing at the docks.

"Hello, young Creeden," he said to Noname. "We are glad to have you both back safe and sound." Then his eyes fell on Eine. He cocked his head to one side and gave her a little bow.

"I'm Eine. I'm from Thela," she told him. It was the first time she had said that aloud and it felt good. It felt important. Reen looked at Anda in surprise.

"She escaped with us and has her own story to tell," Anda told him. "For now, let us be on our way. I'm anxious to be home!"

"I'm sure you are!" Reen led them down off the train platform and into the village. Eine looked back as they went and saw that the villagers were convening in a little huddle. Then they dispersed, unhappily, making their way back to their houses.

***

The important buildings within Enahala were plated with solid, iridescent shell, imported from the Lelon Sea. The rest were built of polished white stone. The entire city appeared white at first, but a large part of it was actually shimmering with pale colors due to the shell plating, and that explained its brilliance in the sun. Everything was rounded because Enahalans were not fond of sharp angles.

Noname explained this to Eine, after they had followed Reen and Anda along a simple trail for several miles through the tall grass, and found themselves at the base of a gleaming white city wall. Above it, the enormous rounded towers glistened like a mirage. Eine stood staring upwards, open-mouthed.

It was like a city of clouds.

Reen led them along the base of the wall, chatting with Anda as he went. There didn't seem to be a gate in the wall anywhere. "…and what do you suppose they did then?" he was telling Anda. "They contacted the General of Trainways and claimed that we were imposing on them. Imposing! It's a simple wooden platform!"

"Well, it *is* their land, Reen," Anda replied, sounding irritated.

"Here we are." The older man reached a place in the wall that looked just as smooth as the rest, and fitted his hand into a place Eine couldn't quite see. He pushed and a hidden door opened - a polished white door that blended in perfectly with the wall. Reen led them through, as Eine looked back at Noname, dumbfounded. He winked at her.

"Bet you're scared, kid."

The four of them passed into a long narrow hall and then stepped out through the other side. The stone path at their feet immediately rose up from the ground before them and curved its way gracefully up and around the side of the nearest gleaming building. There were no supports beneath it and no rails on either side; it was a floating walkway. Eine glanced around, wildly. They were all around. Walkways rose and twisted as far as she could see, upwards around the buildings. She felt paralyzed for an instant, filled with a strange anxiety.

"I hate these things," Noname grumbled mentally. Eine barely reacted at all. She was craning her neck to see people up above, walking along the pathways effortlessly. Several of them wore white coats like Reen, but some wore pastel colors and some even glittered a little. There was almost no one on the ground before them. Reen was already mounting the rising path in front of them.

"Welcome to Enahala, Eine," Anda said, with a proud smile.

"I'll take you to your rooms and then you can meet us in the council hall for a meal, at two-marks," Reen declared, walking ahead. Eine stepped onto the walkway and was surprised to feel a rough, almost sticky surface under her feet. She realized that the stone had been treated with something to prevent slipping. The cleverness of the whole thing took her breath away.

"It's not glue, Eine, don't fall off," Noname said behind her. She nodded, uncertainly. Anda was already getting ahead of them, chatting with Reen.

"How does it stay up? If it's not magic?" she demanded. Noname shrugged and glanced up at the brilliant buildings overhead.

"Anda's people are good architects, probably the best. They designed them so that they hold. I don't know how." Eine continued on, peering down over the side, as they climbed higher. "But it gets really tiring after awhile, that's for sure," he added. "You can't beat Enahalans for their leg muscle."

"But what about when they're sick? Or injured? Do they have wider ones for auto-cars?"

"No, no, they have elevators. Little platforms that are lifted up by ropes and pullies. But it's considered cheating, I think…"

In the buildings they passed, there were long, oval-shaped windows and arched doors that opened out onto the airy pathways. The paths often split so that one side could wrap upwards around one tower while the other stretched out towards a different one. A gray-haired couple strode across a path that passed underneath them; Eine looked up and spotted an old man with a cane up above, shuffling along. As they curved upwards around the building to their left, she saw a white-haired lady pass by on another path, who smiled at them. Eine smiled back. There seemed to be many elderly people walking along with no trouble.

Her own legs were beginning to ache when Reen and Anda stopped ahead at one of the arched door. Eine and Noname were both huffing for breath as they joined the Enahalans at the door. Reen gave them a superior smile.

"This is a spare room for the young lady," he said, sliding open the smooth door. "I'm afraid we only prepared a chamber for the Creeden." Eine noticed this second use of Noname's homeland as a title, and then realized with a smile that it was only natural. The Enahalan certainly did not know his name.

She stepped inside the door and found herself in a small, round room, with a domed ceiling. It was dark and warm, and the walls were hung with soft-looking draperies. There was a large mat on the stone floor that cushioned her feet. A low bed covered in blankets stretched along one wall, while the other wall was fitted with two stone basins, one very large and one small.

"Someone will come and help you get ready for the meal," Reen reassured her. "In the meantime, make yourself comfortable." He was already turning away, back onto the main portion of the path. Eine leaned back out the doorway, feeling anxious. Anda was following Reen, but Noname stood there looking back at her, his eyebrows raised.

"Is it okay?" he asked.

"Where are you going to be? And Anda?" she asked. The idea of being shut up in a separate room from them was a little unnerving. Noname cocked his head at her and smiled his boyish smile, which was more reassuring than Reen's strange comment about someone coming.

"Anda!" Noname called up the path. "How far away will I be?" Anda said something she couldn't hear, and then Noname told her, "Just around the corner, kid." She nodded and watched him head back up the path. She was reminded of that feeling she'd had before, that she didn't want him to be very far away. Confused, she closed the door and stood there a second, staring around at her room.

When her eyes adjusted to the darkness, she noticed a round white disc set in the wall near the door. She inspected it for a moment and then tentatively tapped it. The room sprang into light. Eine cringed, and almost fell over backwards. She would've landed into the large basin behind her, which she could now see had a pump handle and a spout on one end, and a round drain in the bottom. The small basin had a miniature version of the pump and spout, but it held a large round hole at its center.

Fascinated, Eine spun around and studied the room in the bright light. The floor covering and the draperies on the rounded walls were a deep red. She padded over to the bed and ran her hand carefully over the blankets and cushions. They were various deep blues and greens, and they were feathery soft under her fingers. Was this what Anda's people slept on? Was this what she was meant to sleep on tonight? Eine took a step backwards and shook her head. It didn't seem right somehow. Maybe she would just curl up on the mat on the floor.

She sat down on it now and gazed around the room again. Anda's people had all this comfort and yet they risked their lives trying to stop the Indigo. It was an amazing thought. She tucked her legs up and rested her chin on her knees, feeling a small glow inside her. It was an amazing and hopeful thought.

TWELVE

A light tapping on the door broke Eine from her reverie. She got up quickly and slid it open, revealing a plump, middle-aged woman with tidy, graying hair and blue eyes. She wore a white dress that buttoned up the side like Reen's trousers, with a light blue apron over it.

"Hello, my dear," she said with a smile. Then she hesitated and glanced down at Eine's cloak and bare feet. Her smile faded. "Oh…I see you've been traveling!" she added. "Well, not to worry, we'll have you all cleaned up in no time."

"Cleaned up?" Eine asked, taking a step backwards.

"Oh, yes. You'll be gleaming in time for supper. Now let's get this tub filled." The lady bustled past her and rolled up her sleeves. She grabbed hold of the pump handle on the large basin and began to pump vigorously. Eine stared as a flood of water suddenly came pouring out of the spout. The water was coming from inside the wall, it seemed, or possibly from the floor. She had always wondered what the insides of the Thelans' houses were like. This seemed like something they must have, since they were usually clean.

"There now," the woman said, plugging up the drain at the bottom. She pulled her arm out of the water and shook it, glancing back at Eine. "Don't be shy, dear, go ahead and get out of those clothes."

"Oh!" Eine exclaimed. "No, I'll just wash underneath, thank

you. Thank you for running the water."

"Don't be silly! Come here."

On impulse, Eine recoiled and turned to run, but the woman was quick. She had the green cloak untied and Eine's under-shift up over her head before she could stop her. Eine shrieked and shoved the woman away. She fell over backwards with a hard thump. Then the two of them glared at each other with equal astonishment, Eine hugging her naked self and the woman's apron falling off.

After a moment, Eine turned and climbed frantically into the basin. Thankfully, the water was warm. She cowered under it and stared at the woman over the side.

"Well, goodness!" the woman snapped. She got up slowly and stood there, a few feet from the tub, rubbing her hip. "Why didn't you just beat me with that club?" she demanded, gesturing at Eine's table leg that had fallen from her cloak.

"I'm sorry," Eine murmured.

"I should hope so!" The woman shook her head and approached the basin wearily. "I'm not trying to hurt you, child. You just can't take a bath with your clothes on."

Eine stretched her legs out cautiously until her toes touched the end of the basin. The warm water was beginning to relax her a bit. She looked down at herself and noticed the streaks of dirt here and there. She had never seen so much of her skin at once. How pale it all was, and in some places, it was clear enough to see the workings underneath. A lot of her was covered in fine, very light-colored hair.

"What a wild little thing," the woman murmured. She was pulling out a scrub brush and a square cloth from behind the basin. Eine took the cloth from her without meeting her eyes. She wondered if she really belonged there, as she accepted a glop of sweet-smelling liquid and rubbed it into her skin.

"What is the other basin for?" she ventured. The woman stopped scrubbing her back and gave her a look.

"That's for relieving yourself, child. Please don't tell me I have to explain *that*."

***

Eine sat on the bed a little while later, wrapped in a blanket, as the woman, whose name was Eten, combed out her hair. She was beginning to feel lulled into falling asleep. Everything was soothing: the scrubbing, the towel-rubbing, and the comb sliding through her tangles.

"…just as light as my dress, or nearly so," Eten was saying, admiringly. "Never seen hair like yours, my dear, especially now it's clean."

"Mmm," Eine said, sleepily.

"Especially with eyes so dark." Eten took the black ribbon which had been tied around Eine's wrist and placed it over her head, tying it underneath her hair.

"Now, let's see what's in the closet here." The woman stowed the comb in her apron pocket and pulled aside the drapery from one section of the room. Eine looked and saw that there was clothing hanging inside of a recessed part of the wall. She watched, surprised, as Eten poked through them. "Let me see. You certainly need some real under clothes…"

Several long moments later, Eine found herself swaddled in a long, pale blue dress, with a darker blue cord tied low around the waist. The under clothes had turned out to consist of a pair of short pants and a strange contraption that hooked around her small chest, but Eine had put up a huge fight over the latter and won. Eten shoved a pair of white boots over her tough feet and she wiggled her toes inside them, feeling cramped.

There was a knock on the door, just as Eine said firmly, "I want to wear my green cloak." It was nice to be clean but there were entirely too many changes going on. Eten had beaten and brushed the thing to death, before hanging it up on a hook.

"Yes, I know you do," she said with a sigh. She went to the door as Eine quickly snatched her cloak. Eten opened the door and Eine saw that it was Noname; she hurried forward, pulling on her cloak, but then she stumbled in the boots. She fell dramatically, with the cloak half on, and landed sprawled on her hands and knees.

"How does anyone walk in these?" she demanded. She glared up at Noname and saw that he was staring at her, his mouth open. He didn't move or say a word.

"Well, neither of you have any manners!" Eten blurted. "If you won't help her up, son, I suppose I'll have to do it." She reached out a hand to Eine, but Noname stepped forward and beat her to it.

"Sorry, I just…" His voice faded out as he helped her to her feet, and his eyes flew over the blue dress and her bright hair. Then he broke into a grin. "You're so clean!" he exclaimed.She laughed, despite the fact that her knees were stinging from hitting the ground. She noticed that he was cleaner as well. His short hair seemed lighter and the little stubble of a beard that he'd grown was gone. He also wore a collared Enahalan shirt, underneath his brown jacket.

"Did someone come and bathe you too?" Eine asked him. He laughed his short, raspy laugh and shook his head.

"No, but I wouldn't have objected," he said, grinning wider. Eten cleared her throat and he gave her a mock frightened look. "Depending on the person…!"

"Yes, well, I believe I'm done here," Eten said, removing her apron. "I hope you enjoy your visit." She clipped the end of the last word fiercely before marching out the door. Eine followed her quickly, pulling her cloak all the way on.

"Thank you, Eten!" she called. There was a muffled reply from the woman as she walked away down the path. Eine looked back at Noname, who was standing with his arms folded, watching her.

"Why did they send someone to clean me up, but not you?" she asked.

"Have you ever seen a bathtub, Eine?" he asked. She shook her head and pulled her hood up, feeling embarrassed. "Come on, Anda is waiting for us, and I'm starved." He stepped outside and Eine hesitated, glancing down at the table leg on the floor. After a moment, she grabbed it and tied it back onto her cloak cord.

An enthusiastic Anda, wearing a new white coat, met the two of them on the path a few moments later. Then he led them through a dizzying array of white stone walkways, chattering and pointing things out as they went. Eine missed most of it because she was concentrating on walking in her stiff boots. If she wanted to peek over the side or look up at the towers above, she had to stop walking altogether. Soon, they were approaching one of the iridescent buildings that gave Enahala its look of glass and clouds. Adding to the effect were large, arched windows filled with glass in different pastel-colored panes. It was absolutely beautiful.

"And here, of course, is the council hall," Anda said, striding ahead.

Eine followed slowly in her boots as he and Noname approached a great, yawning archway that was the entrance to the council hall. The walkway widened as it reached the open doors, and several people emerged, talking and gesturing. It suddenly struck Eine that she had not seen a single person younger than middle-aged. The three men that passed them now, just like everyone she had seen so far, were each at least as old as Anda. She didn't have long to wonder about it though, before they were inside the beautiful building, walking along a long hall that glittered all around them. The high ceiling and rounded walls were glossed with something clear and shiny. Eine's head swiveled around and around, trying to take it all in.

"What do you think we're eating?" Noname asked Anda. "I hope it's a roast."

Eine's stomach rumbled as if in agreement, even though she wasn't sure what a roast was.

"I don't know, Ney, but we're a bit late. It's just past two-mark," Anda told him. Noname glanced over at Eine and she gave him a bewildered look.

"It's their time system. It's complicated, I don't really understand it," he said.

Anda turned a corner in the hall and they came upon a large circular room, which was filled with the multi-colored windows. It held three long tables set out in a row, loaded with dishes and glasses. They were also loaded with dinner guests, and Eine hesitated in the doorway, intimidated by the sight. She understood now why Eten had gone to all the trouble she had.

The council dinner party was finely dressed in white and pastel colors. The dinnerware was not tin or glass, like the plates and cups Eine had seen back in the Thelan marketplace. It was of a metal that shone brightly and reflected faces like mirrors. The voices of the diners rose and fell, layering over themselves and rising up towards the ceiling, way up above. Eine glanced up and spotted a glowing glass structure hanging from the ceiling.

"Are you coming?" Noname asked her. She realized that she was still standing in the doorway, while Anda had wandered off. She nodded and tried to smile confidently. "Come on, this way." She followed him around the first two tables, staring unabashedly at the guests. Once again, there were no young people; all the heads were gray or white, or even bald. Of course, no one was wearing a hood but Eine. Several people glanced up and watched them with open curiosity. Eine bumped into Noname when he stopped, and she blushed.

"Have a seat, friends," Anda said, happily. There were two empty seats next to him so they sat. Quite a few others at the long table turned and stared. Eine looked away, and watched as several new people entered the room, carrying covered trays. "So Eine, what do you think of our council hall?" Anda asked her. A few guests leaned in to listen.

"It's…amazing," she said, keeping her voice low.

"But a little overdone, right?" Noname asked, lightly. The listeners scowled or huffed at this, and Eine shook her head at him. "A little too polished? A bit too bright?" he prompted. She elbowed him to be quiet.

"If you keep that up, Ney, I'll tell them to take your food away," Anda told him with a smile.

The food arrived, and Eine was astonished all over again. The hot food on the train was nothing compared to the items that Anda helped load onto her plate. There was cooked meat that smelled so delicious, she practically swooned. There were spicy vegetables that she'd never seen, soft bread covered in butter, beans and rice in a rich sauce, and lots of leafy salads. She ate and she listened, as the dinner guests chattered, mostly in Enahalan.

"Should be interesting tomorrow, eh?" a man with a bushy white beard asked Anda, in Thelan. He had a very lively expression and sharp eyes. "Let us hope we've gained some useful information."

"Indeed," Anda said. "Have the others returned?"

"Idder came back as scheduled, but not Levane," the woman next to him said, quietly. Eine swallowed and looked over at her. Someone else had come back from Thela?

"No word at all from him?" Anda asked, worried. The bearded man shook his head. Eine's heart sank, as the Hunters' announcement came rushing back to her. They *had* caught a foreigner.

"Erano, how did Idder get back?" Noname asked, with his mouth full.

"We don't know yet," the bearded man said. "But they say he's returned with some strange pet that had to be stabled. I'm sure he'll enlighten us at the council."

The sound of laughter from another table caught Eine's attention. It sounded youthful, and it was a pretty sound. Between the many heads in between, Eine caught a glimpse of the face of a young woman, amid the older Enahalans. She was smiling and laughing at someone who was speaking to her. Eine would have guessed that she was a visitor, but she did have the Enahalan blue eyes, which stood out against her dark hair. She wore a fitted white coat like many others.

"Calthin is still acting the bull," Erano was telling Anda. "He doesn't want us to continue."

"Oh, we'll deal with him as we always do," Anda replied.

The sun was setting outside the tinted windows, casting colored shadows about the room. Eine admired the sight, and set down her fork, feeling incredibly full. She sighed with pleasure and glanced at Noname, who was getting another piece of bread.

"Why are there hardly any people our age here?" she asked him, quietly.

"*Our* age?" he said, with an air of insult. She glared at him.

"I am seven*teen*," she snapped. He took a gulp of his drink but she could see that he was smiling.

"I am *twenty*," he said back. "And I rest my case." Eine rolled her eyes. "There is a reason, Eine, and a very good one. But if I get into it now, someone will get upset, so I'll tell you later," he told her, more seriously. "I hope you're not full. We have dessert after this."

***

After slices of a sweet, green substance had been passed around, and several other dinner guests had chatted with Anda and stared at Eine, the three of them stood outside in the cool night air, beneath a maze of brilliant stars. Eine took hold of Noname's sleeve, so she wouldn't fall, and tilted her head back to gaze up at the sky. She smiled.

"Well, we'll be back here bright and early," Anda said, buttoning up his coat.

"How early?" Noname asked warily.

"Seven-on-the-mark," he replied and then smiled as Noname appeared to be working that out. A moment later, the younger man frowned. "Eine, we will come and get you, my dear." She looked down from her star-gazing and nodded. "Don't be intimidated by the council, but just tell them whatever you can. Every bit of your inside knowledge is helpful."

THIRTEEN

Eine had the dream again that night. The floating lights were back, in the dark woods that had become so familiar now. They fluttered closer to her this time. They swirled all around her and she found herself smiling up at them. *"Eine,"* the voice was calling. *"...the stone..."*

She woke up suddenly to the sound of a knock at the door. "Eine?" It was Noname's voice. Bleary-eyed, she slid out of the soft bed and felt a pain in her lower back. It was strange to sleep on something that wasn't hard and flat.

"I'm coming," she called out. She had slept in a long sheer shift that she had found in the closet. Now she pulled back the closet drapes and poked through the pale-colored dresses. They were of several different sizes, but she found a small, green one this time. She tugged it on quickly and stepped into the white boots, yawning.

"What are you doing in there, kid?" Noname asked. She scowled and slid open the door to face him. He smiled, but he looked sleepy as well. The morning was still mostly dark. "You look radiant in the morning! Come on, Anda's waiting." Eine put her cloak on and tied on the table leg again, feeling grumpy. She was also hungry, which amazed her when she thought about all the food they had eaten the night before.

She followed him out onto the pathway, sometimes hustling and sometimes slowing down so she wouldn't trip in the boots. They met Anda at the open doorway to the council hall, which didn't sparkle in the lack of sunlight. It stood silent and forbidding in the dark instead. Anda waved them inside quickly, and this time the halls were fairly dark, with just a few lanterns glowing in the corners. Eine felt both drowsy and anxious, her appetite gone. This was the council where she would have to speak about Thela. She suddenly realized that she hadn't pulled her hood up when she'd left her room, and she did so now, instinctively, worried. The people here were depending on her to provide useful information.

She was afraid that her narrow little world wouldn't present them with much.

Voices preceded their approach to another large chamber, echoing down the hall towards them. In another moment, they had stepped in through another archway, and then Eine saw a long, curved table, gilded and engraved with graceful patterns. It was occupied by six very old Enahalans, who sat in chairs that were equally ornate and golden. They each wore a gold-colored sash over their white or pastel coats.

Anda signaled for her and Noname to follow, and they passed the golden table and joined the crowd that faced it. Here was where the voices were coming from, as people rustled about and whispered to each other, in their rows of simple chairs. There were no windows in this room, but gold-colored curtains hung at intervals along the walls, and another large light fixture dangled from above.

Glancing down from the ceiling, Eine noticed a pair of long white chutes that ran down one corner of the room. There was a small flap door set into each of them at about eye level, and one chute was distinguished by a metal hand-crank. She wandered what all of it was for.

There were several empty seats in the very first row and the three of them took their places there. The six ancient faces that gazed back at them from the golden table were silent and grave. There were three men and three women, and most of them were frail and hunched over, their heads shaking. All of them were snowy-haired, blue-eyed and rail-thin.

After a moment, another man about Anda's age entered the room and walked towards the front row. He was tall and willowy like Anda but, to Eine's surprise, a few years younger. His hair was longer and it curled in blond wisps; he also walked with a pronounced limp. His face was gaunt and lined as he shook hands with Anda and sat down next to him. Eine realized he must be the third foreigner in Thela, the one named Idder.

One of the old men at the golden table suddenly rang a bell, establishing silence all around the room. He cleared his throat and scratched his trembling head. Then he said something in Enahalan that rang out over the crowd. He had a surprisingly deep voice that resonated. Everyone but Eine murmured something back, respectfully.

"Three out of four of our brave volunteers have returned," the old man said in Thelan. "And we are joined by a native Thelan herself, a demi-Laxen." He paused and Eine felt a hundred pairs of eyes on her. "We will hear their testimony from their time in Enahala." He folded his wrinkled hands while the woman next to him spoke up. Her white braid of hair was so long that it wrapped several times around her head.

"First, we will question the Axten, Idder Bay," she declared, in a wobbly voice. All eyes turned to the man next to Anda, whom Eine had not realized was not from Enahala. He stood up and nodded solemnly. "Where did you arrive inside the city walls?" the woman asked.

"I was sent to an industrial area, where there were glass and tin factories," Idder replied. His accent was certainly different; there was a lilt to his voice that made the end of every phrase turn upwards. "I managed to sneak into a glass factory as it was closing for the night. I hid myself in a storage room and then later took the uniform of one of the cleaners, to disguise myself."

"Who oversaw the workers?" a different man at the table asked. This one had a long white mustache and a heavy brow.

"Members of the Indigo, in their blue uniforms. They were always on guard." Idder paused and frowned for a moment. "I could never manage to see how they came and went. They were simply there, or they weren't."

Eine recalled with a shudder how the Indigo man who had taken Graf had vanished into thin air. She glanced at Anda but he was listening to Idder intently.

"Please describe the Indigo," the deep-voiced man ordered.

"They are ordinary men. They appear Thelan, or at least no marked features suggest that they are foreign. Their uniforms are all in one piece, with attached hoods and a cord tied around the waist like a belt. The cloth is a deep, blue-purple like the color indigo."

Eine felt her gut twist involuntarily.

"Did you ever see them harm anyone?" another elder asked.

"Oh, yes. They bullied the workers if any of them slowed down or stumbled. I saw them strike a few, or shove them out of the way," Idder told them. "But I never noticed if anyone disappeared. I didn't see anyone taken."

"Can you describe the factory? And the tasks of the workers?"

"The factory was very sparse. Just the three furnaces, the marver for rolling the glass, and the glassblowers' benches. There was not enough air. It was very hot," Idder told them. "The cleaners went around sweeping up all the dust. We would start on the top floor and finish at the bottom, sweeping the dust out the doors. There was a break-time, during which they were given bread… We were each paid one Thelan coin at the end of the day. At night, I would return to the storage closet until the other workers had gone. Then I did some investigating on my own. I discovered two trap-doors on the first floor, all of which were locked." Noname looked up at that, intrigued. "I never saw them being used during the day." Idder shook his head. "Nothing else peculiar."

"How many days did you spend thus?" the deep-voiced old man asked.

"Four. And on the fifth day, I was supposed to meet Levane near the west wall." Idder stopped here, as if it were difficult, and cleared his throat. "I left the factory with the other workers, and followed several towards their brick houses. I passed through a network of alleyways between these buildings, past the market at the center, eventually finding myself at what used to be the western tin mines. It's now just a weathered expanse of dust, with some sand dunes."

Eine listened in wonder, unaware of what that part of the city was like.

"I set out across that emptiness in the dark, but I hadn't gotten very far, before the Hunters came for me." He sighed.

"They had Levane already. They had captured him at the wall somehow. As you know, they are great brutes on giant horses…very frightening. Before I knew it, I was running for my life. I was just running…" His voice faded out and Anda placed a hand on his back, encouraging him. Eine could almost feel the ache in her stomach at the thought of the Hunters.

"They caught me too," Idder said quietly. "I was dragged along for awhile, back into the city, and then something happened to the horse that was carrying me. It stumbled or tripped, and its rider dropped me. I landed on pavement and then I ran, as fast as I could! I was amidst some larger buildings, and didn't know what they were. But I found a building with an open window and crawled inside." The council members leaned forward. "It was a stable, full of the Hunters' beasts." Several members looked disappointed. "There were oversized versions of many different creatures, just like their giant horses. I suppose they use them for food. I don't understand where the Hunters find them so large."

"Is that where you captured the beast that you brought here?" the wobbly-voiced woman asked. There was a hint of disdain in her voice.

"Yes. That is where I met Elawder. The stable had a skylight with a grid across it. My people are good with animals, so I climbed up to the skylight to remove the grid and then coaxed Elawder to fly us straight out of it," Idder told them. A moment of confused silence followed.

"Are you telling me, Idder Bay," the deep-voiced council member demanded, "that you flew out of Thela on the back of a giant goose?"

At that, Noname suddenly began to laugh, completely disrupting the solemn atmosphere. Eine grinned and looked at Anda, whose eyes twinkled.

"Quiet, please!" the gold table occupants snapped.

"Indeed. He's a magnificent animal," Idder said, proudly. "He flew me out over the dust dunes and straight over the city wall. I owe him my life. Unfortunately, we were spotted by the Hunters who threw spears at us, and I was struck in the leg." He winced, looking down at his wounded limb. "But Elawder didn't fall. He flew us right over the wall and to freedom." Idder smiled then, for the first time, with obvious relief.

The council members at the table glanced at each other in disbelief. "How did you know the animal's name?" one of them asked.

"I named him," Idder said, surprised. There were a few titters in the crowd, but they were shushed again. "But more importantly, I'd like to alert the council to what I saw on our flight out." All the old heads turned back to him eagerly. "I saw a small group of people far out among the dunes." Eine stared at him. "I believe they were hiding. They disappeared under something that was camouflaged well. I couldn't be sure. But one of them reached up towards us as we passed, as if trying to signal us."

Eine gasped, staring. Were there Demi's and others hiding out on the western side of the city?! If only she had known!

"That is my whole tale," Idder said then, sounding tired.

"Thank you," the deep-voice man boomed, and then the crowd suddenly applauded loudly, startling Eine. She clapped along with them, still distracted by the idea of the people hiding in the dunes. Could there even be a full-blooded Laxen among them?

"We will break now for the morning meal," Deep-Voice announced. "And then we will hear from our other two volunteers."

***

Eine followed Anda and Noname out with the crowd into the same dining hall from the night before. They were fed fruit and a soft, sweet bread, as well as a hot bitter drink of which Eine could only take tiny sips. Her eyes flew over the tables in the room as she ate, wondering what questions the council would ask her. She heard Anda refer to the gold table Enahalans as the Elders, and wondered again why there were so few younger people in the city.

She noticed an overweight man at the end of their table who seemed to be studying Anda intently. He was balding except for white and gray tuffs of hair on the sides of his head, and his blue eyes were heavy-lidded. He caught Eine's glance and nodded coldly, then looked away.

It occurred to her then that she had yet to hear anyone's thoughts in Enahala. She had gotten past the point of being frightened by it, which was a good step forward. If only she could figure out how to control it.

When the tables were cleared, the council rose and made their way back to the room with the golden table. The elder Enahalans were already seated there, looking expectant, and Eine

117

wandered if they had eaten at all. She sat in her seat next to Noname once more and tried to turn her ears inward, hoping for a stray thought.

The elder with the deep voice again addressed the crowd in Enahalan, and was answered. Then he spoke in Thelan again: "Now we will hear the testimony of our kinsman Anda Leona." Anda stood up obediently and bowed his head towards the table.

"I was sent just inside the southern wall, into an area which is known as the Docks," he volunteered.

"This is where the underground river comes through?" an elder with a mustache asked. Anda nodded.

"I found a merchant's abandoned tent in which I could hide and observe. This is where the merchants trade for foreign goods to sell in the city. The merchants travel from the city center along a paved road that circuits the tin mines. They come by foot, pushing carts full of mostly tin and glass goods. At the docks, they camp out in makeshift shacks or even tents, until the Hunters emerge early in the morning and unlock the grate over the entrance to the river. These particular Hunters appear to live there at the docks, and are occasionally relieved by others who ride out from the city."

As Anda re-explained the way the trading system worked, Eine thought about how little she had actually seen of the area, since she and Noname had arrived in the dark, and then been shuttled through, hidden, inside the merchant's cart.

"But no Indigo appeared in this area?" another elder man, who wore large spectacles, asked.

"No, I saw only Hunters and merchants," Anda said. "I was there for four days until the Creeden arrived, with our young friend Eine." All of the elders at the table turned to stare at Eine again and she felt a rush of nerves. Would she be questioned next?

At that moment, someone's thoughts actually reached her from the crowd: *"I can't imagine how she survived...So strange to see a Laxen up close again."* Eine frowned, and turned around to look behind her. Curious stares met her own, and she turned back. Why was it strange to see a Laxen up close, here? She realized then that she had not yet noticed a Laxen in Enahala. There had been no buzzing in her head. Was that unusual?

"And so, how did the three of you manage to escape?" Deep-Voice asked Anda.

"Our plan was to slip in through the grate and travel out of the city with the exported goods in the river," he replied. "When you have no flying beasts, you must go *under* the wall." A few people in the crowd chuckled. "I knew there was a decent-sized ledge inside the tunnel that extended all the way through to the end, thanks to an overheard conversation about how it was built. The Creeden and I apprehended a merchant and borrowed his clothing and his cart. He was left unharmed, only startled. Then with my two companions hiding in the cart, I posed as the merchant and strode to the grate to drop my goods. We had devised a manner of distracting the Hunter at the grate, of course.

All did not go as planned, however, due to the fact that Hunters from the city center were already in pursuit of my companions. They arrived at the docks as I was setting out, and issued an order for all merchants and carts to undergo a search. As the others began to line up, I continued on, hoping to be perceived as a daft old man who had not heard the announcement. The others began to call to me, good-hearted people, afraid of what I was getting myself into. I reached the grate and the Hunter on duty bellowed like a beast, and brandished his whip." Anda turned slightly pale at the memory. "But I gave the signal, and at that moment, Ne - the Creeden shot down a wagon full of stacked tin bars, which created an ear-shattering racket. I lifted the crate and pushed in the cart, flinging myself in afterwards."

He stopped there and the elders leaned forward expectantly. "And then you fell down into the water?" the be-spectacled man exclaimed.

"That we did, and proceeded to make our way along the tunnel ledge to the outside world," Anda replied. "That is my full tale." He bowed his head. After a second, the crowd burst into applause as they had done for Idder.

Eine shook her head, thinking about the giant rats in the tunnel and the bandits in the woods outside. She wondered what adventures Idder had experienced on his way home. A few moments later, it was Noname's turn to talk, and Eine watched with interest as he stood up and cleared his throat. He seemed a bit uncomfortable.

"I was sent into the heart of the city," he told the elders. "I found myself in the middle of pouring rain in a dirty alley, where broken furniture and garbage was lying around. I was thrilled to be there." Eine grinned. "The stories about the rain are true. It rains almost non-stop in the city center, but it clears up once you get past the factories." There were some murmurs from the crowd.

"Who did you encounter in that area?" the mustached man asked.

"There are three major types of people in the city," Noname explained. "You have the merchants, the factory workers and tin miners, and then you have the 'Dredges', who live on the street."

"In the rain?"

"Everyone wears a hood but everyone is still sopping wet most of the time. I think the Dredges are the result of there not being enough work since the Indigo took over, because there aren't any shops or schools or businesses anymore. We knew that Indigo closed everything down. Also, as I discovered since I met Eine, there are some part-Laxens hiding out on the streets. It sounds like maybe Idder spotted some as well." He frowned and cleared his throat again. "The other Thelans live in the brick houses that Idder described, with all the windows shuttered tight."

"How does anyone get food?" the wobbly-voiced woman asked him.

"The merchants set up a daily market in the city, selling only dried meat, mostly dried fruit and bread. They also sell the local tin and glass, which I guess the people use in their homes. The Dredges steal what they can from the stalls," Noname told them. It was strange for Eine to listen to someone else describing her life. "I managed to sneak around unnoticed for three days, and during that time, I spotted several Indigo, passing through. The people all parted around them. They ducked their heads and got out of the way."

"Did you see where the Indigo went?"

"Most of the time, if I followed them, I lost them. I did see a trap door, just like Idder, in one of the alleys." The council members murmured again. "One man, I was able to follow to someone's home, and then he banged on the door and spoke to someone inside. He went in afterward and I never saw him come back." Noname shook his head. "I waited the rest of the day."

"Are you suggesting that they have secret passageways around the city?" Deep-Voice asked.

"I think it sounds likely. It may be that they have their headquarters underground."

Eine's ears pricked up at this. She had never imagined such

a thing. The old heads at the golden table were nodding in agreement.

"How did you meet the Thelan, Eine?" the mustached man asked. Noname smirked and glanced down at Eine in her chair. She scowled at him, ready to hear herself called a child who wouldn't leave him alone.

"The Hunters made an announcement that foreign spies were in the city, ordering everyone to turn them in. This must have been after they caught Levane, and lost Idder. Eine came across me on my way through the alleys to meet Anda. I was fighting off a Dredge who was trying to steal my bread, and she helped. Then I tried to brush her off and we had a fight as well." He looked sheepish. "She's very strong. She had me figured out and she wanted to come with me." The elders studied Eine again.

"How did she know who you were?" the mustached man asked, disapprovingly.

"She heard my thoughts," Noname said, and a series of gasps rose up in the crowd. "Don't worry, she can't do it all the time." Eine smiled politely up at the elders. Their expressions were wary. "Anyway, we left the city center and crossed through the factories but somehow the Hunters found us. Eine had a run-in with an Indigo member, which she can tell you about, and that may have been what tipped them off. We ran out into the tin mines and plunged in and out of quicksand with their horses thundering after us." Noname's voice was much calmer than Idder's or even Anda's had been while describing the Hunters. He was also beginning to sound impatient to be through with the story. "But the quicksand also gave the Hunters problems, so we managed to get away. We made it to the docks and joined Anda on the fifth day, as planned."

"How did you escape the quicksand?" Deep-Voice asked.

"She pulled us both out," Noname said, a bit grudgingly. "After that, my story is the same as Anda's." The council nodded and he sat down again, happy to be finished. The crowd applauded once more. Eine felt her heartbeat pick up speed as the elderly council members turned their attention to her.

"And now, we'd like to hear from our visitor," Deep-Voice intoned.

Eine gathered herself and stood up, facing the golden table.

She wondered if she should push back her hood, but she was afraid her hands would shake, so she kept them still. The elders whispered to each other for a few moments as if planning their questions.

Then Eine was inundated with several different minds from the crowd.

"Such a tiny little thing."

"I thought quicksand was a myth."

"However did she survive?"

"Must be difficult to hide strength like that."

"It is so odd that Creedens won't tell you their names."

There were so many at once, that she shook her head, trying to clear it.

"Damn Anda and his arrogance! I'll kill him!"

Eine turned around, startled, and stared out at the crowd. The last "voice" had been filled with actual hatred. Someone here in the audience truly despised Anda. It worried her. She turned back a moment later and saw that Noname was staring at her.

"Are you all right?" he asked, quietly. Her eyes flew towards the elders who were watching her, concerned. Everyone was watching. It was ridiculous.

"What do you want to know?" she asked, feeling breathless.

FOURTEEN

"What is your full name and age, child?" the woman with braids wobbled out.

"Eine...of Thela," she said, simply. "I'm seventeen."

"Do you know any of the history of your family?"

"No. Only that I'm a demi-Laxen, and I'm not sure how I know. I just remember it, I guess."

"So you don't know which parent was Laxen?" the man with spectacles asked. She shook her head. "Or what happened to them?" She shook her head again.

"What is your first memory?" Deep-Voice asked.

Eine thought about the humming she had remembered, but it didn't seem very useful. "There was an old woman who told me to cover my head," she offered, instead. "She gave me a hooded cloak. I think she knew what I was."

"Why would you need to cover your head?"

"Because I look a little different," she said. She hesitated, and then pulled her hood back for them to see. There was a moment of silence from the table, and some murmurs from the crowd. "There is also a dream I have of a woman's voice calling me. I think it might be my mother."

"That suggests the mother is the Laxen," the bespectacled man said, looking at the others. The man with the deep voice

123

waved a hand, as if to say it was speculation.

"What are your other Laxen qualities, aside from your strength and mind-reading? And how did you hide them from the Indigo?"

"The hardest thing to hide was the fact that I don't weigh very much," Eine told them. "I learned to copy the way other people walked, to act like I was heavier. It's true that I can sometimes hear people's thoughts, but I can't seem to control it."

"What do the Thelans think of the Indigo?" a woman asked, who hadn't spoken before. She was very thin and frail, with large, sad-looking eyes. "Do they have a theory for why the city was taken over, and the Laxens killed?"

"Maybe some do," Eine said, thoughtfully. "But the Dredges are afraid to even speak of them. We – they don't speak of them at all." Eine suddenly remembered Graf and she glanced down at Anda. He gave her an encouraging smile. "There was a boy, a foreign boy, in the city," she exclaimed. "I met him just before I met Noname."

A confused pause followed this sentence, and then the crowd began to laugh. Eine looked around, confused. Did they not believe her? Noname caught her eye and gave her a solemn wink. Then it dawned on her what she had said. "Oh," she said, feeling herself blush. "I mean…the Creeden."

"A foreign boy?" Deep-Voice repeated, as the laughter faded. "How is this possible?"

"Anda says he might be from Belgin – "

"Belgir," Anda corrected softly.

"Belgir," Eine amended. "I told them that he didn't say the 't's on the end of his words." As she finished speaking, she noticed the elders were staring at her in open amazement. The crowd behind her had become very quiet. The entire room, in just a few seconds, had become incredibly still. Eine felt suddenly anxious.

"You met a…Belgin child in Thela?" Deep-Voice asked, slowly.

"Belgir," Eine said, before she could stop herself, and Anda chuckled behind her.

"No, no, if he's *from* Belgir, he's Belgin," the elder said, shaking his head. "I'm sorry, but surely you are mistaken?"

"How in gods' sake did she *find him?!"*

Eine stiffened, and looked back over her shoulder at the crowd. It was the same angry voice as before, and this time it was a little frightening. All the faces she could see were curious and surprised. Did someone here know about Graf?

"How had this child gotten there, did he say?" the wobbly-voiced woman asked.

"Um…he didn't know. Something had happened to his memory." Eine stopped just short of telling them that Anda had mentioned Enahalan memory drugs. She had a feeling that he should be the one to bring that up. "And then while we were walking through the alleys, an Indigo man appeared out of nowhere, and took him away." She felt suddenly tired, as the council absorbed this news. It had been a long speech for her, this 'testimony', and the confusion of all the intruding thoughts was exhausting.

"Appeared out of nowhere?" the man with spectacles prompted her.

"He appeared and disappeared, just like Anda can do," Eine said wearily. "Then I found Noname and the rest of my story is the same." She sat down, abruptly.

"Thank you, my child, we will have much to discuss tomorrow," Deep-Voice said, sounding overwhelmed himself. "We'll end the council here for today."

The crowd behind Eine burst into applause, as she looked at Anda and Noname. The clapping was louder than it had been for any other speech, and she cringed a little at the volume. Noname leaned in close to her and muttered, "You 'heard' someone, didn't you?"

She nodded and told him, "I need to speak to you two right away."

***

Anda was quiet as he listened to Eine's description of the strange, angry thoughts. The mental voice had been so distorted with hate that she didn't think she'd recognize its owner if he spoke aloud in a normal tone. Anda looked grave, but not very surprised.

"You know who it is?" Noname asked him.

"I have my suspicions, Ney," he replied. The three of them sat in Noname's room, which Eine had discovered was much larger than her own, perhaps because Reen had called hers a spare room. Noname's was also circular and draped with long wall hangings, but they were a deep blue instead of red, and his bath basins were in a separate compartment. There were also low, padded seats along two of the walls. Eine sat on one of them now and stretched her legs out, feeling relieved to be out of the formal council.

"Eine," Anda said, sounding serious. "Is there no connection you can make to determine how your mind-reading is triggered? That is the key to controlling it."

"Is there something that happens every time you hear someone?" Noname asked. Eine thought about it for a few moments, trying to remember the way it had happened in the council.

"It always…surprises me," she said, feeling discouraged.

"Think about it," Anda told her. "I think it'll come." He stood up then and stretched, his long arms reaching up towards the domed ceiling. "Well, I must go home and take care of a few things. We'll have dinner again at the council hall, but until then, Eine, you should see some of the city. Ney, you should take her around a bit."

"Sure," Noname said. "Let's get some lunch. I'm starving."

Eine stood up eagerly, happy to see more of Enahala.

"I'll never understand how you can eat so much, Ney," Anda said, leading them out. Eine and Noname walked out onto the pathway together and watched Anda as he set off in a different direction, into the afternoon sun.

"What's his house like?" Eine asked, wondering if it were anything like the rooms they were staying in.

"It's a little white cottage, kind of in a dome shape," Noname told her. "It's perfect for an old bachelor like him. He's got an old-fashioned firepit and an old *garina* – it's an Enahalan instrument with all these buttons and levers. It sounds awful but he loves it." He paused and studied her for a second. "Have you ever heard music, Eine?"

"A few times," she said. "Some children in Thela have little grinder boxes. They turn the handles and tinkling sounds come out."

"Hmm." He sounded unimpressed.

"So not everyone here lives in a tower," Eine said, thinking about the description of Anda's house.

"Yes, there's a garden area with some freestanding units like his. It used to be for families, but that's not really an issue anymore…" Noname looked around them for a moment, as if trying to decide where to go.

"What do you mean?"

"Well, that's what I was talking about earlier." He chose a walkway that veered off to the right, and then lowered his voice, walking ahead. "Enahala has a problem with stagnation," he told her. "Maybe you could tell by the way they treat the Meyjans that they're a bit self-important. They think…a lot of their own race."

"What do you mean, stagnation?" Eine asked. She stumbled over her boots and he caught her arm.

"I mean, they've bred so much within their own kind that they aren't having children anymore."

She stared up at him, confused. "Not at all?"

"Very rarely. That's why there are so many old people, Eine. It's a big deal, it means they're…dying out. But they refuse to accept it, or at least not openly." Noname shook his head. "Anda's different, of course. He's been out in the world much more than a lot of them."

"But I don't understand how breeding with only Enahalans keeps them from having children," Eine said.

"Oh, well, I can't explain it like Anda could, but it has to do with genes, or what we're made up of, inside," he told her. "We inherit them from our parents, and I guess if a group of people keep inheriting the same kind of genes, then sometimes things can go wrong."

Eine was quiet for a moment, remembering what the red-haired Laxen had told them on the train. Scientists thought there was a Laxen *gene*. Noname stopped and gave her a curious look, his eyebrows raised. There was a smirk in there somewhere that he was just barely hiding.

"You do know how babies are made, right?" he asked. Eine blushed furiously and nodded. "Just vaguely though, right? Not really?" He was right about that, but she wasn't going to admit it. On impulse, she gave him a hard shove. He grinned, and grabbed onto her arms. "I'm sorry! Don't push me off the path!"

"But the Enahalans can't die out. They're great people!" Eine exclaimed. Noname put a finger to his lips and she shook her arms free. "They're the ones leading an investigation into the Indigo. They're trying to save Thela!" He nodded, growing serious.

"Have you noticed there aren't any Laxens?" he asked quietly. "They stopped being born here even before the regular birthrate dropped. There are a few left, but the Enahalans really feel their loss. Most of the beauty of the city was designed by Laxens." He gestured ahead at one of the iridescent towers coming into view. "So if something is killing them, they want to help stop it."

Eine gazed up at the beautiful building before them and frowned, trying to understand. "Anda said all the magic in the world is done by Laxens," she murmured. "What are we? Where did we come from?"

Noname nodded again at the building and smiled. "There's a place where you could find some ideas about that, if you had nothing better to do with your time. I'll show you."

The walkway they were on sloped directly across to meet the large, double doors in the sparkling building. As Eine watched, an elderly man with a single eye-glass emerged, carrying an armful of books. He nodded as they passed, eyeing them with interest. Noname reached out and grabbed a stout handle on one of the doors, pulling it open.

Inside, Eine saw a great, cavernous room that stretched across the whole width of the tower. It was well-lit with many elaborate light fixtures, and through the center, there wound a massive spiral staircase with gold railings. All along the white stone walls, stretching up to the high ceiling, were cases and cases of books. There were people scaling these cases on rolling ladders, and others were lounging on padded seats throughout the enormous space, reading.

"This is the library," Noname told her. "Enahala's famous for its collection." Eine followed him inside, for the first time feeling in full her inability to read. There were so *many* books here. "So let's see, what would Anda say?" Noname said, striding across the polished floor. He was promptly shushed by a middle-aged woman who was bent over a scroll. He added in a whisper, "No library outside of a university can compare with this one."

Eine smiled, looking around at all the serious expressions, peering over pages. "But then again, they think 'a lot' of themselves here," she whispered back, and he grinned.

"Don't repeat that." He led her over to the elaborate railing that curled around the staircase. Eine leaned over it and looked down; to her surprise, she found herself staring down into another floor of the library below. She marveled at the sheer size of it.

"What's in the books?" she asked.

"Everything, Eine. History, stories, drawings, instructions." He looked up over their heads and Eine saw the next floor above through the stairwell. "Theories, maps, explanations," he said, sounding thoughtful. "We had a library in Creede, but it was very small. I used to like to read the stories from the Old-World times."

Eine looked back at him, intrigued. "Stories from before the Laxens?" She felt a nervous, excited feeling in her stomach. "I'd like to read about that."

"We'll come back then. But let's go get a couple of *lalens* to eat." Noname turned and started to walk back towards the door.

"I bet Loneela will like that one." Eine spun around, staring at the quiet readers. No one was looking at them in an obvious way. Anda's words came back to her. What was causing it to happen? After a moment, she hurried after Noname.

***

Lalens turned out to be portions of meat and melted cheese, wrapped up in thick lettuce leaves. Noname bought them each one at the open doorway of another white building, one that he said was filled with different kitchens and clothing vendors.

"It's a market," Eine said, amazed. "All inside one building."

"Basically. Here, try it. It's really good." He took a big bite of his *lalen* as Eine struggled to get her hands around the lettuce wrap.

"It's that melted cheese again," she commented. "That's your favorite thing." He smiled but said nothing as she took a bite. It was delicious. She stood gazing at Noname as she chewed, tasting all the flavors, and he watched her, amused. Then she swallowed. "What's next?" she asked.

The next place turned out to require a longer walk. They strolled along another pathway, occasionally stepping onto other branches, or curving around buildings. Eine wondered, as she took bites of the *lalen*, how often Enahalans actually touched the ground. It was a distant shadow below now, especially with the sun settling lower in the sky. At what age did they give in and start using the elevators Noname had mentioned? The elders certainly must. She nodded at people who criss-crossed their way past them, disappearing into arched doorways, or stopping to chat with people they knew.

"I wonder what Anda's thinking about the Belgin boy," Noname said. He finished his food and brushed his hands off. "Tomorrow will be interesting."

"How many days does the council last?" Eine asked.

"Well, tomorrow will be the discussion of our testimonies, and what happens after that depends on what they decide."

"You said there are a few Laxens still here, right? So… why don't they come to the council? Don't they want to be involved in stopping the Indigo?"

Noname frowned and took another bite of meat and cheese. "I'm not sure. I mean, not just any Enahalan can be in the council. Everyone there is a descendent of the first council. That's the way it works. But Laxens would be welcome, I'm sure, in this case. Maybe they're afraid to get involved."

As Noname spoke, Eine heard the faintest strain of a melody in the distance. She tilted her head to one side and listened. "*Nivick*," Noname said in Creeden, with a grin. "They're rehearsing. Perfect timing."

He led the way towards a shimmering building up ahead, which was not a tower at all. Eine realized with a start that it was almost entirely open to the elements; it had a half-roof that curved over only a portion of its interior, and then stopped abruptly. Because of this, a group of people were visible inside despite the distance, and this was the source of the melody that was growing louder, rising and falling. The people were singing. Curious, Eine started walking faster, wondering why a group of people would all be singing together. As they got closer, she realized there were other beautiful sounds accompanying the voices. She gave Noname a questioning look.

"This is the concert hall," he said, leading her closer. The open building was soon blotting out the sun, overlooking them. Noname found a place along the low wall where they could lean over and look inside. The sun was setting behind the building, but the view revealed a swath of padded seats that faced the group of performers. A few people sat in the seats, listening, as the singers stopped abruptly and then started up again. Around them, in a semi-circle, were other performers manipulating various contraptions; there were objects that were squeezed, tubes that were blown into, and rows of levers that were pushed in different combinations. These were the sources of the music, and the combined sounds swam through Eine's head, flashing with colors and shapes, and feelings.

"How are they doing it?" she breathed. "What is it?"

"Watch," Noname said, grinning. The curved wall behind the musicians was beginning to glow faintly. Eine gasped as the glow changed color, swirling first into blue and then green. The colors danced along the wall in rhythm with the music. They flashed in pinks and yellows; they swam in little rivers down the wall in purple and then in red.

"Two Laxens run the concerts," Noname told her. "One of them has the ability to create colors from sounds. And sometimes vice versa, I think. I forget how it works."

"It's beautiful! It's like…what the sounds make me see in my mind," Eine exclaimed. He smiled at her.

"I thought you'd like it," he said. Then he put his hand over her hand, where it rested on the wall. Eine couldn't speak for a moment. She just stood there, listening, totally absorbed. The singing would sometimes drop to a sensitive murmur, but then it would shoot up to the skies, ringing like bells, with the music crashing underneath it.

"Do you understand the words?" she asked, turning to him. There was a soft look on his face as his eyes drifted from hers back out towards the performers.

"It's about the idea of the spirit. The part of you that lives on after your body dies," he replied. "They're singing about the idea that there's an after-life." Eine blinked at him. What idea was this? Did people really believe that? She turned it over in her mind, confused. How could they possibly know?

The sun slipped down behind the half-roof of the concert hall, casting everything before them in shadow. Eine realized that Noname's hand was still over hers, and she liked it there. It felt very warm and solid. It was hard to imagine there was something else inside his body, something that would keep living after he died.

"Do you believe that?" she asked him. He nodded.

"I think so."

"But what…is the after-life like?"

Noname laughed. "I haven't been there, kid. But the idea is that the spirit is the person without a body. So it's just a being, that floats or flies... I imagine a world of floating lights." He shrugged and looked embarrassed. "Some people believe that fireflies are actually souls. Not that you know what fireflies are either."

Eine realized she was still holding the end of the *lalen* in her other hand. She raised it up to her mouth and took a last, absent bite. She was going to have to learn how to read. If there were ideas as incredible as this floating around, then she wanted to know about them. She was in the right place to do that, now that she knew about the library.

Maybe she could stay here, after the council ended. She remembered her earlier concern about that and felt hopeful. Would they let her keep her room? Or could she find a corner somewhere else, somewhere where she wouldn't be any trouble?

But would Noname stay? She looked up at him and his eyes darted away quickly, as if he'd been watching her and didn't want her to know. Where would he go when the council was over? Would he stay here, since he was part of their mission against the Indigo? She wanted him to stay. She wasn't sure exactly why, but it was a strong feeling. She looked at their hands on the wall and, on a sudden impulse, raised her fingers up so that they slipped between his. His larger fingers curled around hers and she felt an unexpected rush of happiness, nerves, embarrassment. His brown eyes were on her again, she knew without looking. She pulled her hand away suddenly, feeling her face grow warm.

She met Noname's eyes and he gazed at her steadily. "Can you read my mind?" he asked, in a low voice. *"She looks like an angel."*

The music ended with the loud bang of a hollow drum, and they both flinched. Eine stared back out at the musicians. A nasal sound blared and was followed by the performers' voices.

"I'll never get that right!"

"We all came in late there."

"I could do the whole last triplet again."

Noname cleared his throat and she turned to face him, feeling breathless. What was an angel? He gave her a small smile and then jerked his head. "Come on. Let's go get Anda."

FIFTEEN

At dinner this time, Eine noticed that she was beginning to recognize many faces. She spotted the young woman again, who was standing up talking to Idder Bay enthusiastically. She was thin but also very curvy, and her blue eyes flashed in her animated face. Eine thought it must be a shame for a pretty woman of her age, which she guessed was in her mid-twenties, to live in a city of aging men. But perhaps she didn't want to marry and have a family.

The idea dawned on Eine suddenly, that since she had left Thela, marriage and family were an option for her as well. Startled, she stared down at the mix of meat and vegetables on her plate. Those were things she had never thought about before. She hadn't admitted it to herself, but she had always imagined that she wouldn't survive for very long. So the future was not of much concern.

…But if she stayed here, in Enahala? She would be in the same position as this dark-haired woman, surrounded by elderly people. She frowned, unsure of whether that mattered to her or not. It was good to be somewhere safe, around kind people, and with the opportunity to learn so much.

"He's *nicktu*," Noname was telling Anda, as he drank from his glass. "What's that in Enahalan? *Malena?*" Eine watched him discreetly, remembering the flood of nerves she had felt at the concert hall. His fingers intertwined in hers. She wondered again about the word 'angel'.

"What is it, 'confused'? *Malena* is 'confused'," Anda told Noname.

"No, *nicktu* is stupid."

Eine looked away, as Anda replied with the Enahalan translation. She decided to focus on his suggestion about her mind-reading ability. How had she felt just before she'd heard Noname? Nervous. And what about during the council, when all those thoughts had reached her at once? She had been nervous, because it was her turn to tell her story.

Eine gasped. What about the time before that? She had heard Anda just before the train took off. She had felt excited and nervous! She put down her fork and looked at Anda, but he and Noname were laughing about something now. Was it…anxiety that caused her to hear thoughts? Was that something she could control? She closed her eyes and wondered if she could make herself nervous. She imagined that Noname was staring at her now, the way that he had at the concert hall. She concentrated on it, imagining the feel of his fingers again, and his words. She felt a thrill tingle all over.

She focused on it, willed it to get stronger. Her heart began to pound.

"But what good will all of this talking do? How will it help?"

Eine's eyes popped open. She discovered that she was facing a gray-haired man at another table, who was nodding and listening to the woman next to him. He looked as if he were distracted, not paying attention to her. She kept her eyes on him a moment, clenching her fists, but she didn't hear anything else. She frowned and looked back at Noname, realizing that the feeling was gone. He was staring back at her and she blushed.

"What's wrong?" he asked.

"I was…trying to read minds," she muttered, feeling embarrassed. He grinned.

"I'm trying to fly right now. It's not working out either." Eine smiled and he looked very happy with himself. She felt a rush of happiness too, looking at him.

"Are you the Creeden?" a soft voice asked from behind. Both Noname and Eine turned to see the dark-haired, young woman standing there, with a tentative smile. Noname looked at her for a moment, as if mesmerized. Then he pushed back his chair and offered her his hand.

"I am. It's nice to meet you," he said politely. The woman smiled wider and it lit up her whole, lovely face. She shook his hand.

"I'm Loneela. My father is Agin, one of the elders in the council." She offered her hand to Eine and Eine shook it, although she felt an odd, sinking feeling. "And you are the Thelan. Congratulations on your escape!"

"Thank you."

"Which one is Agin?" Noname asked her.

"The one wearing those ridiculous old spectacles," she said with a laugh. "I tease him about them all the time but of course, I'm the only one who would care that they're old-fashioned."

"What do the modern ones look like?" Eine asked. She had never looked closely at the spectacles that had been sold at the Thelan market. Loneela looked surprised.

"I have some right here." She pulled a tiny pair from a pocket in her long coat and showed them to Eine. The glasses in the frames were each about half as large as the ones her father were, and the frames were thin wires.

"Those are from Inowa, aren't they?" Noname said, with a smirk. "That's probably why he doesn't want to wear them." Loneela's pretty face clouded but she nodded.

"Yes, you know how it is. If it's not Enahalan…" She sighed and put the glasses away. Noname looked as if he regretted mentioning it. He frowned and looked down at his plate. "Well, I will see you at the council tomorrow," Loneela said, smiling at him again. "Goodnight!"

"Goodnight," Noname said. He watched her walk away for a moment. Eine understood that the woman's charms had made an impression. The sinking in her chest felt heavier. But why did she mind? *Did* she mind? She suddenly felt a small panicky feeling.

Noname cleared his throat and turned back to his dinner, without comment.

***

The next morning, the council began again at seven-on-the-mark. Eine followed Noname and Anda into the main room with a feeling of foreboding. The arrangement of the gilded table and the audience's chairs had been altered; everything was now turned to face the open center of the room. Eine sat with her companions and examined the faces in the crowd, wondering what they were thinking. Most people seemed eager, expectant.

After the greeting in Enahalan, the deep-voiced elder signaled to someone standing near the door. "We have been constructing a map of Thela, as it is now, based on the testimonies of our volunteers," he rumbled. The person by the door stepped outside and then returned, pushing a wheeled stand into the room. Stretched across the top of it was a large rectangular canvas. The man postioned the map in the middle of the room, and then Eine found herself staring at a detailed layout of her homeland.

Thela had been painted from above in mostly grays and blacks. It was wheel-shaped and the city wall was a thick dark circle on the outer edges. Inside, there was a wide ring of gray, over which was printed, in neat letters, TIN MINES to the south and the east, and SAND DUNES, to the north and the west. Near the wall to the south lay a long curved section marked THE DOCKS. Inside the ring of tin mines and dunes, there were the factories to the east, the Hunters' stables to the west, and the long, low buildings and alleys in between.

There were several areas around the stables and the brick buildings that were shaded over in a way that suggested they were unknown. Eine realized at once that the Hunters' platform and the market were missing. She thought she could pinpoint roughly where they would be, if asked.

"Many thanks to Loneela Indane for the artwork," Deep-Voice intoned.

Eine followed the heads that turned around her and saw Loneela smiling and nodding. She felt herself frown.

"Due to the descriptions of the trapdoors in the city, and the frequent disappearances of the Indigo, it has been suggested that the order's headquarters are underground," the woman with the braided hair trebled.

"However there are still sections of the city that are yet to be infiltrated," Deep-Voice said, nodding at the map. "We must discuss today whether we shall send in more volunteers, with specific coordinates in these locations, or whether we should examine our options for exploring the underground areas of Thela."

"*Iwalahen*," Anda said immediately, and everyone turned to face him. The single word had sounded like a polite question. The elders nodded at him and he stood up, approaching the map stand at the center of the room. There were quite a few whispers throughout the room as he did.

"I wish to discuss the issue that was raised by Eine of Thela in her testimony," Anda said, projecting his voice across the room. Eine looked at Noname and he nodded. Here was the business of Graf and his inexplicable presence in Thela.

"You are referring to the Belgin boy," said the man named Agin, who wore his unwieldy spectacles from before. Eine saw now that his features were fine and symmetrical like Loneela's, only creased and spotted with age.

"Yes, I think it's the most urgent issue at hand," Anda said. "As Eine mentioned, the boy had no recollection of why or how he had come to be in Thela. Apparently, his memory would return for a moment, just long enough to remember a sibling, for example, and then disappear again." He cleared his throat, looking grave. "This is highly suggestive of a memory drug."

This time, the council burst forth with many unhappy voices, and obvious disapproval.

"I realize this is an inflammatory statement," Anda told them.

"Indeed," Agin remarked. "You believe an Enahalan is involved in smuggling a child into the city? What would be the motive?"

"*Iwalahen*," a throaty voice rose up. A man stood up from a seat somewhere in the middle of the crowd, and Eine recognized him as the overweight man with the heavy eyes who had been watching Anda at the first dinner. He looked amused now as the elders nodded at him, and he strode out to the center of the room.

"Well, Leona, I must say it's good to see you back safe and sound," the man said, in a tight voice.

"Calthin," Anda greeted him. "Do you wish to object to my argument?" There were a few titters from the crowd, and Eine remembered the conversation she'd overheard about someone named Calthin at that same dinner. '*Calthin is acting the bull again.*'

"Yes, that is an accurate guess, based on our previous

debates," the man said with a smile. "I'll do my usual digging for the truth. I believe you're taking a very large leap to your conclusions." Anda nodded as if to encourage him. "I must remind everyone here that Enahalans are no longer the only masters of the memory drug. *If* the boy is from Belgir, it seems much more logical to assume that the Belgins have developed a memory drug of their own."

"Yes – "

"But we're not even sure this boy is from Belgir, are we?" Calthin addressed the table. "Have we heard the boy's name?"

"It is only Graf, I'm afraid," Anda said. Calthin smiled.

"We have a common name, and a description of his accent from someone who, at the time, had never spoken to anyone outside of Thela. And this description has been interpreted by our good friend Anda, who is never without a good, controversial theory." The crowd chuckled.

Eine looked at Noname in protest but he only raised his eyebrows, unconcerned.

"I once thought having a voice of constant dissent was good for the council," Anda said lightly. "Nowadays I admit, it has grown tedious." This time there was open laughter. Deep-Voice cleared his throat loudly and silence returned. "First I'd like to remind everyone here of something as well: our native memory drug is particularly useful for concealing information until the time is right, or rather, until the right listener has been located." Calthin cocked an eyebrow at him. "A child, who has been given information which can't possibly escape his lips until he reaches a certain contact, would make an inconspicuous messenger."

Calthin nodded at this. "Agreed. However, it's much more likely that this is a child who, through malnutrition and a terrible life on the streets, has developed brain damage, or is repressing unpleasant memories."

"That was my first point," Anda told him. "Now hear my second: Noname's description of the Indigo disappearing becomes even more alarming when combined with Eine's story of how Graf was taken in front of her. Her own comparison to my fading trick is another reason of concern. As we all know, fading is a skill many Enahalans have mastered."

"Let us hear about this incident from Eine again," the mustached elder suggested. The others nodded. Eine was dismayed at the sudden, expectant quiet that was directed her way. She stood up quickly though and walked over towards the two men in the center of the room. She wanted to help Anda, and she knew she could.

Calthin gave her a wide, leery smile and she frowned back at him. "Go ahead, child," he said sweetly. Eine felt like she'd truly had enough of being called a child. Anda was the only one she'd allow it from, from now on.

"I was walking with Graf in the alleys," she told him, keeping her voice cool. "And there was no one else around, anywhere. We were talking softly." She swallowed, feeling a little more confident. "And then a member of the Indigo appeared directly in front of us, like magic." Anda nodded at her, smiling. "I grabbed hold of Graf, but he grabbed him from me, and then he disappeared again. It was like he'd never been there."

"Are you certain, Eine, that this man had no time to slip away through a hidden door? A trap door, even?" Anda asked.

"Yes."

"Now, Calthin, and all of the council, I present my second point. I believe the Indigo have learned our art of 'fading'. This is a tricky thing to do without the help of an Enahalan." Anda allowed his words to settle upon the crowd and make a quiet impression.

Calthin cleared his throat and addressed the golden table. "Again, I'm afraid I must insist that this is testimony from a child who has been exposed to very little advances in machinery, or technology, and it is being interpreted by someone with an agenda," he declared.

"I'm not a child," Eine retorted. There was a surprised pause, and everyone stared at her. "And I'm not stupid or blind," she added. "I saw Anda fade in the woods, on our way here, and this was the same thing."

"My dear, I understand your conviction -" Calthin began, patiently.

"What agenda do you suppose I have, Calthin?" Anda interrupted. "Perhaps you can enlighten us in that area."

"Oh, don't pretend that we aren't all aware of your criticism of our great people, Anda Leona!" the other man declared. "Wouldn't it serve your purpose very well to find that there was a corrupt group in Enahala? One that tainted the rest of us and our honorable way of life?"

There were some sounds of agreement from the crowd, and Eine looked around at them, disgusted. Were they really going to accuse Anda of inventing this?

Anda was quiet for a moment, his blue eyes piercing Calthin, who stood there triumphantly. When he spoke again, it was with a cool steadiness. "My dislike for a certain, specific characteristic of our culture does not justify your accusation. Do I need to remind you of the dangers of nationalism? Isn't our present predictament enough of a warning?" The crowd stirred again, but more quietly. Eine looked at Calthin, but his features were hard to read. He was simply watching Anda closely. "Please consider the example of the Pinnacle," Anda continued. "We have seen the destruction that supreme arrogance and self-importance can cause. Not only was the loss of Andliss felt around the world, but my Creeden friend tells me that scholars have come to suspect that Indigo himself may be an Andliss survivor."

This prompted a flurry of excitement and surprise around the room. Eine noticed that the elders at the table looked grave.

"This council once had a list of the known Andlissians whose remains were never accounted for," Anda continued. "There has always been the possibility that someone who did survive might take revenge."

"This is a decided change of subject," Calthin declared.

"I believe I've made my point," Anda said stiffly. "The evidence remains. There are strong signs of an Enahalan influence in Thela and it must be taken into account, before we decide on our next plan of action."

"*Iwalahen*," a pleasant voice spoke up. Eine looked in surprise to see Loneela rising up and waiting for her nod of approval from the elders. The dark-haired woman joined the three of them in the center. Eine turned, uncertainly, and then went back to her seat. Noname was watching Loneela.

"Anda Leona," she said, her tone encouraging. "I would like to know what you believe would be the intentions behind your suspected alliance between Enahala and the Indigo."

Anda regarded her seriously. "One thing we know for sure about Indigo, is that in order to exterminate Laxens in such large numbers, he must have a source of some unknown power. This alone must be tempting enough for some to ally themselves with him. Power is very seductive."

"I agree," Loneela told him. "And do you have any ideas as to who the allies would be?"

"Oh, yes, let us name names!" Calthin exclaimed, indignant. "Let us start a hunt for the traitor, and point the finger at our enemies! This is all very convenient, isn't it, to cause trouble for those we dislike?" He appealed to the elders at the table, only some of whom seemed to be in agreement.

"Let's not be so hasty, Calthin," Agin said mildly. "We're not asking this question of the entire council, only Anda."

"A man who has never shown spite," the braided-haired woman chimed in.

Eine smiled at this, especially as she heard sounds of assent from all around the room. If they resented his criticism of their pride, they would at least admit that Anda was a kind man. She saw that Calthin's face had flushed a dark red, however. He settled his lidded eyes onto Anda's face with a look that turned Eine's blood cold. It reminded her suddenly of the vicious "voice" that had cursed her friend the day before.

Had it been Calthin that she'd heard? Eine looked to Anda, alarmed, but he was observing his opponent calmly. Was Calthin the traitor that Anda suspected? Was Anda attempting to out him in front of everyone?

"I have no wish to make accusations now," Anda declared. "I only wanted to put us on guard. If Indigo has been alerted to our actions in Thela by an Enahalan connection, will he retaliate? Will his destruction extend beyond his city walls?"

"It is always wise to be on our guard," Deep-Voice spoke up. "But if there were members in the council that were in league with Indigo, how would we keep any decisions quiet?"

Eine closed her eyes and tried to focus on the real feelings of anxiety that were growing inside her. She clenched her stomach, letting the tension settle there. If ever there was a time for her ability to show up, it was now.

"Please remember, we are still speaking of a hypothetical situation," Calthin was saying.

"It is better to be prepared," Anda replied.

"Let us have some water," Calthin said then, as if aside to someone. Eine listened with her eyes closed, gripping the arms of her chair. She felt a faint strain of the man's anger, but no clear thoughts. She could sense some desperation. "Thank you," she heard him say.

Eine's eyes popped open to see Calthin handing a glass bottle of water to Anda. His fingers fumbled over the mouth of the bottle for just one moment. Then a red-hot conviction shot through her. *"This will stop your interfering!"*

"Don't drink it!" Eine shrieked, jumping to her feet. Everyone gasped. Startled, Anda dropped the water bottle. It smashed onto the polished floor, where the water bubbled strangely white.

Calthin gave Eine one furious glance and then lunged for Anda, knocking him down to the ground. Noname yelled and sprang to his feet. Eine ran straight into the middle of the room and grabbed hold of Calthin by his collar. She jerked him up and then flung him backwards, sending him crashing like a sandbag into the wall. Then Noname was at her side, with his gun drawn.

Eine looked down, shaking, and saw that Loneela was kneeling by Anda. Others burst forth from their seats now and joined her, encircling him. "I'm all right!" he exclaimed. "Thank you, I'm all right!"

"Calthin Umb!" Deep-Voice roared.

"I don't believe it!" the sad-eyed elder woman wailed.

Calthin had scrambled to his feet, but Noname was on him in a moment, aiming at his head. "Get down, you *inuckit*," he growled. The heavyset man crumpled to the ground again and covered his face.

"The water," people were crying out. "Was it poisoned?"

"Yes," Anda said, and his voice trembled. "Eine knew it." Eine sank down next to him, feeling tired, and a little confused. The people around him stepped back and let her in, eyeing her in fascination.

"The Laxen read his thoughts!"

"She saved his life!"

Anda sat up slowly and took Eine's hand in his. "Thank you, dear friend," he told her, his eyes very bright. She squeezed his hand.

"Did Calthin use Graf to tell the Indigo about Enahala's plans?" she asked. The council grew quiet around her, listening. Anda sighed.

"I'm afraid so. And gods know what else."

SIXTEEN

Calthin Umb was escorted away by several Enahalans who arrived shortly, wearing white caps that marked them as officials. Then the council was issued a recess, at which point everyone in the room began talking at top volume about what they had just seen. Noname helped Anda to his feet and, taking Eine's arm, he led the two of them away from the commotion. They stopped at the foot of one of the stained glass windows, and then Eine was surprised to see Noname push it open like a door. Outside was a small ledge with a protective railing; the three of them stepped out onto it, and were greeted by a clear breeze.

"Do you think Calthin is working alone?" Noname asked Anda. His scarred face was grim in a way that Eine had never seen. It frightened her.

"I suspect not, but I can't be certain." Anda sighed and placed his hands on the railing. The view before them was magnificent: the white towers and walkways gleaming and casting shadows in the setting sun. Then there was the great drop below. Eine took a step back from the rail. "I'm still in such shock, Ney. I knew Calthin was self-serving and untrustworthy. But I never imagined him a murderer!"

"He…hates you," Eine said, hesitantly. She felt sorry for saying it, especially when she saw the pain on Anda's face. But she needed to explain. "I felt his anger."

"My foolish old rival," Anda muttered, shaking his head. "We studied together, long ago. And now they will put him to sleep."

"To sleep?" Eine asked.

"Permanently," Noname told her.

"They will give him a truth drug first, to find out what he has gotten us into," Anda said, his eyes out towards the view. "It's not perfect, but it will help."

Permanent sleep. It sounded to Eine like a peaceful death at least. She looked at Noname thoughtfully. And then would Calthin's spirit live on? Would it float away like the lights in her dreams? She gasped suddenly.

Was that what the floating lights in her dreams were meant to be?

"Did you make it happen, Eine?" Noname asked, interrupting her thoughts. "Or is Anda here just extremely lucky?"

"I did it," she admitted. "I think I'm starting to understand it."

"Excuse me," a familiar voice came from behind them. Loneela joined them on the balcony, looking concerned. "My father asked me to find out if Anda would like to retire for the day."

"No, my dear, if the council plans to continue after this break, then I will be a part of it," Anda replied. "They will return with Calthin's confession before long, and I'd like to hear it."

"Yes, and then we'll need all the sharp minds that the council has, to help us decide what to do next," she said. She smiled her lovely smile at him. "I'm so glad you're all right."

Anda's weathered face reddened a little, as if he were flattered, and he smiled back.

"I have two mighty soldiers that keep me safe," he said, cheerfully. Eine grinned and Noname rolled his eyes.

"It seems to me that this one is all you need," Loneela said and gave Eine a playful wink. Eine glanced at Noname, embarrassed. He folded his arms across his chest, his brown eyes on Loneela. "The Creeden just tags along, doesn't he?"

"Yes, I'm just decorative," he said in a flat voice. Loneela laughed and he softened, realizing she was just teasing. He grinned suddenly, and added, "They use me to distract the women." Anda snorted at that and shook his head.

"We *don't* keep him around for the lessons in modesty he provides," he retorted. Loneela giggled and Noname winked at her. Eine felt her gut twist suddenly; she turned away and leaned on the rail of the balcony, oblivious now to the great height. She let the wind cool her face, realizing it was very hot. What was all this winking for? Why was everyone so playful all of a sudden?

"Well, there must be some poor girl at home in Creede," Loneela was saying, "who would take issue with that kind of work."

"I haven't found a girl who would put up with me yet," Noname said, with mock sadness.

"Ah. Well, you won't find much luck here in Enahala. We're all old maids here."

"There are a few exceptions that I can see." Loneela made a sound of protest and laughed.

"Yes, I'm afraid it's my duty to marry well above my age," she murmured. "We must keep the great Enahalan race going."

"That's a shame," Noname said, sincerely. "But he'll be a lucky man."

Loneela smiled. "How can I accept such compliments from someone whose name I don't even know? Creedens are so mysterious."

Eine looked over at Anda and saw that he was staring out at the city, not listening. She reached over and put her arm through his. "Let's go back inside," she said quietly. He looked up, surprised, as if he'd forgotten that anyone else was there. Then he nodded and they walked back in through the door-window. Eine saw from the corner of her eye that Noname watched them go, but she couldn't read his expression.

Inside the council room, the crowd had half-cleared, and the remainder was divided into animated little groups. The chairs had been turned out of the neat circle they'd formed before and were now askew all across the room. The bearded man named Erano, who had spoken to Anda at the first council dinner, now approached him and Eine, looking excited.

"Anda, I've heard something extraordinary!" he whispered. "Someone has alerted Illeen and Binden of the situation, and they are coming to speak at the council!"

"Really?" Anda exclaimed. "Well, that is something." Eine

raised her eyebrows in a question and realized that it was an expression she was picking up from Noname. She frowned. "They are Laxens, Eine," Anda told her. "Two of the very few left here, I'm afraid."

"Do they run the concert hall?" she asked, eagerly.

"Yes, Illeen does the color show there."

Eine looked back over her shoulder to tell Noname, but he was still out on the ledge talking to Loneela. They were laughing again. She suddenly felt very tired. She stepped away from Anda and found a seat that was set apart from any of the others. She remembered now what she had 'heard' in the library. *"I bet Loneela will like that one."* The poor woman probably desperately wanted to marry someone close to her own age. Maybe Noname and Loneela would get married, and then Noname would stay in Enahala. Shouldn't that be a good thing? Why did she feel upset?

If they fell in love, would he tell her his name? It was hard to imagine him as anything but Noname now, or Ney. Eine felt a sudden strong desire to know his real name. But she would never know it, if he fell in love with Loneela. Or anyone else.

She watched idly as a man approached the pair of chutes in the corner and turned the handle-crank for several long moments. He opened the little door afterwards and removed a glass cylinder with a rolled-up paper inside. Then he carried it out of the council room.

Eine decided that she would leave Enahala if Noname got married. She didn't know why or where she would go, but she felt certain of it. She had taken care of herself before and she could do it again.

A few moments later, the two of them reentered the room. With her eyes on the floor, Eine noticed Loneela brush by in her white coat and boots. Then she heard Noname pulling a chair over. He sat down next to her and she looked up. He was studying her face, with a small smile on his own. He looked smug.

"What's the matter, Eine?" he asked. His smile irritated her.

"Did I say something was the matter?" she demanded. He grinned wider and looked away.

"Loneela's a nice girl, isn't she?" he said, glancing over at Anda. Eine sighed.

"Very much so," she said, honestly.

"Very much on the hunt." He looked back at her with a

different smile, a reassuring one. She felt confused. "But you can't blame her," he added.

At that moment, a bell sounded. The council was restarting. Eine watched as the people quickly stood and began moving their chairs back into the circle. She followed suit, pushing thoughts of Loneela out of her head. Anda joined them as she and Noname settled in, surrounded by the scraping of chairs and excited whispers. The elders reentered the room a moment later and took their places at the table.

Then two Laxens walked into the room. The buzzing went off immediately in Eine's head. She turned to stare at them, just as the rest of the crowd did, but their eyes immediately met hers as well. They were both men. One was tall and thin with long, graying blond hair, tied into a knot behind his head. He had the typical blue Enahalan eyes and he wore a belted white tunic over light gray trousers. The other was shorter, broad-shouldered, and well-muscled with dark eyes and short dark hair speckled with gray. He wore a pale green vest and pants in the same color, with heavy boots.

"Good afternoon, Illeen and Binden," Deep-Voice greeted them. "We thank you for joining us."

"Good afternoon, Kahl," the long-haired man said, in a quiet voice. The other one merely nodded. He turned his dark eyes back to Eine and thought, quite directly at her, *"I didn't think there was any one left in Thela."* Eine gasped. He could send his thoughts to her? She swallowed, intimidated, and nodded at him.

The two of them found seats in the front and sat quietly. Deep-Voice, whose name Eine now knew was Kahl, held up a curled sheet of paper that she realized must have arrived through the wall chute. He addressed the council. "Calthin Umb has told us an interesting tale. As some of you may know, he traveled to Inowa two months ago to attend a scientific conference. It was there that he met a man who was inquiring after some rather unusual laboratory materials, which he said were for his master. He somehow made Calthin curious enough to slip him a truth drug, and then admitted that he was a member of the Indigo. It would seem that their leader is a student of experimental science." He paused, letting everyone absorb this. "He apparently studied a great deal about the Pinnacle's creation of the Hunters, after he hired them, and used some of that knowledge to breed the giant animals that Idder Bay discovered in the city."

...And most likely the giant rats in the tunnel underneath, Eine realized.

"But this Indigo member did not know his leader's identity, so that was all Calthin could learn. But he gave the man a message for his master, that he could be his liason with the outside world, if it were so desired. A communication was set up between them that continued until today. While pretending to be on a holiday in Etainland, he met with several Indigo members in Belgir." Kahl paused here, sounding weary. "He did indeed teach them Enahalan fading. The Belgin boy was kidnapped at random, so that Calthin could send him with news of our investigation. It was the most secure method, thanks to our advances in memory drugs. He hired a Kry to mind-send the boy into the city."

The two Laxens shared a look of disgust at the words 'Kry'. Eine looked inquisitively at Noname and he whispered, "Mercenary Laxens. Tell you later."

Kahl looked down at the paper in his wrinkled hands. "By now, we can rightly assume that the boy has told Indigo himself that Enahala is in full investigation of his activities. We must be aware that Indigo has every reason to strike back."

The room broke out into loud exclamations.

"This adds a sense of urgency to our decision-making," the wobbly-voiced woman declared. "It is no longer safe to send in more volunteers."

"We have two clear options," Kahl added. "Do we cancel our operations and wait for a possible attack, or do we make the bolder choice, and strike first?"

Eine's heart leapt into her throat as she listened.

"In either case," the mustached man spoke up, "we can appeal to our neighbors for help. There are many who would send forces in our defense, and some who would send them to join our army."

"Let us now hear your opinions and questions," Kahl declared. The room fell abruptly silent as everyone turned the matter over in their minds. As the tension spread over her, Eine caught hold of it, and let herself be flooded with fragments of thoughts.

"...to go to war! We've been at peace for decades..."
"...could come for us in our beds! We'd live in fear..."

"...would we know where to send the soldiers?"
"Who knows what we would be fighting?"
"...must defend ourselves at all costs..."

A physical voice cut through the melee and commanded everyone's attention. *"Iwalahen,"* the dark-eyed Laxen said. The council members nodded and he walked purposely out into the center of the room.

"Iwalahen," his friend repeated, and then floated gracefully over to join him.

All of the blond man's movements flowed like water. He was so elegant it was hard for Eine to take her eyes off him. As she stared, she felt a wave of discomfort and unhappiness roll off of the both of them, mingling with the light buzz in her head.

"We have avoided coming here, perhaps for too long," the blond man said, after a moment. "It's hard to explain why." He looked at his companion but the latter said nothing. "I have terrible nightmares about the Indigo... I dream that they're coming here, that soon they'll be everywhere." He stopped and turned a shade paler.

"I had a Laxen cousin in Thela," the other man spoke up. His voice was thicker and deeper, as Eine had heard his thoughts. "When the Indigo took over, I never heard from him again. I went to see for myself. The city was closed off and there was no way in or out."

Eine felt her hands clenching together.

"But I for one can not hide any longer," the blond said, casting his blue gaze out over the crowd. "I can not sit still and let my nightmares come true. So if there is reason to believe that the Indigo will come here..."

"Then we want to fight," the other declared. The force of the words was felt by everyone in the room. "We vote to attack first."

***

It was several hours later, and long past sunset, that the council finally came to a close. There was a hurried lunch that most everyone ate in their seats and no mention of dinner. Many people spoke and there were countless disagreements, but as it went on and on, it became clear that most people were in favor of striking first. When it came down to it, the idea of an attack on

149

Enahala - especially by an order whose power source was completely unknown and unheard of - was too frightening to accept. The discussion after that fell to the details of how and when. Notices had to be sent immediately to gather forces. It had to be determined if the Creeden Laxen, Oln, could mind-send an army into Thela in small groups. The target locations inside the city had to be narrowed down.

Several Enahalan soldiers, wearing white caps like the ones who had taken away Calthin, were called in and the map of Thela was analyzed and covered in marks. These soldiers were not much younger than Anda, but they were well-muscled and in good shape. It was a military operation now; there would be no more formal councils.

Somehow, as tense as it all was, Eine dozed off at one point, and dreamed about the voice calling her in the woods. She awoke once to hear Anda and Noname discussing Andliss and Indigo's fascination with the Pinnacle. Then she drifted off again. She was awoken again much later by Noname, lifting her up like a child, still talking seriously with Anda. Startled, she looked around them and saw that the crowd was making its slow, haphazard way out the door.

"Is it over?" she mumbled. Noname looked down at her, a troubled expression on his face.

"It's just beginning, Eine," he said, sounding worried. He carried her towards the door and then Loneela approached, her features lit up with excitement.

Eine cringed and wiggled in Noname's arms. "Put me down," she said. He didn't hear her; he was looking at Loneela. "I'm not a child - put me down!" she snapped. Noname gave her a stunned look and practically dropped her. Her feet stung as she landed and she glared at him. He snarled back at her, his brown eyes hurt and angry.

"Anda! All three of you," Loneela exclaimed. "You must come and eat with us at my father's house. Everyone is hungry, and there'll be more discussion. Several other elders are coming."

"Absolutely," Noname said, in a sharp voice that made Eine look up at him. "Anda, what do you say?" Anda looked tired but he nodded and smiled at Loneela.

"We are honored to attend, my dear."

Eine stood there, exhausted, and stared at Loneela as she turned around, urging them to follow. She could not imagine listening to her chatter with Noname, or hearing any more about the strategy of attack, or even enduring polite company, whether or not there was food.

"I'm just going to go back to my room," she said, as they passed through the door. Anda looked surprised, but Noname didn't. He raised his eyebrows at her, coolly.

"Do you even know how to get back there?" he asked. She frowned, realizing that she didn't.

"Ney, why don't you walk her back? Loneela and I will meet you at the crossing by the library," Anda said, as Loneela turned back to listen. She nodded at this, but she did not smile. Noname said nothing and walked past Eine, headed towards the entrance hall. Nothing glittered in the building now that the sun had set and the night sky was cloudy. Eine lagged behind him down the hall, but she caught up with him outside on the path. She saw with a start that the white walkways glowed dimly in the darkness, making them easier to see.

"It's a good thing they don't have children, in one way," she said, stepping carefully. "They'd fall off of these all the time."

"Not if they were raised to be used to it," Noname muttered. It was true that children could get used to most things. Eine and the others in Thela were proof of that. "I'm sure Loneela has excellent balance," he added, pointedly. Eine felt stung. She was certain he was angry with her now, and she was confused about why. They fell silent then for the rest of the walk, until she saw that they were drawing near to the building which housed her room. She could recognize which door was hers; maybe she should go on alone.

Then she remembered the serious debates through which they had sat all day, and she felt ashamed that she and Noname were arguing now. Whatever it was about was silly. They should be talking about what was important.

She sighed. "Well, maybe that will help her fight," she mused.

"What?" he asked.

"Loneela's balance," she explained. "And I have strength…" Noname gave her a sudden horrified look.

"Are you going to *fight her?*" he exclaimed, incredulous. Eine scowled at him. The Creeden word for 'stupid' came back to her, out of nowhere.

"No, *nicktu*! In the attack! I'm talking about when we fight the Indigo." To her own surprise, he laughed. It was a short, loud laugh that shot out into the night around them. "What?" she demanded.

"You think Loneela will fight with the army?" he asked, grinning. "Eine, she's not a soldier. She's not going to fight anyone."

"Oh." Eine felt relieved at the thought. At least she wouldn't see the pretty woman during the fight.

"You're not either, kid," Noname added. "I don't know what you're talking about."

Eine stopped and stared at him. "Why not?"

"Why not?! Because you're half-Laxen! And we're going back into Thela!" He was staring at her now as if she was insane.

"But Illeen and Binden are going," she said.

"But they didn't just escape! And they're men! And they're full grown and Binden is a fighter!" He was getting exasperated now, and louder.

"But I'm stronger!" Eine retorted. "I am stronger than a full grown man!"

"So what?" he yelled back. A low murmur made them both jump. An elderly couple was passing on a pathway nearby, watching them. Noname dropped his voice. "This is a real battle, Eine. You're not a soldier and you'll get hurt. What are you thinking? You're safe here!"

"I'm thinking that this is more my battle than it is yours," Eine told him, feeling herself tense all over. She clenched her fists. "The Indigo killed my parents. They're killing *my* people. I want to help."

"No." His voice was hard and sharp. Eine locked eyes with him, feeling a terrible anger rising up in her throat. "I won't let you do it," he said.

Eine's mouth flew open to scream at him. Then her anger suddenly plucked out his thoughts.

"I can't lose you."

Bewildered, her mouth hung open for a moment. Anger was a kind of anxiety after all. Noname's face was still drawn together, fierce. She hugged herself, aching now to lie down and do anything but argue. She turned away.

"I can find my own way," she said, and felt the double

meaning in the words. She followed the rest of the path by herself, all the way to her door, unsure whether Noname was standing there watching her, or not. Then she let herself in and went to bed.

SEVENTEEN

Eine woke up feeling hungry and unhappy, and confused about both. She lay curled up in the soft bed, gazing up at the curved ceiling. It took a moment to remember that she hadn't eaten dinner, and she'd argued with Noname. She would have lain there longer and mulled over the argument, but the growling in her stomach made her sit up. It occurred to her then that this was her first morning in Enahala where there was no council meeting. Did that mean that no one would come to get her?

Unsettled at the thought, she got up and began to fill the bathtub. She had a few Enahalan coins from Noname, and she thought she could remember where the market building was. A *lalen* sounded wonderful right now. She bathed quickly, even though she was beginning to enjoy the feel of hot water, and then chose another dress from inside the curtained closet. This one was pale pink with a scooped neck. As she pulled it on, she wondered where all the clothing came from. When she had imagined staying in Enahala after the council, she hadn't actually thought about clothes, or money for food. It was upsetting how quickly she'd gotten used to having these things provided for her!

But now she was going back to Thela, albeit with an army, possibly never to return. So maybe it didn't matter. Pushing the thought from her mind, she wrapped up in her cloak and began to tug on the white boots. After a moment, she stopped and pulled them back off. If she wasn't going to the council hall, then she didn't have to dress up. She could grip the curving pathways better with her bare feet anyway.

Feeling more like herself, she stood up eagerly and slid open the door, greeting an overcast morning that dulled the usual brilliance of the city. Wide-eyed, she walked out onto the path and looked around at the city for the first time on her own. As usual, there were smatterings of people out and about, rushing along, looking occupied, or strolling in couples and chatting. A cool breeze was blowing, whistling around the circular buildings, and Eine was glad for the sturdy grip of her bare feet.

She set off in the direction of the market building, and after stopping to ask someone for help once, she found it, descending safely towards the open door of the first shop she could see. It wasn't the *lalens* shop, but an intoxicating scent enveloped her the moment she walked inside.

A man in a big apron was cooking eggs with soft bread. He rolled it up together and wrapped it up in paper; Eine let him count out the coins that Anda had given her, and then sat on a round stool to eat every last bite. When the man turned his back, she actually gave in and licked the paper a little bit, before throwing it out. It still amazed her how much she could eat lately. Her appetite had certainly grown.

She made up her mind afterwards to go straight to the library, and start learning how to read. Now was as good a time as any. Feeling energized, she swept back out into the breezy day and followed the winding paths. She asked for directions again, and before long, spotted the lovely building ahead of her. She thought of Noname as she walked up to the double doors, and felt a sudden twist of emptiness inside. What was he doing today? Was he still angry with her? Was he spending time with Loneela? She sighed, suddenly, remembering the moment outside the concert hall. *'She looks like an angel.'* Perhaps she should look up what an angel was while she was here.

The library was warm and peaceful inside, soothing. People were descending the central staircase, whispering to each other. There weren't as many readers on the seats as before, perhaps because it was still early. Eine padded around on the smooth floor in her bare feet, looking up at the rows and rows of books along the walls. Of course they were in many different languages, she realized. That was daunting.

Should she learn to read in both Enahalan and Thelan?

As she was standing there, considering, a stooped woman with curly white hair approached her, looking curious. "Can I help you, my dear?" she asked softly, and glanced down at Eine's feet.

"Well, I don't know how to start," Eine told her. "I don't know how to read." The woman looked taken back for a moment. Then she wrapped her white shawl around herself more tightly and gestured for Eine to follow. They made a half-circle around the great room before she stopped and, to Eine's concern, began to ascend one of the sliding ladders. She climbed very slowly and deliberately, and Eine stood underneath her, fearful, ready to catch her if she fell.

In a few moments, she was back again, looking satisfied.She handed Eine a small book with a contraption attached to it by a cord. "This is how you start," she told her. "It's Thelan. Put these in your ears and turn the knob here. It will sound out the letters for you."

Eine smiled and studied the ear pieces in wonder.

***

She had been murmuring softly to herself, repeating the recorded sounds and fingering the letters, for over an hour when Anda found her. A large hand rested on her shoulder and she gasped. Pulling the ear pieces out, she gazed up at him as though from far away. She had forgotten where she was. Anda looked worried though, so she shook it off quickly.

"Eine!" he exclaimed in a whisper. "We've been looking for you everywhere!"

"What?"

"We came to your room this morning! Where were you?"

"Oh, I…" Eine stopped and smiled, surprised. They had still come to get her, even though there was no council.

"Have you eaten anything?" Anda asked her. "Ney's gone to see if you somehow found your way to my house."

"I did eat. I bought something at the market and I came here," Eine said, holding the book out. "I thought you were busy."

"Well, we weren't going to just abandon you, child. You could have left us a message." Anda's kind face clouded and he folded his arms, in a huff. Then his blue eyes fell on the book with its listening device. "Ah, you've found a child's lesson book! Very clever," he said, changing his tone. "How is it going so far?"

Eine opened the book back to the page and ran her finger along a sentence. "'The house…is very…small,'" she read. Anda nodded approvingly.

"Let me check it out for you and you can bring it home," he said, taking the book.

"I can take it?" she asked, surprised.

"You can borrow it for five days. That's the way the library works." He led the way to the spiral staircase and began to descend to the lower floor. "And then, if no one else wants it, which I can't imagine anyone would, then you can have it for five days again."

"I'm sorry I didn't leave you a message," Eine told him, following down the stairs. "I mean, I wouldn't know how anyway."

Anda laughed. "Well, that's true, isn't it? You don't know how to write! I suppose you are used to taking care of yourself, after all. But you are welcome to come and eat with me, Eine, and stay whenever you like." They reached the bottom of the stairs and he carried the book over to a desk that was topped with a large, stamping machine. Laying the book inside it, he brought the top down with a loud thunk, and then handed the book back to her.

"Come, let's go and tell Ney you're alive."

Noname was irritable and said little when they met up with him at Anda's house. Anda seemed surprised by his reaction, but Eine was not. He took off before long, claiming that he needed to go train with the Enahalan soldiers. Neither he or Eine said anything about their argument.

Anda's domed cottage was very snug and comfortable. The white walls were left plain, instead of hung with draperies, but there were framed paintings hanging here and there. The large main room held a round pit at the center for building a fire, and above it was a smoke grate in the ceiling that was covered up when not in use. He also had a large round table and several cushioned seats. In the corner stood his *garina*, which reminded Eine of the instruments at the concert hall, except that it was much larger than the ones she'd seen. It had been lovingly polished all over and had its own little seat attached to it.

Eine found a soft, bowl-shaped seat in the corner, and plugged herself back into her reading lessons, as Anda puttered about, taking care of his own business.

The next four or five days passed in the same quiet way. After all the rapid changes that had occurred since Eine had left Thela, it was odd to settle into a routine. But there was something comforting about it too. She slept in her room and ate good, simple meals at Anda's. Then when he went to join Noname in training, or met with other council members for news, she practiced her reading and made trips to the library. Sometimes she concentrated on attempting to read the minds of the others in the library. Whenever she was successful, the results were often about the coming battle.

"It's good we've set supplies aside. Just in case the Indigo do come."

"If only we had more young men to fight."

Eine developed a liking for *kalan*, the bitter hot drink from the council's breakfast, which turned out to be a favorite of Anda's, especially with a little sugar in it. Reading with a full stomach and a warm drink was a wonderful thing. Sometimes she fell asleep in Anda's bowl chair, with books spilling out of her lap. Once, she woke up to see Noname standing there, watching her. He was frowning, his dark brows furrowed, unhappy. Eine sat up quickly but he made a gesture, as if to say, "Carry on." Then he left.

She felt like something was missing. There was no one to laugh at the things she didn't know. There was no one to insist that she needed taking care of. It left her with a strange little ache inside.

In the library, after a week had gone by, Eine found a history book with a chapter on Andliss. Eagerly, she flipped to the right pages and began running her finger across the words. She still read haltingly, and had to skip over the longer words, but she had made enormous progress.

"Andliss was a city of light, especially in the Old-World. The Andlissians, Laxen or not, were gifted with many talents. Art and science prevailed in Andliss and thus there were festivals, conferences, and great works commissioned. Andliss produced the master painter Enoct Ect; the legendary storyteller Alect; the first Harmonic Singing company; the great biologist Rined Secta; and many more...

...A city of impressive engineering and design, Andlissian buildings were open-air and interconnected, in a style that is still copied in other cities... The writings of Alect and others have been re-printed around the world, and become classics...

In the Year of Five Floods, three Laxens from different parts of the world came together to form the Pinnacle, a society that professed Laxens to be a superior race. The full names of the Pinnacle members are not certain. They were each gifted with elemental control, and took to calling themselves the Gale, the Frost and the Flame. They based their philosophy of supremacy on the fact that the first Laxens were believed to be gods, and used this to ask the question what is a god, if not a super-being? Were not the Laxens gods among regular people, deserving of worship?

The group attempted fanatically to recruit others of its kind but was largely ignored by the general public, who sometimes pointed to the works of Andliss as an example of the fact that non-Laxens were not inferior. The group became increasingly outspoken and threatening...

By the Year of the New Star, they had made their decision to destroy Andliss as an example to all. The Flame, who had the ability to ignite objects with his mind, managed to set the entire city ablaze in a single moment. The immense effort killed him, leaving the others to revel in their success, as the world watched in horror. Though rescue attempts were made, the fire so thoroughly disintegrated the city that no survivors were ever found.

The group's remaining members locked themselves inside the caves in the Ice Lands, but they were found and killed by a voluntary league of Laxens. The loss of Andliss remains a painful subject among historians to this day."

Eine sat back and pondered the story. Anda had mentioned that the expression "Great Gods" had come from reactions to the very first Laxens. People were frightened of and awed by those who had special abilities. But what *were* gods? Eine stood up and returned to the history section through which she'd been digging. She found a heavy volume on Old-World legends and carried it easily, one-handed, back to her seat. She noticed someone eyeing her in surprise as she did. She thought of Noname and gave the book a defiant little toss and caught it.

Then she settled in to skim through the stories of the time before the Laxens. To her delight, the book had many pictures, which were labeled as copies of old engravings and paintings. "Before the first Laxens came to be born, the people lived in a very different world..." Eine rested her chin in her hand, reading. In the

Old-World, there had been very little medicine. The average lifespan was only about forty, due to the many diseases that remained incurable until early Laxens invented the common medicines. Living structures were built mostly of wood in those days and were demolished in severe weather; Laxens, with the help of others, devised the methods of making brick from clay and pavement from stone, of soldering metal. Old-World people lived in small villages with very little protection from thieves or wild animals.

There was a full-page, detailed painting of a woman in a dress that seemed made of one long piece of cloth, wrapped around her. She stood near a rough shack, clinging to a basket of nuts, and bracing herself against the growls of an enormous dog that threatened her. The woman was barefoot, and the dwelling behind her reminded Eine of the Mayjans' houses.

"Because they were without the means of preventing so many misfortunes, people of the Old-World developed a great deal of folklore to explain away what they did not understand. Many of the early tales and songs have been carried down into modern times, such as the frightening story of the Blue Stone that 'destroyed everything all around', or the Forgotten Man that haunted forested areas. Some of the beliefs remain strong to this day, especially the theory of the after-life." Eine paused, remembering her conversation with Noname. So that was a very old belief.

"But the most well-known folk ideas of the time were sparked by the births of the first Laxens. As these individuals with various unusual abilities and talents began to crop up among families, they were hailed as 'gods', or magical beings that are not of this world. In the stories, gods did not permanently die, and they had the power to control all of the unknown. In some parts of the world, elaborate systems were set up to venerate these first of a kind, but over time, it became more and more apparent that Laxens were very human. They were not immortal, although most were very difficult to be killed by non-Laxens. They mated with regular people often, and lived as they did, using their abilities to build a better life. They were said to have 'brought the light'."

On the adjacent page was an old engraving that filled Eine with awe. It was of a young girl - or perhaps a fine-featured boy, she couldn't tell - who sat on an outcropping of rocks among several trees. On its back were wings! Eine ran her fingers over the picture, fascinated. Streams of light poured down on the figure from above, casting an aura all around it. The figure had long, light-colored hair and wore a simple shift. There was something very peaceful and lovely about the scene. Underneath the picture were the words, "The most famous work of Laxen Divinity Art, *The Angel*. In reality, no Laxen has been known to bear wings."

Eine sounded out the title of the picture and then gasped. Angel. She stared at the picture again. Her hair did resemble the Laxen in the image. She turned the page quickly and scanned for the word again, in the text.

"…the angels were believed to be messengers. This idea sprang from an uncommon Laxen ability known as transferring or conduition, by which one Laxen can send communication, and sometimes even an action, through another Laxen. This ability is difficult to describe properly because it has so many variations."

"Eine!"

She jumped about a foot in her chair. Spinning around, she saw Noname standing in the door of the library. He was wearing a new coat that she hadn't seen before, one with leather flaps on the shoulders. It made him look broader-shouldered and more formidable. "Eine!" he called again, looking urgent.

Everyone in the room promptly hissed at him, "Shhhhh!!!!"

Noname broke into a broad grin at that, and Eine smiled back automatically. It seemed like ages since she'd seen him smile. She got up quickly and closed the book. When she reached the door, he was standing there watching her, an excited look on his scarred face. "The army has started arriving," he told her. "They're flying in right now."

***

The airships were landing in a large field that ran behind the garden area where Anda lived. Eine had never seen anything so amazing. There were three great balloons in the sky, descending to the ground, as carefully as if a giant, invisible hand were setting them down. Hanging beneath them were large, oblong structures that were lined with round windows. The ships varied quite a bit in their shapes, and the balloons were different colors: gray, navy, and maroon. The balloons had a quilted appearance due to the crisscrossing ropes that strapped them to their ships, which had whirling propellers attached in the back.

Eine stood at the edge of the field with Noname, absolutely in awe. Weighted objects were being thrown out of the ships to tether them to the ground. One ship that had landed just as she arrived now revealed a yawning opening – from a hatch that dropped open - and from it spewed forth about fifteen soldiers.

"There are a few groups arriving by horse and auto-car out front," Noname said, looking on approvingly. "We had a good response."

"They're so beautiful," Eine said, startling him. She shaded her eyes and watched as the last airship sank into the grass. He laughed.

"I thought you meant the soldiers for a second."

She grinned. "Where will they all stay?"

"The council is going to have them make camp out here in the fields for tonight," he replied. "We just have to sort everyone out and give them instructions."

"What are the instructions?" she asked.

"We're to go by airship into Creede to meet Oln. He can't travel here because of the fighting there… They need him. Then he'll mind-send the groups into Thela." He cracked his knuckles with a loud pop, making Eine flinch. "We take off the day after tomorrow," he added.

She looked up at him seriously and he gazed back down at her, his brown eyes troubled. "You do know that I'm coming," she said.

"I know that I can't stop you," he told her.

"The council must want me to go, anyway, to help."

"They do," he said, unhappily.

"Good." Eine put her hands in the pockets of her dress and looked back out over the field. She felt a small weight lifted from her heart.

"Loneela gave me this jacket," Noname said. She flinched, as the weight came plunging back. She turned to glare at him, and then saw that there was a decided twinkling in his eyes. He was just barely managing not to smile. "Do you like it?"

"There you two are," Anda's voice boomed from behind them. He joined them with a nod of his head and eyed the soldiers moving about in the field. "I don't think the three of us have been together for more than a second these past few days," he commented. Then he gave Noname a disapproving look. "I thought you weren't going to accept that jacket."

Eine's heart lifted again, and the ups and downs suddenly made her feel dizzy. Noname turned a little red and grinned from ear to ear. "I thought it might have some use after all," he said.

EIGHTEEN

The sun was only just visible over the horizon as Eine followed Noname up the ramp of one of the beautiful airships. The structure that swallowed them up was made of steel and it was covered in decorative etchings. The graceful lines swooped along the outside surface of the giant oblong shape, circling rounded windows with very thick glass. This was an Enahalan airship, so its massive balloon overhead was a brilliant white, with steel-gray cords bound in a mesh pattern across it.

Noname and Anda had come to get Eine while it was still very dark. She had been awake already for awhile, feeling excited and worried. She lay in the soft bed and heard scraps of thoughts from the room next to hers, slipping in due to her nerves. They were dream-thoughts that made little sense. She thought about the picture of the angel in the Old-World book and wondered about the strange ability that an 'angel' Laxen was supposed to have. Conduition. What would it be like to have something pass through you? How did it work?

She got up after a minute and washed her face, and cleaned her teeth the way that Anda had taught her. Sometimes it still felt odd to be so clean all the time. Even her green cloak had been washed recently and it felt softer. She combed out her hair and pulled on the clothes she had set out the night before: the plainest dress she could find in the closet, a gray one that felt sturdier than the others, and the white boots, which wouldn't stay white for long. She wrapped on her cloak and tied the table leg into the cord.

She added a second dress to the small back-bag that Anda had given her, which already held a canteen, dried food, a little whistle like Noname's, and cloth bandages. She had just put her arms through the loops of it when there was the knock on the door.

The soldiers on the airship watched the three of them now as they sat down. The seats ran along the walls facing inward towards an open space in the middle where there was a pile of bags and weapons. The seats swiveled to face the windows as well, and Eine smiled at this. She could watch as they took off. In the ceiling was an open hatch that led to a small round room on the roof of the ship, which was where the pilot stood, controlling the hot flames that Anda had explained made the balloon rise. Eine wished she could go up there and watch, but at the moment, the fourteen soldiers accompanying them were more interesting. Binden was among them and he nodded at Eine, but the others were all so different from each other. After the sameness of the Enahalans, it was fascinating to see.

The council and Enahalan army had convened to divide the men up by strengths. Therefore the group on this ship hailed from all over. There were two dark-skinned men but the shades of their skin were very different from each other. One had liquid black eyes and wore a fitted brown suit; he also wore a necklace and belt made of black stones that matched his eyes. The other wore a green robe with a strange, high collar of diaphanous material that gave his peaceful face a surreal quality.

There were two very tall pale men, almost the size of Hunters. One had white hair, although he appeared to be young, which he wore in a high ponytail. The other's head was shaved clean and he wore gold hoops pierced through his ears. They both wore a flexible mesh of armor that draped over shirts and trousers made of thick cloth.

There was a fiercely muscled woman, her silhouette wrapped in layers of embroidered cloth, whose black hair hung in long braids.Next to her, to Eine's surprise, was a Meyjan man, tiny and stout in a leather-armored outfit.

There were two other Laxens aside from Binden, and Eine had heard there were more of the brave souls in the other ships. One was a waifish young man with pale hair and large green eyes.

He wore all black and his expression was cold and blank, belying his soft features. The other was an older man with wild gray hair and a thick gray beard. He wore a long coat not unlike the Enahalans, although it was brown, and his green eyes were restless and lively.

He gave Eine a long, scrutinizing look and then winked.

There was one more non-Enahalan: a wiry, yellow-skinned woman with short blond hair and long, sharp fingernails, who wore short trousers and a top with no sleeves, as if she were never cold. The rest of the soldiers consisted of three blue-eyed Enahalan soldiers in their white caps. They would almost have been difficult to distinguish from each other, except that one had a gray beard, one wore spectacles that were bound around his head, and the other had bushy gray eyebrows. The three of them studied everyone on the ship and whispered to each other.

Eine swiveled in her seat to look at her two companions. Anda wore a white cap like his kinsmen but he had donned the long blue coat he'd bought at the market outside of Thela, and placed a long staff in the pile of luggage at the ship's center. Noname wore the jacket from Loneela with a black shirt underneath and his usual black trousers. His gun and the bandit's sword were strapped to his belt; his short-cropped hair had grown out a bit since they'd reached Enahala and it somehow gave him a younger look.

He met Eine's gaze and smiled. "Are you ready to fly, Eine?"

As soon as he spoke, there was a roar of fire overhead, spewing hot air up into the balloon. Eine spun around to look outside the window. Several of the soldiers near the open entrance began pulling in the heavy iron ball that weighted the ship. Then one of them cranked a wheel that wound the ramp up and sealed it against the ceiling and the walls.

There was a jerking movement, and then Eine felt an odd sensation in her stomach. She clung to the edge of the circular window, watching as the ground sank slowly beneath them. She looked up and saw the horizon dropping, the sky stretching downward as if to envelop them. Panic struck her. Her stomach lurched and she closed her eyes tight.

"Turn around, kid," Noname told her. "Don't look out till we're level."

She obeyed without a word, swallowing hard. The ship

around them was swaying, and her stomach swayed with it. Was she going to be sick? In front of all these strong soldiers? Was this what flying was like??

Noname took her hand and squeezed it. She looked up at him and saw he was smiling in a knowing way. "Hang in there," he said.

"Have you flown before?" she asked, clenching her teeth.

"A couple times. The first time, I threw up everywhere," he said cheerfully. She groaned and took her hand away. Then she grabbed his back, realizing it helped.

"Why didn't you tell me?"

"I don't know, you're a Demi. I thought you might not feel it!"

Eine cast an embarrassed look at the soldiers across from them. The giant with the white ponytail was smirking at her. The woman with the braids rolled her eyes.

"Find a fixed point and stare at it," the bearded Laxen advised.

"Oh, I forgot she might be sick," Anda said, looking concerned. He started digging in his bag. "Here, I've got some mint tablets. Try sucking on one of these for a little while."

Eine accepted the little tablet and looked back out the window, determined not to miss anything. The white buildings of Enahala were directly below and around them was the city wall. It was so incredibly strange to see them from up above. Straight ahead, to the east, she could see that the plains through which they'd taken the train continued on around the city, and then were interrupted by a large, glittering lake, surrounded by trees. This was the way birds saw the world.

They were traveling east towards Creede, so they would fly right over that water. Eine felt sick again and she closed her eyes for a moment, listening to the soldiers talking. They were speaking in different languages, but Thelan sentences often broke through.

"It's faster by wing-glide."

"Our horses get a better price at Tobin."

"What about this mind-sending? Have you seen it?"

Sucking on the mint was helping. Eine opened her eyes again and saw the brilliant lake flashing by. It was beautiful. She felt truly like a bird, like she could swoop down and drag the tip of one wing in the water. It flew by so fast. Then it was open land again, fluttering by, and the sky blazed a deep blue overhead. On the horizon were mountains shrouded in low clouds. Before them, a collection of buildings was approaching. Eine leaned closer and then a flock of birds suddenly filled the view, startling her.

"That's Etainland," Noname said, and she realized she was still holding his hand. She felt a flood of shyness suddenly, and let go. He didn't seem to notice. "Look at their games arena," he added, pointing.

She looked again and saw that the birds had veered off to the south, flying together in a perfect fleet. Noname was pointing at a massive bowl-shaped structure among the buildings below. The other tiny buildings of Etainland all had a reddish tint to them. They flew by underneath the ship in a rambling, twisting layout, dotted by clusters of trees and a few small lakes.

Eine wished she could capture the images that sped by them. She would never be able to remember them in such detail. Her stomach turned again, despite her excitement.

"Ah, the Etains will win at the Inowan games again, I'm sure," Anda commented, looking out.

"I went to a *hirer* match there once, as a kid," Noname said. "…With my father." He frowned and looked on ahead, past Etainland. There were long dark smudges of green in the distance, and one of the other airships was visible, blowing along ahead of them.

"Are you happy to be going home?" Eine asked him, swallowing. He said nothing for a moment, and then shrugged.

"It's always good to see Oln."

"I wonder if he's still living in the temple?" Anda asked.

"Probably. He'll come out to the landing grounds to meet us," Noname said. They fell silent as the reddish buildings continued to pass by. Eine watched as another airship caught up to them and flew past. It resembled a giant flying beetle, flitting about with propellers spinning. The swaying, floating motion was beginning to seem natural now, as she stared off at the oncoming green land. It lulled her a bit and she found herself yawning. She hadn't slept very well and the trip was going to take a little while. She put her head against the window frame and gazed down through half-closed lids.

"Fever swamp coming up," she heard a soldier say. Then she fell asleep.

***

Eine felt herself plummet several feet. Her eyes snapped open. She was still in her seat, inside the ship.Then everything dropped again, and her head banged against the window. Curses and shouts flew up from the soldiers.

"What's going on?" Noname yelled. Eine looked around, dazed. Several of the taller men, including Binden, leapt out of their seats and banged on the hatch lid. Anda was staring out the window and Eine followed his gaze; she saw with a start that dense, dark trees blanketed the area below them. As she looked, the ship sank again, and her stomach flew into her throat. She gasped and doubled over.

"Don't look out, Eine," Anda said. Noname jumped up with the others as the hatch lid lifted, and a terrified-looking man put his head through.

"The balloon is torn!" he roared and disappeared back through the hatch.

"It's torn?!" several people exclaimed. Eine gasped, still trying not to be sick.

"Are we gonna crash?"

"Are we falling?"

"There is a repair kit!" the bearded Enahalan called over the others. "He will have to scale the ropes and patch it." Eine wasn't alone in shuddering at that thought.

"Does he need help?" Noname asked, staring upwards.

"I am very agile," the woman with the short hair and long nails declared. Her voice was rich and throaty. "I can do it." She crouched down immediately and leapt up towards the open hatch. She caught the edge and swung herself up, disappearing above. Eine felt dizzy just watching her. The ship plummeted again; she grabbed onto Anda and stared out the window. Noname joined her and they saw that the trees below were more distinct, suddenly closer.

"She won't do it in time," the bearded Laxen spoke up. "We need to prepare to land."

"We're over the swamp!" the Meyjan exclaimed in a shrill voice.

"Brace yourselves!" Anda called out.

"We'll hit the trees!"

The ship did something like a pirouette around them. Eine and a few others groaned, nauseated. They were falling to the left now, plunging towards branches and leaves that reached upwards. Noname fell bodily into both Eine and Anda, flattening them into the wall. Suddenly the others were sliding across the floor, crashing into seats and limbs and windows. The pilot fell abruptly down into the ship. Eine threw her arms over her head.

She heard glass shatter and cries from all around. She felt the ship scrape itself across branches, then tumble downwards again. She banged against metal and glass and somebody's arms. The ship tilted sharply. Somebody screamed from far away. The ship snagged and her head jerked backwards - then they fell again, followed by great tearing sounds above.

Eine heard Noname cursing in her ear. Then suddenly they snagged again, and everything stopped. There was an abrupt quiet. With her eyes shut, Eine felt like the darkness was spinning. All was silent for several seconds, and then she became aware of a chorus of insects, from not far away. She opened her eyes a sliver and saw the sleeve of Noname's jacket. He moved and she opened her eyes all the way, to see, above her, the opposite wall of the airship, with its rows of windows and empty seats looking down at her. Everything was dark. The windows were cracked and smothered by branches. The insects' singing was broken by the loud, raucous cry of a bird.

The ship was lying on its side in a tree. All the soldiers lay on the same side, thrown across and battered. Noname's arms were around Eine, from behind, his left elbow protruding through the broken window underneath them. Anda was pinned, directly in front of them, underneath half the body of the giant with the shaved head and earrings. He stared out at them with wide eyes.

"You okay?" Noname asked, sounding hoarse.

"More or less," Anda said, muffled. The large man rolled over slightly, and Anda managed to raise his head.

There was a moan behind them, followed by several others. Eine angled her neck to see through the window beneath her. She saw only branches and dangling shards of glass. There was blood on Noname's sleeve.

"You're hurt," she said, in a dazed voice.

"Just cut from the glass. Scratched."

"Don't move around too much!" a rough, female voice called out. It had to be the woman with the braids. If the ship tipped over, they would most likely start falling again.

"Everyone all right?" another voice asked. It was answered in grumbles. Eine struggled to sit up, as Noname uncurled himself. The air felt thick and humid inside the dim ship. Turning her head, she gazed out through the open door of the pilot's hatch, where weak sunlight filtered in. The material of the balloon was visible outside, woven through and tangled, dangling in flaps.

"The pilot is dead," someone said, calmly. Eine turned to see the thin, pale-haired Laxen crouching over the pilot, whose body was wrapped limply around one of the seats. There were several murmurs among the soldiers. The dark-skinned man with the high collar crawled over to examine him.

"Cracked his head when he fell," he commented and shook his head.

"What about the Gusson woman?" Noname asked, looking at the open hatch.

"She must be lost too."

"I heard her scream."

The group of them fell silent again, as they returned to examining their injuries. Noname sat up next to Eine, holding his arm out carefully, while Anda unwound a bandage from inside his bag. The older man winced as he moved and gritted his teeth.

"Anda, what's the matter?" Noname asked him.

"I'm just sore all over. I suppose it had to be the Calibreen and not the Meyjan who landed on me…"

"Ah, we should send the Meyjan out to examine the balloon," the Enahalan with the bushy eyebrows spoke up. The small man made an indignant sound from somewhere in the huddle of passengers. "Even without the pilot, if we can repair the balloon, we may be able to steer the ship again," the Enahalan added. He had a large, red slash across his forehead from a shard of glass.

"He's the lightest," someone else agreed. "He won't tip the ship over."

"No…he isn't," Eine said, suddenly. Nearly everyone turned to stare at her.

"Eine," Noname warned.

"He isn't the lightest," she insisted, and got up carefully to her feet. "I am. I'll go and look."

"Be careful!" he told her.

"I will," she said, mildly. Now that the shock of the crash had worn off a little, she felt curious about where they had landed. The soldiers had called it a swamp, and she wasn't sure exactly what that meant. It was stifling in the ship anyway, so she needed a little air.

"Of course, of course," the bearded Laxen said, as Eine picked her way over the men. "She's half a Floater." She paused and looked back towards his voice, thinking she'd misheard him. In the dusky light, she spotted the man laying on his side, next to Binden, who was up on his haunches, looking around. The latter met Eine's gaze and nodded.

"A Floater," he sent right into her head. *"A Laxen who can float on air."*

NINETEEN

Eine crept out through the hatch of the ship with Binden's 'words' dancing around in her brain. She had finally received information about her parents, but she barely had time to absorb it now. The sounds of the swamp filled her ears as she crawled out onto a moss-covered tree branch. The birds didn't sing here, the way they had in the forest near Tobin. They cried out at intervals, sounding frightened or angry. Eine was dismayed to discover that the heavy, damp air felt worse outside of the ship.

All around her were bending, willowy trees, draped in dark, soft-looking moss. Looking down, she could just make out a pool of dark water. It didn't seem to be a very long drop to the ground after all. The ship had plunged its way far down the branches of the tree; when Eine looked up, she saw patches of blue sky through dark branches.

The branch she rested on was covered in shredded, white balloon material. She frowned and lifted some of it, uncovering a herd of scattering 'little things'. She dropped it quickly. There was no sign of the pilot's capsule, except for bent and twisted steel around the edges of the hatch opening behind her. It had been torn off entirely in the crash. Eine shuddered. They were lucky to be alive.

She examined the balloon again, wondering if any of the

soldiers could mend the thick white cloth in that state.She was turning around slowly, ready to crawl back inside the ship, when she heard a sudden rustling nearby. She jerked her head up and saw movement in a neighboring tree. She froze, digging her nails into the bark underneath her. Was it some kind of animal? A moment passed and then the figure of a person emerged, crawling out where she could see it. It was the short-haired blonde woman, her face swollen and scratched. Eine sighed with relief.

"The tear was man-made," the woman called across to her. She sounded exhausted. "It was sewn up halfway...so it wouldn't be noticed."

***

A short time afterwards, Eine found herself standing ankle-deep in muddy water, surrounded by the strange noises of the swamp. As far as she could see, between tangled roots and undergrowth buzzing with gnats, the ground was semi-solid, most of it partially submerged in water. The soldiers were climbing down from the tree behind her, some of them dropping with short splashes into the water. Noname stood nearby with his gun drawn, looking around them in the heavy stillness. She could see sweat already beading on his forehead.

"Are you absolutely sure?" Anda was demanding of the blonde woman. "You have no doubt it was sabotage?"

"I would never suggest it otherwise," she said in her velvety voice. With one long fingernail, she drew a line in the air. "It was a clean slit."

Anda turned away, looking very grave. "Thank you, Amlat," he said. One of the Enahalan soldiers - the man with the short gray beard - picked his way across the wet ground towards him.

"What do you think, Leona?" he asked. "Could Calthin have had an accomplice? It could've gotten past the truth drug."

"I'm afraid I don't know."

"Stay out of the water!" the woman with black braids hissed. She was standing balanced on a large tree root, staring down at the murky pools. The other soldiers scoffed at her.

"It's the fever you gotta worry about, Zwit," the Calibreen giant with the white ponytail declared. His voice was deep and hollow. "You can kill whatever's in the water."

Eine's ears pricked up at the word 'fever'. She remembered now that someone had used the phrase 'fever swamp' just before she'd fallen asleep on the ship. She looked over at Noname and Anda, who stood in a discussion with the Enahalans. She joined them, feeling worried, and after a moment, the same Calibreen, the Meyjan, Binden, the bearded Laxen and the man with the iridescent collar, all came squelching over as well. They formed an oddly sized ring around the small group. Eine had grown used to the Laxen buzz in her head, she realized now. Standing close by Binden and the other man, she barely noticed it.

"...But how far is Creede?" the Enahalan with the scratched forehead was asking.

"It must be over five *illilun*," his bearded countryman answered.

"We could march that," Noname said, sounding doubtful.

"We'd never make it!" the Meyjan exclaimed. "We'll all get sick!"

"You can fight it off. It's not death," Noname told him.

"It depends on how long you're exposed to it," the Calibreen replied.

"I am never ill," the bearded Laxen said, cheerfully. "That Kry monster probably won't catch it either." Eine glanced at Binden, completely confused by their conversation. He caught her eye.

"The other Laxen is a Kry, a mercenary," he sent her.

"But what is the fever?" she asked.

"It makes you hallucinate," someone said from behind her. She turned to see the man with the black necklace and belt, standing there with his arms crossed. The stones looked flat now in the dim, swamp light. "It makes your skin crawl and you shiver even though it is hot. Your bones ache. It comes from the spores of the plants here."

The group of them fell silent. Eine glanced up at the trees around them, in disbelief. Was it possible?

"I thought it was a myth," the man with the high collar said, his dark eyes wide.

"No, it's real. I remember Creedens who had it," Noname said, reluctantly.

"Then I say we get moving!" the Meyjan announced. "The faster we're out of here, the better!"

"I agree," Anda said, nodding. He began taking off his

175

jacket and the others started following suit, swinging the unnecessary clothes over their shoulders. The man wearing the black stones whistled at the other soldiers, who had remained on guard near the base of the tree. They began sloshing their way over.

"Creeden," a gruff voice said, and Eine realized it was Binden. She had almost forgotten he could speak out loud. Noname turned to him with raised eyebrows. "If this Oln is powerful enough to mind-send, he may be able to 'hear' me," Binden told him. A few others glanced at him curiously. "I can ask him to come and meet us halfway."

"Good!" Noname exclaimed. "He'll come for sure!"

"Yes, why does he not mind-send himself here? Save us some trouble!" the man with the stones grumbled. Both the bearded Laxen and the Kry snorted. They flinched and glared at each other afterwards, as if disgusted at their own agreement.

"You can't mind-send yourself," the Kry said with a sneer. "There must be a fixed point."

"Oh, excuse me!" the man retorted. "I am not being paid enough to catch swamp fever."

His words reminded Eine that several of the soldiers were hired mercenaries, not just the Kry who offended other Laxens. She wondered what abilities the quiet and cold-faced Laxen had.

Eine caught up to Noname as the group of soldiers began moving east. He waited for her without a word, his mouth set in a thin, worried line. He had tied his jacket around his waist by its sleeves, and pushed up the sleeves of his shirt underneath, revealing the bandage on his left arm. Anda had stuffed his longer coat into his bag, making it a huge bundle, and Eine did the same with her cloak. She felt a temporary relief from the damp heat as she squelched along in just the gray dress and white boots. The going consisted of climbing over large tree roots and through tangled weeds, wading through shallow water or skirting pools of it whenever they could.

Eine was certainly grateful for the Enahalan boots now. Even though her feet felt heavier when the mud sucked at them. She wondered briefly if that was how everyone else felt when they walked, and then the bearded Laxen's words came back to her: *"She's half a Floater."* She remembered now the red-haired woman on the train, who moved as if her feet were barely on the ground. Of course! It was why she was so weightless!

"Do you have an idea who sabotaged the ship?" Noname asked Anda. The older man shook his head.

"I don't have a clue, Ney. That's the most alarming thing about it."

"It definitely makes a difference if they sabotaged all the ships or just ours," Noname said, climbing over a fallen log.

"Exactly," Anda said, unhappily.

Noname looked back at Binden, who was treading through the messy terrain without much effort, nearby. His compact, muscular frame seemed built for it. "Binden, have you heard from Oln yet?" The Laxen shook his head. "Maybe when he does, we'll hear if the other ships crashed," Noname muttered.

Eine waved away some insects that buzzed around her. She felt her hair sticking to the back of her neck and sighed. It was hard to imagine walking for long in these conditions. "How many soldiers are paid to be here?" she asked Noname, partly just to distract herself.

"Four," he told her, lowering his voice a bit. "Amlat, from Gusson. She's a great fighter. Irridi, from the Kinimin Islands, who's complaining already, Sok, the bald Calibreen, and then Salabad, the Kry from Kroland." He paused and helped her up out of a puddle that sank deeper than she'd expected. "He's the one to keep an eye on," he added, under his breath.

Something slithered away in the water just behind Eine. She looked back, and saw Zwit leap away, her braids flying in the air. The two Calibreens near her both laughed.

"What was that?" Eine asked, hurrying after Noname.

"Snake." She had seen drawings of snakes in the library and she shuddered.

"I don't like things in the water!" Zwit grumbled behind them.

"They don't like you either," Sok, the bald Calibreen, told her.

Eine kept her eyes on the water at her feet. "Why is Salabad the one to watch?" she asked Noname quietly.

"He's got a short temper, and he's very fast."

She frowned and glanced around, looking for the Laxen. He wasn't in sight.

"The other Laxen is Wilder from the Ice Lands," Noname

said. "He's a little eccentric - "

"And he has excellent hearing!" Wilder called from far off to the left. Noname looked alarmed for a moment, but the Laxen just waved at them with an amused expression behind his burly beard. Noname grinned and shrugged.

"What are the Ice Lands?" Eine asked.

"My beautiful homeland," Wilder called back, cheerfully.

"They're freezing is what they are," said the high-collared man near him. "It's a backwoods, barren and lonely place." His tone was very matter-of-fact. "Everyone who lives there is insane." Wilder burst out laughing and the other man smiled a crooked smile. "You see, my friend? You are proof!"

"That one is Glace," Noname said, shaking his head. "He's a History Keeper in Garle. They don't write down their stories there. They just teach certain people to remember it all."

"And *that* is insane!" Wilder declared. "Why would you force yourself to memorize something that you can just write down?"

"It's tradition," Glace said amiably.

Eine leaned in closer to Noname and whispered, "And they volunteered to fight?" He nodded.

"What's the first sign of the fever?" Amlat asked behind them.

"Stop bringing it up," the Meyjan demanded.

"I've heard your eyes start to shine," Zwit said.

"No, that is when you start to hallucinate," Irridi objected. "Then your eyes shine bright."

"Irridi's got it already!" the white-haired Calibreen said, laughing. The man's gleaming black eyes narrowed as a few others joined in.

"Oh, you laugh about it, Lon," Irridi snapped. "I signed up for battle, not disease. Let the precious Laxens save themselves." Eine stared back at him, over her shoulder, but he didn't notice.

"Enahala pays well. Just stay alive," Amlat said, lightly.

"They ought to pay my people for all their insults," the Meyjan grumbled.

"At least some of us *are* getting paid," Sok said with a smirk. "Look at these *hiklu* who volunteered."

"*Hiklu*?" Lon growled. Eine looked back again and saw him slam a giant fist into Zok's shoulder. The blow would have knocked anyone else down, but the two Calibreens were the same height and strength.

"It's not our fight. The Indigo's not attacking the rest of us," Sok told him. He coughed afterwards and shoved Lon back.

"Your sword was made by a Laxen! Your house was designed by a Laxen. My sister married one. They *are* the rest of us!"

"You studied history, didn't you?" Zwit asked Sok, who coughed again. "What are you trying to prove? You know we need them."

"I do not trust books," Irridi said, contemptuously. "I will not read them."

Eine saw a weird blur beside him. Suddenly, Salabad was standing there. The soldiers jumped in surprise. The pale, thin Laxen fixed his cold eyes on Irridi. "That explains a lot," he said.

"And now here is one of them, to show us how special he is," the dark-skinned man retorted. Sok started to laugh, and broke into a cough again.

"Shut up, Irridi," Zwit said. "He's a gun for hire too. He's the same as you."

Salabad chuckled unexpectedly. "Oh, I'm not nearly the same as you," he replied. He regarded Sok with an oddly delighted expression. "By the way, the first sign of the fever is a cough."

The soldiers froze and stared at Sok, whose big face turned pale. Salabad chuckled again, and Eine felt a chill down her spine. Noname took her arm then, startling her.

"Come on, move faster," he said. "He'll live."

**

They trekked through the swamp for hours, soaked through with sweat and mud, and scratched with filthy branches. The sun sank slowly into the moss-draped trees, as Sok continued to cough, and others joined him. The soldiers' chatter died down completely. An orchestra of insects filled in the silence, growing louder as the sun set, and Eine listened in awe to the intense whirring and chirping. She wiped her face repeatedly, and finally paused for a moment to dig Anda's black ribbon out of her bag. She tied her hair up with it, in a messy knot. Noname glanced at her as she did, and she thought his eyes seemed bright in the fading daylight. Anda began to cough a few moments later. She felt a worried knot growing in her stomach.

There began to be more movement in the water, quick splashes and stirrings, and more strange cries in the trees. Some of the soldiers lit torches, or pulled out light wands which Eine had never seen, casting dancing shadows over their surroundings. Eine's stomach was growling and her legs were beginning to ache. She stopped again to pull some dried fruit from her bag and carried on, chewing it, and sweating.

Sok began to groan occasionally. Then Zwit started up. The Enahalans, one of whom was walking shakily and hacking often, began to talk about making camp for the night. Eine listened to their murmurs and looked around in the menacing, singing darkness. Where would they sleep? How could anything sleep here? She stepped onto a log and it swam out from under her. She gasped and fell backwards, landing with a splash into warm mud. Someone grabbed her arm and helped her up again; she couldn't even see who it was.

Noname was coughing now, not as hard as the others, but Eine could see him stumbling. She heard a scuffle behind her and turned to see that Lon had picked up the Meyjan, and was carrying him along. Feeling panicky, she reached out and took Noname's hot hand. He murmured something she couldn't hear and squeezed it. She swallowed carefully a few times, expecting to feel a cough coming on, but there was none. She squeezed Noname's hand back and kept moving.

By the time they stopped - at a semisoft rise of land near the base of a giant tree - Eine had started to feel a little dizzy. But she couldn't be sure that it wasn't just from fatigue. She stood holding onto Noname's hand, as he sank wearily to his knees, and the others dropped to the ground, coughing and moaning. Anda crouched near them and took Noname's bag from his shoulders.

"You have a weather blanket, Ney," he said, hoarsely. "I gave you each one." He dug through Noname's bag and Eine did the same with his. She found a tough, scratchy mat rolled up tight and she spread it out on the ground for Anda. The two of them collapsed onto their mats and began to cough again.

Exhausted, Eine found her own and rolled it out next to Noname. A couple light wands stayed on around her, amid the wheezes of the soldiers. Looking out in the patchy light, she spotted three figures sitting up. She could only barely make them out, but she knew they were Binden, Wilder and Salabad. It seemed that Wilder had been right: Laxens didn't catch the fever.

How had it descended on the rest of them so quickly? Eine stared at the ailing bodies that lay nearby. They had all been perfectly healthy.

"No word yet from Oln," Binden sent her. She sighed heavily, feeling the weight of the humidity in her bones. She lay down on her mat and stared up at the flat black sky above. There were no stars. Her heart felt heavy. She closed her eyes and fell deep asleep.

TWENTY

"Eine...the roots! They'll come through you."

Eine awoke with a start. It was pitch dark. The light wands had gone out. The air was so stifling, she could barely breathe for a moment. If it weren't for the insect noises, she would have thought she was trapped inside a box. The thought made her feel panicky, but she lay still and took a deep, hot breath, getting her bearings. She listened, wondering what had woken her up. Was it just her dream? The voice had been clearer this time.

The stone, the roots...? She felt so frustrated with her dreams.

The soldiers coughed in their sleep, tossing uncomfortably on the wet ground. Eine turned her head and saw the shape of Noname lying next to her. She didn't see any of the Laxens sitting up now, to watch, and it worried her. Had they gone to sleep?

Noname mumbled something in Creeden in his sleep and stirred. Eine propped her head up on her elbow, watching him. She would keep watch herself then. Something croaked from not far away, and she listened, apprehensive. Branches shook under the weight of something moving.

"Vikti duk... No..." Noname turned over, his movements jerky. Eine leaned closer to his face and saw in the darkness that his eyelids were fluttering. She felt a cold chill in her heart. Had he gotten sicker?

"Father," he murmured, and sighed heavily.

"Noname," she whispered. "Are you awake?" He stirred but said nothing. She reached out a hand and touched his face, just lightly on his forehead. It was alarmingly hot. She gasped and grabbed him by the shoulder. "Wake up!" she hissed, shaking him.

Noname moaned and opened his eyes all the way. He blinked at Eine as if he didn't see her for several seconds. Something was definitely wrong. She sat up quickly and felt around for her water canteen. The water inside was lukewarm, but she splashed some of it on Noname's face and he shook his head, stunned.

"What?" he asked, hoarsely. He sat up halfway and stared at Eine. "Eine. What are you doing here?"

Eine felt her heart leap into her throat. She stared back at him for a moment, and then she gave him the canteen. "Here, drink this." She heard her own voice sound wobbly, afraid. "You have the fever. We're in the swamp near Creede."

Noname nodded and drank some more water. He poured a little over his face again, and then shivered. "I'm going home," he said, sounding uncertain. "You're coming with me?"

"Yes," Eine told him. She looked around at the sleeping soldiers and wondered what she should do. If she got him out of the swamp, would his fever subside? She could carry him. She could carry him as fast as she could go, anywhere beyond this awful place.

"Good." Noname sighed and lay back down. "We can see Oln there." He shivered again. "It's so cold...*wunit*...Why is it cold?"

"Here!" Eine yanked out her bundled-up cloak and swept it over him. She tucked it in around him, her hands shaking. There was a terrible, hollow feeling in her stomach. He was so sick. He was sick and she didn't know what to do. Should she wake Anda? Should she try to carry them both?

In her anxiety, Eine was suddenly struck with several sleep-thoughts at once, from the soldiers all around her. *"Women...home...when I get paid...Thela...swimming...flying... monsters in the water"* She shook her head fiercely and put her hands over her ears. She concentrated on Noname's face.

"Eine," he breathed. She felt the mental voices fade slowly. He took her hand and held it under the cloak. His fingers were so hot. She knelt there, afraid to move, staring down at him. "Eine, don't go anywhere."

"I won't." She felt a thickness in her throat that she had never felt before. She squeezed his fingers.

"I have the fever," he said then. "It will break. Just stay with me." He sounded a little more lucid, even though his speaking was slow. Eine nodded eagerly, watching his face. He sighed. "Bet you're scared, kid."

She snorted but it came out a bit strangled. He smiled, and it flooded her with relief. She could see the faint whiteness of his teeth in the dark.

"I know, I know… You're not a kid," he said.

"What should I do?" Eine whispered.

"Just keep me talking sense… Ask me all your questions…"

Eine took a shuddering breath and sat back on her heels, feeling the damp air settle on her again. The little things were still rustling. She could not think of a single thing to ask him.

"How did I get my scars?" Noname asked himself. He shivered again and she tucked the cloak in tighter. "When I was fourteen, my best friend and I thought we were *aliktun*…big men, good fighters. We wanted to be soldiers, so we hid in the back of an army rover…that's an auto-car…going into Southern Creede. It was an ambush…long story…they had been sending raids, and we found their headquarters." He coughed. "We thought we would jump out and help." He fell silent for a moment and Eine waited.

"We jumped out… I'm still surprised we were brave enough to do it. But we were easy targets. A soldier grabbed each of us and then we were hostages. My friend tried to fight the man holding him, but he was killed." Eine gasped. "I saw it… My captor slashed me to keep me from doing the same. Three times. In the end, he let me go." His voice faded out. He was staring up at the dark sky, and Eine couldn't read his expression. "I didn't leave the house again for a long time."

"But why were they fighting?" Eine demanded. "Why are they still fighting?"

"The south wants one military rule, over all of Creede. A *tiktivunuk*… The north wants to run itself by our own means. Believe what we want to believe."

"Believe?" Eine asked, confused.

"We believe in an after-life, remember? We have our own

old traditions. Some of our Laxens are still honored, a little like in the Old-World days. Like Oln. He's like a grandfather to us all. He's very old, but he looks young…" As he spoke, a soft light crept through the indistinct branches above. The solid clouds were finally drifting away from the moon. Eine gazed up at it, realizing that it was the first time she had seen it all night. The moonlight was comforting.

"I wonder if…my parents have an after-life," she said. She looked back down at Noname and saw that he was gazing at her. His eyes were bright in the faint moonlight.

"Clouds on the moon," he said quietly. Eine was struck by the fleeting image of two ghostly figures, flying in circles around the moon. She smiled. But she wasn't sure that was what he'd meant. Noname closed his eyes and she felt him rub his thumb against her palm.

***

Eine woke up in a pair of giant arms. She was being carried like a baby, but not by Noname. She blinked in the shrouded sunlight and looked up to see Lon's large face above her, his white shock of hair flattened against his head. He had dark bags under his eyes and he yawned, not noticing that she was awake. Eine turned her head and looked at the others trudging by. Everyone looked rough, pale and sickly, bright-eyed, and still coughing occasionally.

She didn't see Noname and a small fear gripped her. She saw Anda, helping a bleary-eyed Glace walk, his high collar crooked around his neck; the Enahalan looked better than yesterday, but still weak. She saw the Meyjan stumbling along, mumbling to himself; she saw Sok and Amlat, pushing Irridi ahead of them. Wilder was carrying Zwit, who seemed the worst of all. She was alive, but she was limp, her braids dangling down to the muddy ground.

Salabad walked alone, his face expressionless, his hands folded behind his back.

Eine sat up and craned her neck, startling Lon. "Where is Noname?" she asked him. He gave her a blank look. "The Creeden! Where is he?" she demanded.

"Oh, he went ahead a little ways with the Enahalans," Lon told her, sleepily. The relief that flew through Eine was so intense that she almost felt like crying. She put her face into the giant's shoulder, and felt him stiffen in surprise. "We didn't lose him, little halfling," he said, in a kind voice. "We did lose one though." Eine looked back up at him in dismay. She realized that she hadn't spotted Binden either. "The Enahalan with the *lidder* – the eyeglasses - didn't wake up. I didn't know his name."

Eine hadn't known it either. The Enahalans had kept their distance, just as expected. She was relieved that it had not been Binden, but she felt a quiet sadness.

"Eine!" Anda approached them with Glace's arm around his shoulder. "Are you all right, child?"

"I can walk now. Thank you," she told Lon and he set her down. As soon as he did though, she realized she was still dizzy. She felt a little lightheaded. "I'm all right," she told Anda, regardless. It seemed that she could only catch a bit of the fever, but not succumb to it.

"Most of our fevers broke during the night," Anda said with a sigh. "But we'll all catch it again if we don't reach Oln soon."

"This is a terrible place," Glace murmured. "Why don't they cut it all down?"

"It doesn't harm anyone who isn't trekking through it, my friend," Anda told him. "The fever is a kind of defense mechanism for the swamp. All living things have some defense mechanism."

Eine moved to Anda's side and took up Glace's other arm. "Did Binden hear anything from Oln?" she asked.

"Yes, he reached him this morning," Anda said. He looked relieved to let her take most of the burden of Glace's weight. "Oln told him he would meet us at a specific spot, which Ney has gone to find. I hope it's not very far away."

Eine used her free arm to root through her bag and pull out something to eat. A moment later, she heard splashing footsteps ahead. A bird cawed furiously as Noname, Binden and the two remaining soldiers from Enahala emerged from the curtains of dangling moss before them. Noname looked a thousand times better, only a bit pale. He had taken off his shirt and wore it tied around his waist instead of his jacket. His torso was brown and ridged with lean muscle.

Eine's cloak was thrown over his shoulder. He met her eyes for a moment, and then he looked away, nervously. "We found it," he said, still sounding a little hoarse. "It's an old shrine, a ruin."

"And it's safe from the fever," Binden added. "Oln told me

the plants that grow around it don't release the toxin." Several sighs of relief flew through the group. "He'll be there by nightfall."

"Let's go," Glace said, emphatically. He attempted to start out on his own and Eine followed quickly, holding his arm.

The word spread fast throughout the soldiers and revived a bit of their energy. Binden took hold of Glace and relieved Eine. Noname gave her a small smile and then fell into step with Anda, patting him on the back. Eine felt another little rush of euphoria that he was safe and well. Everything was all right, for now. She looked around to see if anyone else needed help, and saw the Meyjan stumble not far behind. She started to call out to him, only to remember that she didn't know his name. Just like the Enahalan who had died.

"Meyjan," she said, tentatively. "Do you need help?" The little man looked up at her suspiciously, his face pale and sweating. She offered him her arm. He hesitated for a moment and then accepted it, leaning his light weight on her with relief.

"Thank you, miss," he said, gruffly.

"I'm Eine. What's your name?" she asked him. He stared up at her, astonished. Eine heard Wilder cackle with laughter behind them. She glanced back at him, confused.

"Poor man is used to Enahalan snobbery! No one ever bothers to ask his name!" the Laxen called, chuckling. "He's just half a man. Send him out to check the balloon! Run a train through his village!"

Eine turned back to see that the Meyjan's face had gone red. He pursed his lips and scowled.

"Enahalans don't know much about the rest of the world," Amlat commented from nearby. "Everyone knows Meyjans are good little fighters."

"Because you can not see what is attacking you," Irridi said with a snort. Amlat and Wilder laughed.

"Well, I live in Enahala now," Eine told the Meyjan, and as she spoke, she savored the words. "And I don't think you're half a man."

The little man puffed out with pride, still flushing. "My name is Ejan," he declared. "Ejan Best-Blade." Eine smiled and nodded. She looked up ahead and saw that Anda was beaming back at her, his blue eyes sparkling.

They kept up a steady pace for the rest of the day, a few soldiers getting better and a few others feeling worse again. Eine's dizziness faded away but it left her with a throbbing headache. She felt exhausted by the time the sun began to set. Ejan had recovered some more strength by that time and no longer needed her help. She concentrated on climbing over the sprawling, muddy terrain, one step at a time.

Someone had just lit the first torch when the Enahalans at the front turned and waved to announce that they had arrived. Everyone pushed forward, anxious to reach the fever-free zone. Eine followed behind Anda and Noname into a clearing that revealed a low hill. The darkening sky opened up overhead, relieving them of some of the swamp's heaviness, and letting the last rays of the sinking sun fall upon a strange cluster of stones at the top of the hill. The ground was actually solid under Eine's feet and it felt like a luxury.

The soldiers staggered up the small hill, assembling around the structure at the top. It consisted of one and a half stone walls that were draped with creeping vines and half-submerged in undergrowth. The complete wall stood as tall as the Calibreens' heads, while the other had crumbled about halfway up, leaving crevasses for insects to scurry through. There were faded symbols carved into the full wall, forming several lines across its surface.

"What is it?" Lon asked Noname.

"Old-World people used to build these," he said, setting his bag and Eine's cloak down onto the muddy grass. "It was a shrine to one of the first Laxens."

"A shrine to a Laxen!" Irridi snorted. He dropped wearily onto the ground and the others followed.

"Fascinating!" Wilder declared. He moved forward to examine the stones, and Anda and Glace joined him, the latter adjusting his History Keeper collar.

"I have heard about these," he said, sounding much stronger than he had that morning.

"What language is that engraving in?" Anda wondered aloud. "Possibly an old form of Creeden? Let me see."

Eine felt curious about the shrine as well, but she was too tired to investigate with them. She rolled out her mat and lay down on her back, feeling her headache lessen. She gazed up at the purplish sky, which seemed almost strangely large, now that it wasn't covered by branches.

Noname lay his mat down next to her and sat on it, looking down at her. His expression was wistful. "Are you all right?" he asked, softly. She nodded.

"Just tired."

"Oln will be here soon. You should eat and rest." He produced his own packet of dried fruit and Eine accepted several pieces. "Thank you...for letting me babble on and on last night," he said, sheepishly.

Eine smiled. "Do you even remember what you said?" she asked.

"Yes, *everything*." He gave her a steady look and she suddenly felt jittery, confused. Was there something special that he'd said? Not that she could recall. She liked how he looked sitting there, shirtless and muddy, but healthy. Strong and kind, his brown eyes moving over her tangled hair and the torn gray dress that clung to her haphazardly. She felt nervous and happy, and she closed her eyes, still smiling. His fingers wove slowly into her open hand, and the touch of his skin flooded her with tingles.

"This is the symbol for the blue stone!"

Eine opened her eyes and raised her head to look at Glace by the stone wall. He and Anda were peering at the symbols on the wall, while Wilder stood on the other side of it, poking around.

"What is it?" Noname asked, following her gaze.

"I've heard this story," the dark-skinned man was thinking. Eine felt a vague fear in his mind. *"But is it true?"*

Eine frowned, laying her head back down. The blue stone. Why was that familiar?

"Ney, is this ancient Creeden after all?" Anda asked, over his shoulder. "I can't make heads or tails of this writing." Noname stood up and stepped over to join them. Eine looked at Glace expectantly, but he said nothing. He looked afraid.

"Yes, it's *Hiktu*," Noname said, running his fingers over the letters. "Not very many people spoke that dialect. This part means 'here lies...' but then I don't know. Something about mining?"

"Ore," Glace spoke up, sounding reluctant. "Here lies the ore to be mined."

"And this is 'death' here... 'Death for gods,'" Noname finished. He shook his head. "That's not right, obviously."

Glace shivered and hugged himself. Eine watched him,

reaching out for his thoughts. *"'The blue stone came from an ore in the ground. It destroyed everything all around.' That's how the story goes. ...'Until the day a messenger broke it down.' But it can't be true."*

At that moment, Wilder appeared from the other side of the wall and the sight of him gave Eine an odd, tugging feeling. It reminded her of the sensation in her ears when the Inowan Laxen on the train had heard Noname from afar. Wilder put his hands on his hips and stared at Glace with his sharp green eyes. "I just got the strangest old story in my head," he declared. "I don't even think I've heard it before."

Several of the other soldiers called out, interrupting him. Eine turned to see them pointing at the sky. A large, dark shape was approaching, floating over the treetops towards them. A moment of fear struck her, but then she realized it was a balloon, a smaller version of an airship balloon. Dangling from beneath it was a large basket.

"Oln!" Noname exclaimed. He threw up his arms and waved, smiling. The balloon came steadily forward, as they all watched, and then it began to sink in short, smooth drops. Someone inside the basket was moving about, controlling its descent.

"Thank gods we're getting out of here at last," Sok said, as he and the others got to their feet. "I'd rather be in Thela!"

Eine stood up and hurried over to Noname's side, as the balloon drifted lightly down into the clearing. She strained to see Oln as the basket touched the ground. He climbed over the side with ease, and she could see that he was tall and thin; he strode over to them on long, graceful legs. Suddenly, that familiar buzzing struck Eine with a force she had never felt before. She cringed, astonished, as Noname met Oln mid-stride and they hugged. Eine could see now that the Laxen had tanned skin like Noname and brown hair that fell to his chin, and a narrow, pointed face with large, dark eyes. He wore a vest that fastened with oval-shaped buttons that glinted in the moonlight, and his boots had buckles with the same reflective stones.

Oln stepped back from Noname and the two of them launched into a stream of Creeden. It was the most of the language that Eine had heard yet, and the clicking sounds were fascinating. Oln had a deep, calm voice that eclipsed Noname's lighter, husky one.

"Where is Binden Levone?" Oln asked in Thelan suddenly, and he looked around at the group of weary soldiers that stood watching him. Binden stepped forward and the two Laxens shook hands. "I'm glad you were able to reach me," Oln told him. "Although…" He turned his head, as if listening to something. "There is another communicator here, isn't there? There's a very faint impression." He looked directly at Eine, surprising her. "You can receive but not send," he commented. "How odd."

"Oln, this is Eine from Thela," Noname spoke up. "She's a Demi."

"Oh yes, the Thelan…" Oln stepped closer, his deep voice saddened. "The council informed me of her." He gazed down at Eine and she looked up him, almost entranced, feeling the buzzing dancing in her head. He had a chiseled, pointed nose and a small mouth, and fine eyebrows over his dramatic eyes. He was a powerful Laxen. The feel of him was intense.

Was this what the Laxens in the Pinnacle had been like?

"Thank you for helping us," Eine murmured. Oln tilted his head to the side, studying her.

"Eine is your name. Are you perhaps the child of Einelin Wess?" he asked. "She married a Thelan." Eine felt a sudden yearning in her stomach. She stared at him, unable to speak.

"Eine doesn't know her parents," Noname said quickly. "She's an orphan."

Oln nodded and sighed, folding his arms. "Yes, Einelin is gone. I tried to contact her several times and I could not detect her. We went to school in Inowa together."

"What was she like?" Eine managed to ask.

"White-gold hair just like you. She was a Floater, and she had a special affinity to trees. She could make them grow out of anything. The roots would just spring out of whatever substance she chose. And so of course, she married a carpenter." Oln laughed, a deep, pleasant laugh. "Andle was his name, and he was very strong and able, and quick to laugh. He was a storyteller as well. He collected old stories." He blinked as if coming out of a dream, and then saw Anda for the first time, standing off to the side. "Anda Leona!" he exclaimed and went to embrace him.

Eine stepped back, her stomach doing a gentle loop. Noname caught her eye, and he smiled wide. If Oln was right…

then she had just heard the names of her parents. She listened, overwhelmed, to Oln and Anda greeting each other, and to the soldiers grumbling impatiently around them. Einelin Wess had had the ability to grow trees at will. She thought of the forest in her dream and smiled, amazed. Was that her mother's after-life? Was she a floating light in the woods? Eine felt herself make a small sound of protest, of disbelief. She felt tears sting her eyes, and she looked at Noname in awe. He gazed back at her, his brown eyes soft.

Her mother was reaching her from beyond death, through her dreams. All this time. But what had she said? Eine frowned, remembering. There were three things now. The roots, the stone…and "it's through you". She had no idea what it meant.

TWENTY-ONE

"I hate to interrupt!" Sok's voice boomed. "But are we going to get out of this cursed swamp?" Several other soldiers made noises of agreement. Oln had been right about the clearing being free of the fever plants. The group of them already seemed much stronger. Even Zwit was standing and looked alert.

Oln raised a hand in their direction, acknowledging them, and then turned to the Enahalan soldiers who stood near Anda. "They must divide themselves into their groups. As I told the council, I can send no more than five at a time." The two men nodded and began to direct the soldiers. There were only thirteen of them now that one of the Enahalans was gone, so they divided into three groups of four, leaving Salabad standing alone.

"What about the other airships?" Noname asked Oln. He sounded tense now. The time had come to return to Thela, whether they were ready for it or not. It didn't quite seem real yet to Eine. "Did they make it to Creede?"

"Yes, and the soldiers are in Thela now, so good luck to them. You must tell me into which part of the city each group must go."

As Anda began explaining, something bright caught Eine's eye near the shrine. She turned to look and drew in a quick breath. A fluid string of lights hovered around the stone walls. They were floating lights, dropping and rising, darting back and forth. Just like in her dream!

"Noname!" she exclaimed, breathless. He looked and then smiled, a tight, worried smile.

"Fireflies, Eine. They're bugs that glow." He cracked his knuckles as he had on the landing field in Enahala.

"Oh." She stared at the beautiful sight, recognizing their movements now as insect-like. She had heard the word before, in Enahala. Noname had mentioned that people thought fireflies were souls, and she could see how. Enchanted, she moved towards them, taking slow steps. The fireflies flitted away, but not completely, circling back as if they were drawn to the old shrine. Eine stood there and watched them, feeling strangely happy. She felt like she was inside her dream again, the dream that her mother sent her. Einelin Wess.

"Eine," Noname called her. She made a move to go, and then hesitated. A cluster of fireflies alighted upon the engraved symbols on the stone. They scuttled around and flitted their wings in a hungry little mass of light. Eine felt struck by the sight. Glace's strange fear came back to her, as she stared at the engraved letters, illuminated by the insects.

"Eine, we're going!" Noname called again. She turned, reluctantly, and saw that the soldiers and Oln were standing at arms, looking solemn and ready. Oln's head was bowed, as if in concentration. Eine shook off the strange sensation and hurried to join them.

She stood next to Noname and Anda who had joined Salabad, and pulled on her green cloak, despite the stifling air. It still had not really sunk in that she was returning to Thela. The four of them were being sent to the factories, she knew, to investigate the trap doors that Idder Bay had seen. Everything had been planned and finalized. She pulled her hood over her face, and felt her heart sink slowly as she re-tied her table leg into the cloak's cord. A gloom settled over her as she looked up and stared at Oln. She was a Dredge again. She was going back. Her heart began to beat faster.

Why? Why had she decided to do this? Why was she going back? She closed her eyes and pictured the warmth and comfort of the library in Enahala. She imagined herself in Anda's chair, with her books. Listening to music at the concert hall. She could have stayed.

She glanced up at Noname and saw that his jaw was clenched. He met her eyes with a steely expression. If she had stayed, he would have come here without her, to fight *for* her. She could never have let that happen.

Whatever happened now, she knew that she would never be the same fearful person she had been when Noname found her. Everything had changed. She was not going back to the same life she had lived.

"Please…clear your thoughts," Oln said quietly. Eine closed her eyes again, feeling like the request was meant for her. She breathed in and out, and gazed at the blackness inside her eyelids. She realized she had been clenching her fists, and relaxed her hands. For a long moment, everything was still. Then she heard a light sound, a rustling. There were a few more moments of stillness, and then she heard it again. Were the groups disappearing around her? She kept her eyes closed tight, suddenly afraid. What would it feel like?

The blackness gave a little spin. Eine tilted and shifted. Then she was on her hands and knees, on solid pavement. Pavement scattered with grains of sand. Her sweat was suddenly cold. A grimness took hold as she opened her eyes, and saw her hands resting flat on that familiar surface. Her booted feet couldn't feel the pavement this time, only her hands. She was back in Thela.

Eine looked up and saw the others kneeling around her. Silently, they got to their feet, staring around at their surroundings. It was only familiar to Eine and Noname, the sight of the tall factories in the dark. The cloud-covered sky above, with no stars. The silence. To her left, she could make out the low tin roofs of the first brick buildings. The sight brought forth a flood of memories and images. Eine shook her head, trying to drown them out.

Noname stood motionless, listening, with his hand on his gun. He jerked his chin at the rest of them and moved forward. They followed, making their way towards the northern-most factory. Eine expected to feel the Hunters at any minute. Salabad moved out to the front, and she noticed suddenly that he carried no weapon. She had little time to marvel at this before they reached the factory door, where the Laxen picked the lock in a couple of quick movements. He pushed it open and slipped inside. Then he turned back and gestured for them to follow.

Eine felt an odd thrill at being inside of one of the factories. It was too dark to see much as she crept in behind Noname, with Anda behind her. They moved through a narrow hallway and into a large room with long tables. There was a dust in the air that made Eine suddenly need to sneeze – she clamped her fingers down over her nose. Noname was circling the room, investigating the floor, while Salabad stood still, holding his head up as if he were listening. Eine wondered if he had extraordinary hearing like Wilder. She glanced at Anda and saw that he was also holding his nose. She took a careful breath through her mouth, trying not to cough on the dust either.

After a few seconds, Noname moved towards a door across the room, and the rest of them followed. There were no windows in the factories and the dark was intense; the next room revealed only indistinct shapes of the equipment. Eine peered at them curiously, trying to remember how Idder Bay had described what the workers did.

Something ran over her foot and she gasped. Everyone spun around, gripping their weapons. It was a rat. Eine shook her head at them in the darkness, and Anda put a reassuring hand on her arm. Then they moved on into another room.

Here, Noname froze and gestured towards the floor. He had found one of the trap doors. Anda crouched down to investigate. Eine held her breath as he signaled to Salabad to look at the lock. The Laxen knelt down to do so, and then Eine saw that Noname was watching her. She couldn't see his expression in the dark, but he stepped towards her and slid his arm around her. He felt warm and solid against her, his heart beating quickly. She put her arm around his waist and rested her head against his shoulder. If only they could stay this way, and everything else could disappear.

Salabad stood up abruptly, staring at the door in the far wall. Everyone froze. Eine listened, but everything was painfully quiet. The Kry stepped soundlessly across the room, his eyes on the door.He stopped and cocked his head. Eine felt her heart pounding in her chest. What was he doing? What was going on?

Salabad turned to look at them in the dark. "They knew we were coming," he said, at a normal volume. His voice was as cold and calm as ever. "They're already here."

The door suddenly burst open and the Indigo swarmed into the room. Eine screamed silently, her mouth dropping open but making no sound. Gunfire exploded and she dropped to her knees, with Anda at her side. There was a loud crash in front of them; Noname had thrown a table onto its side, to use as a shield. He dropped into a crouch, and started firing over it. Shots rang out against the walls above Eine's head. She gasped, looking up. How had they known? She felt helpless, pressed against the wall.

Several loud cries rang out from the other side of the table. Eine realized that Salabad was out there with the Indigo. She peered around the side, and spotted a figure darting back and forth at an incredible speed, striking the others across their heads, knocking their guns to the ground. He had almost as much chance of getting shot by Noname as by the Indigo, except for his incredible speed.

One moment Anda was next to her and then he wasn't. She looked out again and caught a glimpse of him fading in and out among the Indigo. Noname immediately stopped firing and ducked behind the table. He swore under his breath. The gunfire was lessening on the other side as well; the distractions were working. Noname grabbed Eine's arm, startling her. Then he pushed the table forward, in the direction of the door they had come through. He was moving their shield towards the door. Eine copied him, sliding the table much faster.

Anda appeared beside her again, looking shaken. She clasped his hand. Noname jumped up and started firing again.

An Indigo man suddenly leapt over the table. He crashed down on top of Eine and Anda, knocking them backwards. Eine's head struck against the floor and she saw stars for an instant. She reached out immediately and grabbed a blue-sleeved arm; she twisted it, and felt the bone snap. There was a pained cry, before another man dropped down on top of them. Noname twisted around and shot him. Another one hopped over the table. The Indigo were charging them.

Eine threw out her fists, as hard as she could. She felt the crack of a nose, the snap of a rib. She bent an arm in half; she crunched the arch of a foot. They were fighting in such a tight space, on their knees, huddled behind the table. Her heart was hammering in her chest as if it would burst through. She saw Noname striking someone with his gun; he had run out of his ammunition. Gun shots began to ring out overhead again. Was Salabad all right?

Eine lunged for someone who was wrestling with Anda and threw her arms around his waist. She crouched, and flung him bodily over the table, back out into the gunfire. For an instant, the fighting froze, and all eyes behind the table stared at her. Then it started up again.

Someone grabbed Eine by the arms and tried to pin them back. She yanked herself free and turned to slam her fist into his face. But something sharp stuck her in the arm. She yelped even as she landed her blow, and the Indigo man dropped like a stone. She stared at her arm and saw that her sleeve had been shoved up, but she couldn't see a wound. She saw Anda beating back another man and reached to help, catching the man's wrist and snapping it. He roared and Eine let go.

Then the room suddenly did a spin.

Eine gasped and sat back on her heels. The room spun again, around her, in a sickening swing. It was as if she were back on the airship. She planted her hands on the floor in front of her. Everything was blurry. She saw Anda fighting someone in a dark haze. What was wrong? Why was she dizzy?

Then someone's arms were around her, gripping tight. Her eyelids were drooping. Her limbs were heavy; she could barely move. She heard a scraping of metal, and a wooden creak.

"Noname!" she shrieked. Then she was pushed very hard. And everything went black.

***

Eine drifted through a silky blackness for what felt like days. She saw snatches of images – Noname's eyes, the council hall, fireflies in the swamp. She heard an impossibly faint humming, and Anda's voice singing. *"...And the light will return from beyond..."* The Old-World song.

Where was she? She felt as if she were climbing up from the depths of a great well. Or she was coming around the corner at the end of the tunnel... The Docks...

Eine opened her eyes with an effort. Her eyelids were heavy as stone. She saw a smooth white ceiling above her. White. Was she in Enahala? She blinked in slow motion and looked around without turning her head. She could see only the ceiling. No, there was part of an object in the corner of her right eye, behind her, above her. She could feel a hard surface underneath her.

A terrible realization sunk in. She could not move a muscle.

She couldn't lift her head; she couldn't turn it. Eine's heart stopped, horror filling her. Her fingers, her legs… She had no control over anything. Was she tied down? She couldn't feel any restraints. She started to breathe heavily, panicky.

Where was she? What had happened? The factory and the fighting. She had been fighting, and then she'd gotten dizzy. That was all she could remember.

"Eine?" a small voice asked. She flinched at the sudden sound. Something creaked overhead, and the object just out of view moved. "Are you awake?" The voice was familiar.

She tried to move her mouth and it worked, but painfully slowly. Her jaw opened as if it were a rusted metal hinge. "Uh," she managed weakly.

"Eine, you're awake!" the voice exclaimed. It was definitely familiar. It was a little boy. "Is me, Graf! Eine, is me!"

Graf! It was Graf! Eine wanted to move, to bolt up and look around. But nothing happened. "Graf," she murmured.

"Yeah, is me! Are you all righ'?" he asked.

"I can't… move." She rolled her eyes around, trying to see him.

"I know," he said, surprising her. His voice sounded hollow. "Is a drug they give you."

"How?" she breathed. "Did you see?"

"No. One of the others told me." The words wavered a bit. "There's always somebody here, for a little while…until they come geh them."

Eine closed her eyes, a cold fear gripping her. She knew now where she was. She had been taken by the Indigo. The stab in her arm in the factory – they had given her a drug and then grabbed her. She was in the headquarters.

Where were the others? She began to panic again, gasping for air. Did they know where she was? She saw Noname's face for a moment, as it would have looked when he'd realized she was gone. Grief stabbed her like a knife. The ceiling above became blurry with tears. The creaking sounded again and she saw the object move as if it were swinging. She blinked rapidly, pulling herself back together. Graf was here; he was alive. But what had they done to him?

"Are you all right?" she asked, blinking away tears. They

crept sideways down her cheeks. It was easier to speak now, at least. "Where are you?"

"I'm up here," Graf said, forlornly. "I'm in a cage, like a bird."

"In a cage?!"

"I'll tell you wha' happened," he said. There were a few more creaks and a rattle. Eine wished desperately that she could see him. "They bra me to a room and they asked me some questions. I said I don' know, I don' know, over and over again. And then someone else came in and he said something like 'Deliver', and then I juss started saying all kinds of things! I juss talked and talked abow all kinds of stuff, Eine. I don' even know wha' ih was abow."

Eine sighed, remembering all that had been said about memory drugs in Enahala. "Then what happened?"

"Then ih was like I woke up, and they were saying, 'Wha' does he wan' us to do with him?' Then they took me here." Graf sounded worn out, suddenly, as if telling the story had taken a lot of energy. How well Eine remembered that feeling. He wasn't getting enough food. "I've been here since then."

"Do they bring you food?" she asked, feeling miserable.

"Sometimes. I think they forgeh I'm in here."

It was a holding room. The Indigo drugged their captives and left them here, temporarily. They had left Graf here too, as if they didn't know what to do with him. At least they hadn't killed him.

Eine gritted her teeth and strained all of her muscles. It was like being trapped in a block of ice, only without the cold. She groaned and let go, frustrated.

"I'm sorry they caw you, Eine," Graf said, in a very small voice. She swallowed, trying hard to think.

"How long do you think I have?" she asked. He creaked about in his cage.

"You woke up pretty fass. They're usually asleep for awhile, and then righ' after they wake up, somebody comes."

Eine tried to think clearly, her heart pounding. Perhaps waking up faster than the others meant that she was less susceptible to the drug. Or had they just given her less of it? She struggled to move again. Surely the fighting up above would distract them, and give her more time.

"I keep trying to pick this lock, buh I gah nothing to do ih with," Graf was saying. "If I could juss geh down, I could drag you or something... Buh the other door's locked."

Eine closed her eyes again and concentrated, focusing on her right hand. She thought about her fingers, and settled on her first finger. If she could get that to move, it would be a start.

"Did the Indigo...say anything...when they left me?" she asked, straining.

"Yeah, they were talking abow foreigners all over the city," Graf told her. "Wha's going on, Eine?"

"I came with an...army from Enahala." Eine stopped and took a breath. Her finger hadn't budged, but there was a distant tingling in it.

"An army?!" Graf exclaimed. Eine shushed him automatically, and then realized that there was probably no point.

"Don't you remember anything now?" she asked. The memory drug must have long worn off.

"Yeah, I remember," he said, sounding bitter. "Somebody tricked me. They picked me up in an auto-car, saying my father sen' for me. I knew something was wrong." He fell silent and Eine wished she could see him, alone and small in his cage. "My father used to talk abow Thela too. I remember. Are you a Laxen, Eine?"

"I'm a Demi," she said, feeling tired. She steadied herself and then focused again on her first finger.

"And the Indigo killed your parents," he mumbled. She grunted in reply. There was definitely a tingling sensation growing in her hand. "So you wen' and gah an army to come back and figh' them?" he asked, suddenly in awe. Eine burst out laughing, surprising herself. Her concentration snapped and she gave up for a moment, feeling a bit hysterical. "Wha's funny?" Graf demanded.

"I just never thought of it that way, I guess." She sighed, and then wiggled her fingers.

"You juss moved your fingers!"

Eine held her breath for a second, incredulous. Then she moved them again, all five of them stiff and slow as if they were brand new. She tried moving her other hand, but it was still frozen. "Okay, little by little," she muttered and steeled herself again.

"Maybe laughing helps," Graf commented. A loud thump sounded from somewhere far away and he made a nervous sound. Eine listened as several smaller booms followed, like someone running down a hall.

"What does the outside look like?" she asked, focusing again. This time the tingling was coming faster. The drug was definitely wearing off.

"Is all why' tunnels. Just all these why' hallways and Indigo people moving around. You know when tha' man grabbed me, we disappeared buh nah really? I could still see you. We juss moved ow of sigh' or something," Graf said, marveling. "And then he pulled me through a door and we wen' down a trap door and all these steps… I think we migh' be underground."

Eine's left hand was free now and she wiggled it in excitement. The sensation was spreading all over. She moved her feet back and forth, hope rising in her chest.

"You're moving your fee!" Graf exclaimed. She shushed him again, smiling. If she could just get Graf out of his cage before anyone came, then he might have a chance. She struggled for a few more moments, bending her knees, rolling her head around. Graf was creaking excitedly in his cage. She arched her back for a second and then finally pulled herself up. She was sitting up. She felt weak and numb all over.

She turned her head and saw an empty, white room all around her. It was not the soft white of Enahala, but a harsher, brighter hue. She was sitting on a white table in the center. In the corner, up very high, was a large domed cage hanging from a heavy chain, and from inside peered Graf's little face.

TWENTY-TWO

There were two other tables in the room that were empty, and there was a light dangling from the middle of the ceiling, which cast the corners in shadow. That was all.

"Are you all righ'?" Graf asked, his green eyes wide. He looked thin and pale as he stared down at Eine, clinging to the bars. She could make out a filthy rag hanging from the metal base of the cage around him, but nothing else from that angle. The door of the cage was flush with the bars and a rusted metal lock held it closed.

All she had to do was get up there. More heavy sounds came from nearby and they both cringed. Then Eine got to her feet awkwardly, gauging the distance from the table to the bottom of the cage. It was a distance she could jump when she wasn't stiff and dizzy from a paralyzing drug. She wasn't sure about it now.

"If I jump, can you help me hold on?" she asked Graf. He nodded eagerly. She planted her feet and sprang up as hard as she could. Her fingers just missed the cage. She landed in a stinging crouch on the ground underneath. There were more noises outside; it sounded like many people were moving down a hall.

"Is too high," Graf wailed. Eine shook her head, climbing back up onto the table. She stood there a moment, steadying herself, and then tried again. This time, she caught hold. Graf cried out and grabbed her hands. The whole cage swung backwards and scraped against the white wall. Eine gripped the metal edge as she swung with it, her body going limp. Her feet slapped against the wall, and then they swung back.

"I gah you!" Graf said. She struggled to pull herself up as the cage swung towards the wall again. She got her elbows through the bars and then finally her knees up onto the base. Graf hugged her tightly through the bars. Eine squeezed him back, relieved. He was skin and bones. He smelled terrible. She could see now the mess that was inside the cage and she closed her eyes.

"I have to break the lock," she said and let him go. Someone was yelling now outside. Something crashed like glass shattering, as she twisted the lock with all her might.

"Wha' we going to do, Eine?" Graf asked in a half-whisper.

"We're going to break the door open too," she grunted, working the rusted metal loose. "And then we're going to run." She struggled for another minute and then the metal snapped, crumbling into rusty bits. Then she crawled down quickly until she was dangling again. She let herself drop, landing more smoothly this time. She waved up at Graf as he pushed the door open and looked down at her. "Come on, I'll catch you!"

There was a sudden loud rattle at the room door. Graf gasped and then jumped as if he'd been stung. Eine caught him, a smelly heap of bones. She shoved him down to the floor behind the table. "When they carry me out, run out the door!" she whispered. He stared back at her with enormous eyes.

"Wha' do you mean?"

"Just do it!" She flung herself onto the table, just as the door opened. Then she closed her eyes.

Fast, angry footsteps stormed into the room. "Get her to Indigo and then get back out there!" a man's voice ordered. A woman's arms grabbed Eine roughly and pulled her off the table. She let herself go limp.

"Why doesn't he leave?" the woman asked. "Why is he staying down there?" They were opening the door again. Eine held her breath. *Please run, Graf.*

"He's a madman," the man snapped. Then he suddenly gasped. "Hey!"

Eine heard little feet running pell-mell past them. Her heart leapt. Maybe he would get away. Maybe they'd ignore him.

"That was the rat in the cage," the woman said. "Someone

will catch him." The door closed behind them. Eine peered through her eyelashes and saw white walls, hanging lights above. There were voices echoing off the walls up ahead. The man ran off ahead, leaving the woman behind, his blue uniform passing through Eine's narrow line of sight.

"How did they get in?" her carrier mumbled to herself. Eine opened her eyes wider and rolled them around. Her captive was alone now. Should she run for it now? Should she wait until she saw a doorway? "This was never supposed to happen!" the woman went on.

Eine's stomach suddenly buckled in a terrible, familiar way. Hunters. She clenched up all over, and the Indigo woman stared down at her, her dark eyes wide, angry. There were sudden shouts up ahead of them. The woman's head jerked up to see, and then Eine sprang from her grasp, cracking her on the skull with one flailing arm.

She ran for it, with no idea where she was going, her stomach churning. She was running down a white hall. Everything was rounded, like inside a tunnel.

Down the hall, she spotted a group of blue uniforms headed straight for her. They were running; one of them pointed right at her. The Hunters' horn blasted overhead. She heard thundering footsteps. Eine spun around and saw another hallway to the right. She ducked into it and ran, her boots smacking on the polished floor. Where could she go? How could she get out of here?

Gunfire suddenly flared up behind her, and she skidded to a stop. Were the foreign soldiers inside? Shouting rang out again and then the sound of clashing metal. It was hard to tell which direction it was coming from now. Eine turned around quickly, out of breath. The hallway she was in now was marked with several small doors lined up in a row. They ran along the middle of the wall. There was something disturbing about them.

Then Eine heard a gun shot that sounded very much like Noname's gun. Her heart leapt into her throat. He was here! They had found her! She shot back down the hall towards the sound. A Hunter bellowed and someone cried out. There was a fight taking place in the hall she had just left. In a few seconds, she burst back out into it. She almost ran straight into Wilder as he ran a sword through the belly of a Hunter.

Eine stumbled backwards, horrified. Behind Wilder, Amlat and a stranger in black robes were fighting back to back. More soldiers she didn't know were plunging ahead and falling back against both Hunters and blue uniforms. Everyone was bloody. Gun shots blasted the walls, forcing everyone to duck repeatedly. Frantic, Eine grabbed a piece of metal armor from the floor and held it up over her head.

All around her, the shouts and groans were terrifying. She thought numbly of Graf, somewhere in these halls, and hoped he had escaped. She had done what she could for him. She had to help the others now. This was why she had come. Her heart was hammering. Sweat was slipping down the sides of her face. Her hands felt clammy and numb.

Numb was good.

Eine closed her eyes and stepped out into the mayhem. A Hunter roared at her and raised his whip - she hit him square in the knee with all her might and he fell, knocking down others. Someone fired nearby and she ducked under her shield. Then an Indigo man struck her on the head and she stumbled backwards. She fell into another one and smashed into him with her shield. Then she rushed back towards the other man and struck him the same way. She dropped back under the shield afterwards, panting.

Where was Noname? Was he fighting somewhere else?

Suddenly the floor dropped out from under her. She flew up over the fighting, grabbed by the hood of her cloak by a Hunter. She lost her breath. Her heart stopped as her feet swung out ahead of her. Then she crashed into several bodies, slamming them into the wall. She fell to the ground at the feet of soldiers and Indigo, her bones rattled and bruised. Someone leapt over her a second later and landed without a sound. Eine pulled herself up, wincing, and saw that it was Salabad. He stood there for one moment, dark and sleek in his black clothes, squinting at the battle with narrowed eyes. The next moment, he was a blur.

Eine jumped to her feet and tried to see him. He was flying back and forth through the crowd, inducing startled screams everywhere. When Noname had said he was fast, it had been an understatement.

Suddenly, Eine saw Anda wrestling with a tall Indigo man off to one side. She shoved her way to him and caught hold of the man's arm. She yanked it backward; the man winced and Anda knocked him out with his long wooden staff.

"Eine!" Noname's voice yelled. She spun around, just as Anda grabbed her hand. She couldn't see him.

"I'm here!" she called. A Hunter's whip cracked down between her and Anda.Their hands came apart. Eine swung a fist at the brute's side, but then someone threw their arms around her, pulling her backwards. She writhed and broke free. Then she was grabbed again and yanked off the ground. She was suddenly blinded by limbs and faces all around. What was happening? She screamed and kicked. Her captor stumbled.

"Eine!" Noname cried again. Then whoever had grabbed her was running. He burst out of the fight and ran down the other hallway. It was so fast. Eine clawed at him frantically.

"One more Laxen out of the way!" the man growled. He yanked open one of the little doors in the wall, revealing a dark yawning hole. Then he shoved Eine headfirst towards it. She screamed again and caught hold of the sides, pushing herself backwards. Down the hole in front of her was a narrow, steep slope: a chute. The sight stopped her heart.

"No!" She heard Noname's voice, and a gunshot. The Indigo man grunted, and then flung his full weight into Eine. Her arms snapped backwards; she landed chin-first inside the chute. Then she was sliding, terrifyingly fast, into darkness. The sounds of the battle faded instantly. She rolled to the side, landing on her back, sliding faster. She clawed at the sides to find a handhold, but there was nothing. She flew up several inches and bounced painfully off the side. She spun again, arms and legs striking the smooth walls all around her.

Then she was out, bursting free of the chute and flying. One second of weightlessness. She fell onto a hard metal frame. The pain of the impact shot through her. Her eyes were squeezed shut in agony. Everything was aching, throbbing, bleeding. She stirred limply, one hand reaching out. She felt cold metal all around her.

Eine slowly opened her eyes, afraid to breathe. The light was dim. She was in a cavernous room. She could see metal rails curving overhead and around either side of her. They were all around her, holding her in. She was inside a kind of globe-shaped cage, formed out of many separate rings of metal. Through an opening in the rings, she could make out the end of the chute, high above, from which she had crashed into the contraption she lay inside now. Under her back was a flat metal surface, very cold.

Fear gripped her as if she was going to choke. Where was she?

She looked around, dizzy with pain. There were other chutes lined up above. There were shadowy objects all around, more metal globes…

There was a man standing quietly, not far away. Eine flinched. He was watching her. He was perfectly still, and he wore a modified version of the Indigo uniform. It was looser, hanging from him almost like a cloak. He was small and his hair was a ring of frizz around an aging head.

His eyes gleamed a bit in the low light.

"I am always surprised by the little ones," he said slowly. His voice was even and cool. It sounded light, and more youthful than he looked. "The ones who look so frail, but are not. I find it…perverse."

Eine felt her skin scrawl at the sound of his voice. There was something just under the surface of it, something dangerous. Was this actually him? Was she staring into the face of the man who had killed her parents? The man who had forced her to live on the street and terrorized an entire city?

He was small and intense, not the vicious monster of a man that she had expected, without knowing what to expect. She had never really imagined laying eyes on him. This man instilled in her a different kind of fear. It was a skin-crawling feeling that warned her of utter unpredictability. He was capable of anything. He was insane. He stepped forward calmly, approaching the cage-like structure that held Eine. She shuddered instinctively.

"This is an interesting turn of events," Indigo said, glancing up at the chutes above. Closer now, she could see there was something irregular about his features. Something not quite right. "Calthin and Erano never warned me of a direct attack."

Erano! Eine blinked at the familiar name. Anda's friend at the council?

"I was considering branching out," Indigo muttered, almost to himself. "You make things perfect in one small place, and then you find that it's not enough. You have to go beyond."

Eine felt a tiny flare of anger inside her and grasped onto it, using it for strength. "You made Thela *perfect?*" she forced herself to say. Her teeth were almost chattering. "Is that what you think?"

"Of course. True man must always be in control, little beast. True man without abominable gifts." He reached out a pale hand and spun the metal rings around her. They clicked smoothly. "When false men are allowed to become powerful, to pretend they are gods...!" He bit off the last word and clenched his teeth. He gave the rings around her a hard pull, spinning them rapidly. Eine felt the flat metal underneath her begin to spin slowly with them.

Indigo suddenly grabbed her wrist in a grip like a vise, halting the spinning. She gasped. "Then we must destroy them all," he said, with an eerie intensity. "First, we must uncover the stone," he added in a lighter tone. "For you can snap my wrist like a twig, can't you, little beast?" Eine yanked her hand free and twisted around. But a sudden flash of blue light stopped her.

Indigo had opened a large, rectangular compartment within the contraption, just behind where her head had been. Inside it, filling all the space, was a brilliantly glowing, dark blue gemstone. It was larger than Eine's hand. Blue-purple light pulsed from it and flooded the shadows around them. It lit up Indigo's face and Eine glanced at him, unable to help it.

His face was riddled with burn scars, the flesh lumpy and discolored. Eine winced and looked away. The blue stone caught her attention again immediately.

"You know, there is truth to all those old stories. One day, in my travels, while I was healing, I found a shrine that marked a poisonous ore." He made a quick movement and pulled out shackles from underneath the flat metal beneath her. "And yet it wasn't poisonous for true man."

"No..." Eine got to her knees, unable to take her eyes from the stone. She should run. There was no one else even here. There was something draining about that blue light; it felt strangely like it was pulling at her.

"Oh, yes," Indigo said, taking her wrist again. His hands were cold. Eine felt confused. She struggled to remember something she wanted to say. "Now you lie back down and you start to spin." He sounded like he was talking to a child, telling a story. Eine wilted as he pressed down on her shoulder, and she lay down as he commanded. "The spinning keeps you disoriented. And then the stone does its work."

"How am I...a beast...?" Eine murmured. "...and not the

Hunters?" He was snapping the shackles around each wrist, and then her ankles. He chuckled - a light, unpleasant sound.

"The Hunters are my pets. No one would begrudge a man his pets. They don't hurt anyone unless I tell them too." He smiled at her suddenly, a stiff, unhappy smile. "But your kind… Your kind is an abomination," he said. "And nature has given me a way to end it."

A sliding sound came from above, just as Indigo finished locking Eine in. "Here comes another one," he intoned. Then he reached up and grasped the top rings of the globe-cage, as Eine watched him from inside a fog. He pulled them down with his full strength and the machine began spinning rapidly. Eine began spinning with it.

A familiar voice roared as someone flew out of another chute. There was a crash as someone landed badly onto another spinning rack. Eine heard the sound as if it were very far away. She turned her head for a glimpse, between the spinning bars. It looked like Salabad. They had caught him too. She closed her eyes.

So dizzy. The blue light flashing on the metal.

"There's plenty of the ore to go around," Indigo's voice was saying. "There's only one stone in the story, but I can reproduce them."

The story... Eine opened her eyes, seeing everything flashing by in a blur around her. She could feel the momentum of the spin blowing her hair, her cloak. What was the story? The Old-World story about the blue stone.

"Who are you?" She heard Salabad's voice, thick with pain and anger.

"I'm a survivor." Indigo's voice sounded cheerful. "I was once called Hymax, but I've renamed myself. After my new favorite color."

Eine's thoughts blurred and swam in front of her eyes. She closed them again. All was lost. This was how all the others had died. Her parents. The tree-grower and the storyteller. What was the story? From Glace's thoughts… Eine tried to concentrate, but it slipped away, and Noname's face came back to her, sick with fever and delirious. He was holding her hand. She ached all over. She felt sick to her stomach.

"Have I captured a Kry Laxen? How impressive. You use your aberrations to make yourself rich." Indigo's voice was chilling as he added, "I have known others like you."

The blue stone came from an ore in the ground. It destroyed everything all around.

Eine felt herself growing very tired, weakening. Spinning and spinning. A toxic ore for Laxens... That was it all along. That was how he did it.

There was another sliding sound above. Eine listened idly, sinking into herself. Another Laxen was caught. And so it would go on and on.

It destroyed everything all around...Until one day a messenger broke it down.

A messenger?

Eine heard a crash of metal and someone yelling. She heard the sound of a third person sliding in. The noises were murky, as if she were underwater. She struggled to stay conscious, to focus on something. The thought of Noname buoyed her for a moment. She never knew his name...she would never know it. He had called her an angel.

The image of the angel in the library book came back to her. *"Angels were believed to be messengers. This idea sprang from...conduition, by which one Laxen can send communication, and sometimes even an action, through another Laxen."*

Something about those words triggered a tiny idea inside her, even as it began to grow dark all around. What had her mother said? The roots. The stone. It's through you.

"Eine!" Noname was shouting somewhere far away, in another world. There was distant gunfire. But a messenger could destroy the stone.

"He's dead!"

"Stop this machine! Stop it!"

Gunfire again, closer now. Then the faint sound of sword blades ringing against the blue stone behind her. She couldn't see anything now. She could barely hear it.

There was a sudden, terrible jolt, and the spinning stopped. Eine lurched violently, regaining consciousness for a second. The world was still spinning; the dim room around her was spinning. Someone was breaking her shackles, holding her hand aside and smashing down on the metal with something. Darkness descended again.

"Does that mean you do know what it means?"

"Eine? Yeah, it's like 'a crossing', or 'passage'."

"Eine, hang on!" Noname yelled. She heard other voices, concerned voices. Ejan's… Wilder, Amlat. Her right hand was free. They were working on the other shackles. She had to destroy the stone.

Eine raised her arm feebly, reaching behind her head. She felt the smooth cool surface and it sucked at her fingers, draining her. She took a frail breath and whispered, "Mother."

Something warm surged through her like lightning. She felt the crackling of branches, of twigs and roots, bursting with life through her. The stone shattered with a thousand cracks behind her. Then there was a sudden silence.

Everything was quiet. Eine dropped her arm, her whole body shaking.

Someone swore in Enahalan. It sounded like Anda.

Eine realized her eyes were tightly shut, and she opened them now, expecting to see the same darkness from before. But Noname's face leaned over her, his features worked into a tight knot of fear and worry, and disbelief. He was alive and she was alive. Eine smiled at him, delirious.

"Bet you're scared, kid," she murmured.

He grabbed her up in a fierce hug, lifting her off the machine. "I love you." His voice was rough and shaky. "I love you so much."

TWENTY-THREE

Eine awoke a week later to the sound of laughter, coming from the next room. She lay there a moment, confused, staring at the low curved ceiling of Anda's guest room. She had been dreaming something new. A man was holding her in his arms and humming, rocking back and forth. The tune was the same as the song that Anda had sung in the woods outside of Thela. The one that had popped into his head through Eine.

'The light goes on further than eyes can see...and the light can return from beyond! To defend... The light from beyond will destroy the stone.'

Anda had said he'd never understood that part. Eine wondered with a shock if her father had been contacting her too, in his own way. He'd been a storyteller, Oln had said. He must have known the story.

Eine smiled up at the ceiling, amazed. She heard Noname laugh again and her heart quickened. She threw her feet over the side of the bed and pulled on the soft white robe Anda had given her. Then she stepped out into the main room where the two friends sat at Anda's round table, drinking that bitter *kalan.*

Noname sat with his long legs stretched out. His hair was cropped down close to his scalp again, and his strong arms were bare under a short-sleeved shirt. He smiled and Eine ran to him, impulsively. He had been busy the last two days, planning something secret, so she hadn't seen him as often as usual. He had never left her side, after rescuing her in Thela.

On the way home by airship, he had pulled her onto his lap and kissed her often, his mouth warm and soft, and urgent. He had run his hands through her hair and around her waist, setting her skin on fire, and Eine felt herself melting, her sharp edges softening, her heart bursting. She loved him. It was so simple now that she understood it.

He stood up and put his arm around her now, a mischeivious look in his eye. "Graf has been helping me pick the horses," he said, dropping another clue.

They had scoured the underground headquarters for Graf, after Noname had killed Indigo.He had flung himself down one of the chutes as soon as he broke free of attackers, and he had shot Indigo with all the rounds left in his gun. Eine had insisted on searching for Graf herself, despite her weakness, pulling Noname along as the rest of the soldiers took prisoners of the remaining Indigo men. She had found Graf hiding in a closet with a handful of bread he had stolen, miraculously, in the middle of all the fighting. They had sent word to his family in Belgir, but he was happy to follow Noname around Enahala in the meantime.

They had left Thela in disarray, with the surviving Indigo and the Hunters shut up in cells in the underground headquarters. The airship of soldiers that had landed in the sand dunes had armed the group of partial Laxens they had indeed found there. The group was temporarily in charge now, tough survivors that they were; the rest of the Thelans were still recovering from their disbelief and shock at their sudden freedom.

Back in Enahala, it had been discovered that Erano had disappeared. He had abandoned his family when the news of Indigo's death had been received, and slipped out of the city. Evidence was discovered that proved he had sabotaged the airship which carried Anda, in revenge for Calthin's death. His betrayal was a dark cloud over the victory, as was the loss of many soldiers. Salabad had survived and was being treated in Enahala's hospital, along with Amlat and Sot. Kind Lon had been killed and Zwit; Ejan went home to Meyja a hero, and Wilder had returned to his beloved Ice Lands.

Irridi had left with a new-found appreciation for Laxens, after he heard the story of how Eine destroyed the Indigo stone.

The news had caused quite a commotion in Enahala. Her conduition ability was exotic enough, but the idea that the source of the transfer had come from beyond the grave…? Many people refused to believe it, claiming that Eine must have some previously unknown element of her mother's tree-growing ability inside her. But others took it as a reaffirmation of what they already believed.

Anda and Glace had brought back all traces of blue stone from Thela to be examined. The toxic ore was an ancient material from deep in the ground, but the reason it only affected Laxens - drained them of their energy until they died - was a mystery. Binden and Illeen had taken a strong interest in the project.

"I have just received an announcement that you may be very interested in," Anda told Eine now, as she wondered why Noname needed horses. He smiled and held up a piece of paper, clearing his throat. "It seems our friend Loneela Indane has become engaged to one of our foreign soldiers. Apparently, Agin is very unhappy about it. Among others."

Noname laughed. "Oh no, she's going to taint the gene pool."

"Yes. Here's hoping it starts a trend," Anda said with a sigh. He stood up and carried his drink into the little kitchen in the back of the house.

Noname glanced at Eine and grinned. "Now you have nothing to worry about," he said, smirking. Eine rolled her eyes and blushed at the same time. "I thought she'd still be waiting around for me when I got back - "

"Shut up," she told him. He laughed, looking very pleased with himself. Then he wrapped an arm around her waist and kissed her on the top of her head.

"You never had anything to worry about," he said softly. Eine felt a throb of intense happiness. She couldn't imagine ever getting used to the feeling.

"Did you know already? Back then?" she asked.

"I thought so but I wasn't sure. …And I didn't know how you felt."

Eine thought about how confused she had been and she smiled, embarrassed.

***

A few days later, Eine followed Noname out through a

small door in the seamless city wall, just as they had entered Enahala the first time. Outside, she saw two horses waiting, one a lovely white with brown markings and the other one gleaming black. Their reins were held by a smiling, gray-haired stable man, and their saddle bags were packed full. She glanced up at Noname uncertainly. This was the surprise he had been working on, but it was still a mystery.

"Where are we going?" she asked.

"The first part is a horseback ride across the Gold Plains to Tobin," he said, smiling. "The storm season is over," he added quickly.

"All the way to Tobin?" Eine exclaimed. "I've never even ridden a horse."

"Then that's the first new thing I'll teach you on this trip. Then we get on a train and head out for the Kinimin Islands."

Eine felt a rush of excitement. She was going to see more of the world, a world that had once seemed forever lost to her. "And we'll see your sister!" she guessed.

"And I'll teach you how to swim." He stopped, looking sheepish and mischievous at the same time. "And other things." He leaned in and kissed her, in a way that made her knees nearly fold underneath her.

"And then we'll come back?" she whispered. Enahala felt like home now. He nodded, resting his forehead on hers, squeezing her tight. They stood there for a moment, holding each other. "Aren't you supposed to tell me your name now?" she asked, shyly.

"I told you, in the swamp," he said.

"You did?" Startled, Eine thought back to the muddled conversation they'd had while he lay raging with the fever. Noname grinned, watching her. "You said some things in Creeden, but I wouldn't know…"

"Clouds on the Moon," he said. His expression was more serious now, wistful. "That's what it is in Thelan."

"Clouds on the Moon," Eine repeated, surprised. She remembered him saying it now, as she'd knelt over him. "Why?"

"My mother said that on the night I arrived, there was the worst storm ever…but I shone through."

Eine looked into his kind, scarred face and thought about the first time she had seen him, back in the dark life she had led on the streets of Thela. "I know what she means," she whispered.

ABOUT THE AUTHOR

Simone Snaith is an author and a singer-songwriter in Los Angeles. Her other available books are **"The Fairville Woods"** young adult series: *From The Ashes* and *Through The Eyes*. She is represented by Michael Bourret at Dystel & Goderich. Find out more at http://www.simonesnaith.com.

For more information about the cover artist, please visit: http://www.audreyknight.com

5-5-15

Made in the USA
San Bernardino, CA
14 April 2015